The Riding Master

By

Alexandrea Weis

This is a work of fiction. Names, characters, places, and incidents are products of the author's imagination or are used fictitiously and are not to be construed as real. Any resemblance to actual events, locations, organizations, or person, living or dead, is entirely coincidental.

Copyright © Alexandrea Weis 2014
2nd Edition WEBA Publishing, LLC, March, 2015

Licensing Notes

All rights reserved. No part of this book may be used or reproduced in any manner whatsoever without written permission, except in the case of brief quotations embodied in articles and reviews.
Cover: Book Fabulous Designs

Editor: Maxine Bringenberg

Chapter 1

The golden dust from the fresh hay tickled Rayne Greer's nose as she tossed two flakes into the feeder at the back of the stall. Wiping the itchy remnants from her arms, she turned her attention to the tall thoroughbred nudging up beside her. The slender bay gently pushed her to the side, anxious to tear into the yellow strands dangling from the heavy metal feeder. She patted the gelding's thick neck and let her fingers luxuriate over his silky coat. Ever since Rayne was little, she had loved the feel of a horse. Their powerful muscles bulging beneath that soft covering of fur had never ceased to fascinate her.

Closing her eyes, Rayne drank in the sweet aroma of the hay blended with the earthy scent of wood shavings and the slightly musky essence of horse. Every now and then hints of the freshly cut grass in the paddocks beyond the barn would filter into the stall on the back of a gentle September breeze.

"Isn't that the best smell on earth, Bob?"

"I can't believe you call that horse 'Bob,'" a gruff voice intruded.

Opening her eyes, Rayne frowned. "What's wrong with it?"

"People are named Bob, not horses," a brassy blonde clarified from the stall door.

Round, middle-aged, and wearing beige riding pants along with custom-made riding boots, the woman's long, tanned face was careworn, but wrinkle free.

"He's a Bob, Rebecca," Rayne contended. "Solid, dependable, easy-going, and kind. All Bob-traits."

Rebecca rolled her discerning brown eyes. "Hardly Bob-traits. My last ex was named Bob, and he was a sneaky, conniving, cheating, dishonest bastard."

Rayne ducked beneath the single chain hanging across the stall entrance. "You said the same thing about your first two ex-husbands."

"At least they paid their share in the divorce settlement. Bob still hasn't."

Rayne looked down the shady shed row toward the barn entrance. "Wasn't he the one who bought you this stable and the surrounding land?"

"He sure did," Rebecca admitted with a perturbed snort. "But he never coughed up any cash for me to run it after he ran off with his podiatrist."

"Ex-husbands aren't meant to pay for everything, Rebecca."

"Where is that written in stone?" Rebecca pointed an accusatory finger at Rayne. "Just because you didn't milk yours for a hefty settlement doesn't mean the rest of us can't. And why you didn't take more out of Foster Greer's hide I'll never know. Man's loaded, what with that big lab company he owns. You should have at least fought to get more from him. That way you wouldn't have had to go back to work after the divorce."

"I got enough," Rayne maintained. "Anyway, I like working."

"Nobody likes working, sweetie." Rebecca paused and examined Rayne's slim figure. "You could still get remarried, you know? You have everything a man could want: a smashing figure, the creamy complexion of a cover girl, carved cheekbones a sculptor would envy, gorgeous hazel eyes, and tits that women like me pay plastic surgeons to build."

Rayne reflexively folded her arms over her loose-fitting T-shirt. Ever since puberty she had been extremely self-conscious about her breasts, feeling it was all anyone ever noticed.

Rebecca lowered Rayne's arms to her side. "You've got to show them off, girl. Let them enter the room before you do." She waved her hand over her ample bosom. "Took two boob jobs to get me here, but you got it for free." She then fingered a strand of frizzy, honey-blonde hair that had fallen from Rayne's ponytail. "You just need to get rid of this mousy color though. Go big blonde, like me." She patted her stiff, perfectly styled coif. "Men prefer bold blondes."

Rayne tucked her hair behind her ear, amused by Rebecca's idea of what men idealized. "I'm not interested in getting married again. I have enough money to keep me riding, keep my house, my car, and whatever else I want. What else do I need?"

"A man in your bed, silly." Rebecca cocked a blonde-tinted eyebrow at Rayne. "When was the last time you got laid?"

Rayne's eyes dropped to the shaving-covered ground as the blush rose on her cheeks. Sometimes she wished Rebecca wasn't so outspoken.

"That long, eh?" Rebecca clucked. "Sex isn't something to be embarrassed about, Rayne. You need a man to turn you on, not turn you off like Foster did."

Rayne gaped at her friend. "Foster did not turn me—"

Rebecca raised her hand, cutting her off. "Of course he did. You wouldn't be red if he had turned you on. You would also be a lot more comfortable talking about sex. But I get it. I'm sure what he lacked in the bedroom, he made up for with gifts." She motioned to Rayne's bay thoroughbred. "Like Bob there."

Rayne peered into the stall. "Foster knew how much I loved horses. He was just trying to make me happy."

"And screwing that twenty-two year old waitress? Did that make you happy?"

Rayne shuddered as a rash of bad memories inundated her. "Why do you always bring that up, Rebecca?"

"Because you never talk about it. It's been six months since you signed the divorce papers, Rayne, and all you do is go to work; every other minute of your time you spend here, communing with Bob. It's not healthy for a woman with your looks."

"My looks?" Rayne softly snickered. "You need to stop worrying about me. I'm fine."

"You're not fine. Far from it." Rebecca edged closer, scrutinizing Rayne's hazel eyes. "Sometimes I get the distinct impression you haven't quite wrapped your head around the fact that it's over with Foster. It's like you're waiting for him to come back."

"I'm not waiting for him to come back. I don't want him back. I just want him to…forget it." Rayne's hand sliced across the air, signaling the discussion was over.

"No, I get it. You want him to admit that he was wrong to leave, don't you?" Rebecca lifted the corners of her small, pink-painted mouth. "I know how you feel, Rayne. I've been there. After my first divorce, from Vincent, I desperately wanted to hear the same thing, but it never happened."

Rebecca hooked her arm. "I think I have just the thing for you. Come with me."

Despite Rayne's protests, they started down the aisle toward the doublewide doors at the stable's entrance. As they stepped into the bright Texas sun, Rebecca pulled a pair of Ray-Ban sunglasses from the front pocket of her jodhpurs. Easing the sunglasses over her eyes, Rebecca waved ahead to a red-railed riding ring. "I've got a new riding master starting today. He's teaching the adult beginners class right now." Crunching noises erupted around them as they ambled through a white-shelled parking lot toward the ring. "He's got a lot of experience, has ridden for quite a few big name stables, and used to show the Lone Star Circuit. Plus, he's real easy on the eyes," Rebecca continued.

Rayne came to an abrupt stop, kicking up a few of the shells with her riding boots. "I don't think I like where this is heading."

"You're gonna love him," Rebecca insisted with a tug on Rayne's arm.

"Oh God, Rebecca, please tell me you're not setting me up."

"No, not setting up, per se. Perhaps just giving you a taste of what is out there. He's thirty-four, never been married, owns a consulting firm that works in the oil and gas business, drives a nice BMW, and loves horses." Rebecca flashed a toothsome smile. "See how much you two already have in common?"

"I don't drive a BMW," Rayne scoffed.

Rebecca dragged her closer to the riding ring. "Not to worry; you can drive his."

Beyond the railing, a small group of riders atop horses of varying shapes and colors were decked out in new black boots and lined up in front of the dominating figure of a man wearing faded blue jeans and a dark T-shirt. His face was obscured by the myriad of flicking horsetails in front of him, but every now and then Rayne caught a glimpse of his sinewy, strong arms and long, lean legs. When he waved a tanned arm to the railing, the sunlight scintillated on his stainless watch, making Rayne's insides unexpectedly quiver. She could barely make out the rumbling of his deep voice from the center of the ring as he addressed his riders, but the little she could hear sounded very seductive.

"His name is Trent Newbury," Rebecca began. "He was the riding master at Shelby Stables in Denton, but left because he was looking for a place in Copper Canyon closer to his house in Lewisville. Lisa Shelby, the owner of Shelby Stables, told me he was a damn fine riding master and hated to let him go." Rebecca grunted, sounding more like a man than a woman. "She was also lying through her teeth, but never told me the real reason for the split."

"You suspect there was a problem at Shelby?"

"You know me, Rayne…if the pope came to dinner, I'd suspect him of stealing the silverware. But I hired him because I really need the help. He's going to oversee you and the other instructors, manage the class schedules, organize the horse show arrangements, and deal with the continuous stream of phone calls I get looking for information on lessons. That will free up my time to take care of the other problems around the stables."

Rayne's eyes swerved to the man in the center of the ring as the riders set out for the railing. Even though his eyes were covered with dark sunglasses, she could still make out his thin, cruel lips, square jaw, slightly crooked nose, and black, wavy hair.

"Not bad, huh? Wait until you see his ass," Rebecca commented with a tweak of hope in her voice.

"Rebecca, how do you know he's not gay? Most men in this business are."

"Not this one."

"But how can you be so sure?" Rayne persisted.

"Because I asked him. I wanted to know up front before the rumor mill started."

"Then why don't you take him?" Rayne suggested, half-laughing.

"I've got Murray, and I don't need another complication in my life." Rebecca pointed at Rayne. "But you do."

Rayne bit down on her lower lip. "He wouldn't be interested in me."

"Oh, there she goes again." Rebecca removed her sunglasses. "Honestly, Rayne, when are you going to get over this? You're an interesting, attractive, vibrant woman with a lot to offer. Stop selling yourself short."

Rayne glimpsed the man in the center of the ring. "I think he's more Selene's type. You know, the attractive playboy kind."

The handsome instructor shouted to the students in the class to take their horses to a slow trot.

"He's too smart for her," Rebecca objected. "He would see through Selene's bullshit from a mile away."

"Has he met Selene?"

"Not yet." Rebecca's heavy sigh lingered in the air. "I was hoping to build up my strength for that confrontation. She'll be livid that I hired Trent and not her for the riding master position." Rebecca replaced her sunglasses over her eyes. "The main reason I hired Trent is to handle Selene. I've been getting more and more complaints from the students in her dressage class about her behavior and her language. She's been trying my patience for a while now. I can put up with a lot, but that woman has pushed me to my limits."

Rayne kicked at a few shells on the ground. "You plan on telling her to go?"

"Not exactly. Selene's ex, Judge Kendrick, likes to keep tabs on his former wife's activities. If she misbehaves, he wants to hear about it, so he can use the information to cut back her hefty monthly alimony."

"How would you know about that?" Rayne questioned with a curious tilt of her head.

"Just like your ex pays for Bob, Judge Kendrick pays for that gargantuan beast Selene rides. I've had to call him a few times to remind him when he forgot to pay the bill, and we've become quite friendly. Imagine if I told old Judge Kendrick that I wanted his wife and her pseudo-horse out of my barn. He'd ask a lot of questions," Rebecca grinned, "and I would be compelled to answer them."

"Watch your back, Rebecca. Selene is one vengeful bitch."

Rebecca inched away from the railing. "Don't worry about me, sugarplum. I've tangled with the likes of Selene Kendrick for years, and I've always came out smelling like a rose." She nodded her head to the man in the center of the ring. "You just worry about getting your life in order."

"Forget it, Rebecca. I'm not interested." Rayne abruptly turned toward the barn.

"At least try and be open to new possibilities," Rebecca shouted behind her.

Rayne ignored her friend and hurried to the shade of the barn, anxious to get back to Bob. But nearing the doors of the stable, something made her glance back at the new riding master. A warm sensation stirred in her belly as he purposefully strode around the ring, kicking up dirt as he went. Rayne shook off the notion of getting to know the man. At this point in her life she was convinced men were a waste of time, because in the end they never stayed when things got bad. Being "open to new possibilities," as Rebecca had suggested, was a sure fire way to get hurt, and Rayne had vowed no man would ever hurt her again.

***

It was early evening when Rayne returned to the barn after taking Bob on a long trail ride across the hilly terrain surrounding Southland Stables. She was heading to her tack room with Bob following dutifully behind her when she saw a figure coming down the shed row wearing sunglasses.

His swagger was the first thing that stood out in her mind. The sway of his hips exuded a ruthless overconfidence, but as her eyes traveled up from the curve of his blue jeans to his wide chest and thick, tanned arms, her temperature began to quickly climb. When she was within a few feet of him, his thin lips twisted into a devilish smile, almost a teasing smirk that Rayne found more offensive than alluring.

What an asshole, she thought as he drew near.

She curiously studied the square curve of his jaw and his slightly bent nose. His hair was thick, wavy, almost black, and was in need of a good trim. His sunken cheekbones accentuated the tan on his face, while his high brow was etched with a few worry lines that complimented instead of detracted from his appearance. When he lowered his sunglasses, she noted the way his riveting gray eyes drank in her figure.

Rayne concluded that she could never be interested in such an obvious man. She was used to men ogling her buxom figure; her ex-husband used to do it all the time when they had first started dating. But what was exciting in her twenties, she now found repugnant in her thirties, making her wonder if all the real gentlemen had gone the way of the dodo bird.

"You're Rayne Greer, right?" His voice was a lot smoother than when he had been shouting at his students. Tinged with a lustful, smoky quality that many women would have found alluring, Rayne felt her uneasiness with the man begin to gnaw at her.

Ignoring his engaging eyes, she gathered up Bob's reins. "Yes, I'm Rayne Greer," she flatly stated, deciding to play it cool.

He held out a thick hand to her. "Trent Newbury, the new riding master for Southland Stables. Rebecca Harmon told me about you. She said you were great with kids."

When Bob rubbed his head against her back, eager to move on, Rayne turned away from his outstretched hand to the horse beside her. "Yes, I teach the under twelve and beginners groups for Rebecca on the weekends."

He lowered his hand to his side, unaffected by her snub. "Rebecca told me you showed a lot of potential." He eyed the slender dark bay thoroughbred. "Is this your mount?"

"Yes, he's a racetrack rescue Rebecca sold me a year ago." Rayne rubbed Bob's long neck. "Where's your horse?"

"Don't have one right now. I just sold my mare a few weeks back." He took a step closer to her, making Bob give a short snort of surprise. "He's high spirited," Trent remarked, giving Bob's neck a pat.

"Careful," Rayne warned. "He doesn't like strangers, especially men."

Bob turned his head and tried to nip at Trent's arm.

Trent chuckled. "Where did he learn that trick, from you?"

"No." She shifted uneasily on her feet, uncomfortable with the close proximity of the man. "He was abused by jockeys and trainers when he raced on the track. No man could get near him when Rebecca first bought him. I started working with him in hopes of turning him into a schooling horse. After a time, I opted to buy him...or my ex bought him for me." She noticed the way Bob seemed to calm as Trent's powerful hand glided over his back.

"Ex?" Trent's sharp eyes returned to Rayne. "You're divorced."

Rayne was surprised by the way his slight smile instantly warmed his unsettling features. All of his cocky assurance disappeared and he seemed almost genuine.

"You have the most intriguing eyes," he murmured, staring at her. "There are flecks of gold amid the hazel in them."

Rayne's toes curled in her black riding boots. "I, ah...." She diverted her eyes to Bob. "I'm surprised he's letting you get that close."

"I have a way with horses. They find me...irresistible."

So much for seeming genuine, she reflected. "That must be a great comfort to you," she sharply returned. "Knowing you have such sway over four-legged animals like that. Or were you talking about another kind of animal?"

His eyebrows went up. "Well, well, not only does your horse have spirit, his rider seems to as well."

"Perhaps you are confusing spirit with sarcasm, Mr. Newbury."

He grinned at her, folding his thick arms over his chest. "It's Trent, and I think you're wrong. You have to have a good bit of spirit and wit in order to be sarcastic. Telling people what you think of them takes a hell of a lot of guts, too."

"Guts or stupidity? There's a difference. One usually gets you into trouble, and the other is needed to get you out of it."

Trent's roaring laughter reverberated throughout the shed row. "Wow, you're a little fireball, aren't you?" He unfurled his arms. "Are you always like this? Or is this just for my benefit?"

Rayne's patience with the arrogant man had reached a turning point and she longed for their encounter to end. "Nice meeting you, Trent. I'm sure I'll see you around."

Trent took a step in front of Rayne, blocking her retreat. "Part of my job as riding master is evaluating the skill of the instructors under me. I would like to take a look at you and your horse together in the ring." He patted the horse's thick neck once more, only this time Bob did not seem to mind. "Maybe even watch you take a few jumps with him," he added.

An anxious flutter shook Rayne's hands. "I, um, I'm still doing a lot of flatwork with him. He hasn't really worked on jumps too much yet."

"How do you expect to be ready for the coming show season?"

She lowered her eyes to the stable floor, searching for the words to tell him in a polite way to go to hell.

"Or do you not want to ride for me? Maybe I make you nervous." He leaned toward her. "I'm told I have that effect on people, too."

Her eyes shot to him and the boastful grin that was spreading across his lips made Rayne want to rub his nose in the manure pile behind the barn. She decided to accept his offer, if anything to put him in his place and wipe the cocky smile from his face.

"How does seven tomorrow morning sound? I could meet you in the back jumping ring and show you what I have done with him so far, before my morning class."

His smile fell. "You're sure?"

She tugged on Bob's reins. "Yeah, I'm positive."

"Then I will see you at seven," Trent agreed as his haughty smile returned.

Without another word she turned and led Bob down the shed row to her tack room. Walking along, she could almost feel the aggravating man's eyes boring into her back. Realizing what she had done, she chastised herself for letting Trent Newbury get the better of her.

At her red tack room door, she worked the combination lock as Bob stood calmly behind her, unflustered by any of the events that had just transpired. In a way, Rayne envied her horse's ability to remain placid in the face of certain disaster. That was the bliss of ignorance as she saw it. Bob did not comprehend the danger of crossing paths with the brash Trent Newbury again. But Rayne knew better, and the rush of heat that had overtaken her when the man had first approached worried her immensely. Such feelings were dangerous for any woman.

Her ex-husband had elicited the same reaction when they had first met. He had also been playful and seductive, but as Foster Greer worked his way into her life, her feelings for him had swept her goals and dreams aside. Rayne had sworn after her divorce never to let any man wield that kind of control over her again. Reason enough to stay away from Trent Newbury. But she feared that the advice her head was asserting, her body might not be willing to heed. Swallowing back her self-recriminations, she bolstered those protective walls around her heart. No one was going to get in without a fight, and one thing Rayne had always been was a fighter.

Alexandrea Weis

Chapter 2

The prospect of dealing with Trent had Rayne tossing and turning the entire night. Visions of how the beguiling man would tear her and Bob apart had kept Rayne from getting any sleep. When she finally rose from bed, her body and mind rebelled with exhaustion.

As she saddled Bob for their early morning meeting, a loud, long yawn escaped her lips, making the horse give her a questioning gaze with his soulful brown eyes.

"What? You've never had a restless night?"

Bob turned away as if amused with her explanation.

After checking his girth strap for the fourth time, Rayne figured she had stalled long enough and it was time to head to the jumping ring. Leading Bob from the barn, she mumbled to herself, stiffening her resolve to ignore anything Trent had to say.

"He's an arrogant fool. Just don't listen to a word he says and do exactly what you feel is right."

Bob's ears darted back and forth as he walked beside her, intently listening to her advice.

"We're good and getting better every day no matter what he says, right?" she imparted to Bob, but the horse just clopped along, swishing his long black tail.

Outside in the golden rays of the early morning sun, Rayne mounted Bob's back and secured the strap on her dark gray riding helmet. Tucking her black riding boots into the stirrups, she took up the slack in the leather reins and guided the horse to the shelled-path behind the barn.

As she rode to the jumping ring, she breathed in the hint of fall in the air and felt comforted that the retreating heat of summer meant she could spend more time riding Bob. Rayne turned to the dense line of trees and greenery that marked the edge of the stables and the beginning of the rolling miles of trails. She loved taking in the change of seasons on those wide trails. Escaping on her horse into the breathtaking foliage always invigorated Rayne. But her exuberance was short-lived when she remembered that this was going to be her first fall without Foster.

The image of the attractive older man with thick gray hair, penetrating blue eyes, and a smile that turned every woman's head still filled her with regret. She found it inconceivable that at thirty-one she had been ousted from her comfortable Highland Park mansion by a bony, blonde girl of twenty-two.

"Egotistical, self-important, cheating…." Her ex was forgotten when she spotted Trent leaning against the white railing of the ring. He had his muscular arms folded over his dark blue T-shirt, while his magnetic eyes were zeroed in on her.

She subdued a sudden swirl of nerves by reminding herself that this was just a casual exhibit of skills for a man who was technically her boss. When Bob arrived at the white entrance gate, Trent pushed away from the railing and walked up to the horse.

"Good morning," he greeted, sounding chipper.

His happy mood instantly irked Rayne, who had to stifle yet another yawn.

"I want to start out by doing some basic flatwork, warm him up a bit, and then see how he does over some high jumps. Let's see what he's got." Trent patted the horse's round rump, making Bob turn and give the man a "what was that for" glance.

Rayne glared down at him. "I know what he's got."

Trent's lips lifted into a sheepish smile. "But I don't. I want to see him in action." He pointed to the ring entrance.

"I'm confused," Rayne said, holding Bob back. "Are you here to evaluate me or my horse?"

"Both. You are your horse and he is a reflection of you, and all that you have taught him." He moved toward the gate. "He will give me a good idea of how you work with your students," he added over his shoulder.

"If I had known this was going to be a test...." She gently encouraged Bob forward.

"You would have what...?" He halted at the gate. "Or perhaps you're afraid if I don't like what I see, I'll fire you."

"Rebecca hired me, not you," she lashed out as she entered the ring on Bob.

"And Rebecca's the one who hired me to be the riding master around here...which means if I don't like what I see, I can fire you."

She drew back on the reins, stopping Bob just inside the gate. "Riding master means you supervise, not hire and fire. And why are you being such an ass about this?"

"I'm not the one coming to the ring with a chip on my shoulder. As soon as you rode up, I could tell you were going to give me trouble by the way you slouched in your saddle."

She gawked at him while sitting up in her saddle. "Christ, I haven't even gotten in the ring and you're already evaluating me."

"I'm always evaluating you, bear that in mind." He waved his hand to the ring. "Take him to the rail and start with a slow, sitting trot. Tighten up your legs against the saddle and straighten your back. It will help your seat. You're all over the place in that saddle."

Rayne's hands clenched the reins. "Are you always this…bossy?"

His gray eyes dug into hers. "It's called teaching, not being bossy. I would have thought you knew the difference."

"I didn't come here for a lesson, Trent."

"Well, you're going to get one. Now take to the rail and start getting him to move out. I want to get a look at his gait."

Cursing under her breath, Rayne directed Bob to break into a trot. After making a full circle around the ring, she eyed Trent's reaction. He was nodding his head and carefully evaluating the horse's movements.

"Nice. He's a real pretty mover."

"That's why I wanted him," she replied, feeling a ripple of satisfaction.

"Go to a posting trot," Trent ordered from the center of the ring.

Rayne let the tension in the reins out ever so slightly and squeezed a little harder with her legs. Instantly, Bob understood and quickened his pace. Out of the corner of her eye, Rayne observed Trent, and as she did, she explored the way his T-shirt clung to his wide chest, and the hug of his blue jeans to his hips and thighs. For a brief instant, she pictured him without his clothes, and the distracting concept took her by surprise, making her legs slacken against the saddle. Bob slowed, but she caught her misstep and encouraged him onward. She checked to see if Trent had noticed, but, thankfully, his features remained unchanged.

After twenty minutes of flatwork, with Trent only suggesting some minor changes, Rayne's nerves began to settle.

"That's enough warm up." Trent motioned to the center of the ring, where two white jumps were set up. "Let's put him to work."

Trent went to the first of the fences and placed two red and white-painted bars over each other in the center of the jump, making an "X." When he was done, he stood to the side.

"Take it at a trot."

Rayne guided Bob to the fence, and the horse heartily jumped the crossbars.

"He likes it," Trent expressed behind her.

"He loves to jump," Rayne shouted back.

Trent went to the fence and raised the cups on each side, increasing the height of the jump.

Bob easily barreled over the hurdle, making Rayne smile with pride. She had never admitted it to Trent, but she had taken the horse through his paces over fences in the past, wanting to see how high he could go. Bob's enthusiasm for jumping had been one of the main reasons she had wanted him. In the horse business, if the animal loved to jump, it was a sure sign that he or she would win in the show ring. But blue ribbons had never been Rayne's motivation for wanting Bob. She had seen something in the calm thoroughbred that she had never experienced before; quick intelligence, and a dignified bearing that reminded her more of a person than a horse.

As Trent raised the fence higher, Bob's interest grew. With every jump, Rayne could feel the animal's powerful body push up beneath her, carrying both of them off the ground. That was what Rayne loved about jumping…the coordination between horse and rider, allowing them to come together as one, appearing as if they were floating on air.

"He's impressive," Trent proclaimed after Bob had cleared another high jump.

Rayne guided a sweaty Bob to Trent's side. "The higher you go, the more eager he gets."

Trent patted the horse's frothy neck. "I agree. He seemed to be asleep on the low fences." Trent examined the horse with a new appreciation in his eyes. "I would like to help you get this guy ready for the first show of the season."

"But the first show is at Golden Farms in October," Rayne anxiously asserted. "That's only a month away. You don't think that is too soon?"

Trent shook his head. "Not if you work him hard."

Rayne's hands fidgeted with the reins. "I haven't shown in a very long time. I don't know if I'll be ready."

Trent laughed, smirking up at her. "You'll be ready. You're good, Rayne. You can do it."

"Maybe I don't want to show."

He appeared surprised. "You'd better show. You're an instructor at the stables where I'm riding master. You need to be seen in the show ring. If you look good, then I look good, and we will hopefully get more clients because of that."

A trickle of anger slithered through her. "Fine. I'll try not to disappoint you." She noticed the stainless watch on his wrist. "What time is it?"

"A little past eight," he answered, checking his watch.

Rayne viewed the stables beyond the ring. "I need to get Bob cooled down before my nine o'clock lesson."

"Bob?" Trent's dark eyebrows went up.

She patted her horse's neck. "His name is Bob."

Trent's hearty laughter made her insides hum. "You named your horse 'Bob'?"

"What is it with the name 'Bob'? First, Rebecca gives me crap, now you?" She was about to turn Bob's head away from Trent, but he held on to the reins.

"Don't go away mad, Rayne. I meant nothing by it. But you have to admit, Bob is a funny name for a horse. I hope you come up with a better show name than that." He edged away from Bob's head and up to her. "Perhaps you could let me think of something for you."

Dread coursed through her veins like a formula car on the track at the Indy 500. "Like what? You're not into names like 'Prince something' or 'Chief whatever.' They're so cheesy."

"I promise to give it a great deal of consideration, and it won't be cheesy, I assure you." Trent led Bob to the gate. "Where did you learn to ride?"

Rayne studied the man's muscular back and round butt from atop Bob. "Back in New Orleans at Audubon Stables. It was close to my house. When I was eight, my dad bought my first horse, Jester. He was a tall palomino that was great with kids. I started showing him when I was ten. By the time I was fourteen, I had traded Jasper in for a dark bay jumper named Destiny."

"You ever show in Texas?"

"No, but I did the Louisiana Sugar Circuit. Won two state championships by the time I was seventeen."

He glanced up at her. "Where did you ride in college?"

"Didn't ride in college. I had to give it up."

"Do you mind if I ask why?"

Rayne paused for a moment, considering how much of her past she really needed to share with the man. Then, the slightest crack in her defenses gave way. "My father and younger sister were killed in a car accident during my senior year of high school. My mother kind of lost it, and I sold my horse soon after. We ended up leaving New Orleans and moving in with my grandparents in Dallas."

Trent slowed up, turning to her. "I'm sorry. I had no idea you—"

"Don't worry about it," she interrupted, ignoring the concern in his gray eyes. "It was a long time ago."

He rested his hand on her boot. "How did you get back into riding?"

She gently tapped Bob's sides, uncomfortable with his touch. "My ex, Foster Greer. He wanted me to have a hobby after I gave up my job as a lab technician at his company." She eyed a figure in the distance dressed all in black coming toward them. "He found Southland Stables and asked Rebecca to let me ride her schooling horses. A few weeks later, she let me train the horses she got in from different racetrack rescue organizations. That's how I found Bob. Foster got him as a surprise for me but...." She shrugged. "Later I learned that he had just bought the horse to keep me preoccupied."

"What makes you say that?" Trent questioned, keeping up with the horse.

"About a month after he bought Bob, I found him in bed with someone else."

Trent let go a low whistle. "So that's why you're divorced."

"I didn't see much point to being married after that."

"But you were married to a wealthy man—everyone in Dallas has heard of Greer Laboratories—and still opted for divorce. That's not something you see every day in this town."

Rayne jerked Bob to a sudden stop. "What in the hell is that supposed to mean?"

A woman with sleek black hair pinned back in a long ponytail strutted toward them, her slender hips rolling seductively back and forth.

"I simply meant some women might never have walked away from so much...comfort." Trent's eyes turned to see the woman with the pale skin and stunning features drawing closer. "I've known more than my fair share of women looking for a meal ticket and not a partner."

"Well, get ready," Rayne told him as she quickly dismounted. "Because you're about to meet their union representative."

"Rayne, darling," the woman purred, coming alongside of Bob. "Are you still trying to turn that scrawny creature into something resembling a horse?"

Rayne curbed her anger and just smiled. "What, no hangover this morning, Selene? So glad to see you're up in time to teach your dressage class for a change."

Trent's eyes volleyed back and forth between the two women.

"Not to worry," Selene twittered as she observed Trent's expression. "Rayne and I always tease with each other. It's all in fun." Her black eyes examined Trent with the ferocity of a big cat sizing up its prey. "You must be the new riding master Rebecca talked about." She held out a manicured hand to him. "I'm Selene Kendrick, your dressage instructor."

Trent took her hand and gave it a gentle shake. "Trent Newbury."

"You two seemed very cozy just now." Selene cocked her head seductively to the side and ran her fingers through her silky ponytail.

"Trent was evaluating my abilities," Rayne explained. "Same way he'll be evaluating your technique, Selene."

Selene placed a suggestive hand on Trent's forearm. "Rayne's technique I can understand your needing to evaluate. After all, she is a junior rider; but me...." Her fake laugh pierced the air. "Trent, I assure you I'm as senior a rider as you. Rebecca wanted to give me the position of riding master, but I turned her down."

"Really?" Trent placed his hands behind his back. "Rebecca told me I was the first person she had met who was qualified for the position. Funny, she never mentioned offering it to you."

Selene never let the slight register on her perfectly made-up oval face. "Well, I also only ride dressage, which means I would be of little help to people like Rayne here." She flashed her sharp, little white teeth at Rayne.

Trent's eyes glided over Selene's tight black T-shirt, black riding breeches, and shiny black riding boots. "After your class this morning, perhaps you could give me a demonstration of your technique."

"Me?" Selene's eyebrows rose on her smooth forehead. "Trent, what could you possibly know of dressage? Rebecca told me you're a show jumper."

"Selene, I've shown in numerous three-day event competitions. Was even the Texas State Champion a few years back, so I'm well-versed in every element of dressage." He tipped his head to Rayne. "Rayne impressed me immensely with her riding abilities. I'm hoping for great things from you, as well."

"Perhaps we could get together later in the week." Selene tossed her ponytail about her right shoulder. "When I don't have a class, and I can—"

"You have a class from eight-thirty to nine-thirty." Trent inspected his stainless watch. "I'll meet you here at ten."

"Today?" Selene smiled sweetly, but the irritation shone in her black eyes. "I couldn't possible make it. Teaching a class takes so much out of me."

"Rayne just spent an hour in the ring with me and now has to go and teach two back-to-back children's classes. I don't hear her complaining."

"Rayne's children aren't expert level, like my classes," Selene protested.

Trent gave her a tolerant but unyielding smile. "In that case, how about ten-fifteen? I'll give you an extra fifteen minutes to get ready."

Selene's features drooped, showing her age.

Rayne had never noticed how much older the woman appeared until that moment. She had heard it rumored that Selene was rapidly approaching fifty, but by looking at her lithe figure and smooth face, Rayne assumed the woman was not a day over forty.

"I guess if we need to get this out of the way...." Selene reluctantly nodded her head. "I'll be ready."

"Good," Trent grunted. "Better get to your class." He turned to Rayne. "I'll head back with you to the barn."

They walked away, leaving a red-faced Selene behind. Rayne smugly grinned as Selene sulked to the white gate of the ring they had just left.

"Selene's not used to people telling her what to do. She also never forgets a slight. Be careful with her, Trent."

He gave her a wary side-glance. "That sounds almost as if you care."

"I just don't want to see you get caught up in a power struggle with Selene. She has a way of drawing everyone at the barn into her drama."

"Is that why you two were so hostile with each other back there?"

Rayne shrugged her shoulders while dipping her head to the side. "I knew her way before I started riding at Southland Stables. We frequented the same social circles when I was married to Foster and she was married to Judge Steven Kendrick. We didn't like each other then, either."

"Judge Kendrick?" Trent's eyebrows went up. "*The* Judge Kendrick?"

"Yep. Sits on the appellate court bench and is a real mover and shaker in the Dallas social scene."

"I just can't picture you as part of the trendy Dallas social set," he admitted just as they came to the edge of the barn.

Rayne wheeled around to him as Bob dutifully came to a halt beside her. "I never liked it. Foster was the one who insisted we attend every charity fundraiser and social soiree to help further the interests of his company."

"And what about your interests?"

She was taken aback by the question. "My interests?"

He stepped beneath the shade of the barn. "I have to wonder if you're just another in a long line of single women who ride horses as a way to fill the time in between wealthy husbands. Sort of like Selene." He slowly grinned at her. "I have to admit you have more skill than most of the others I have encountered, but still I—"

"Do you like provoking me? You're a real piece of work, standing there and judging me as if you—"

"I'm glad to see I was right about you," he cut in. "If you were like all the other women I have met in a dozen different stables across Denton County, you wouldn't be angry with me...you would have been defending your lifestyle."

"You've completely lost me. Was all that bullshit some kind of test?"

"In a way." He folded his arms over his chest as his gray eyes studied her. "Most women defend their actions; they don't get mad because they were accused of being a...what's the appropriate term...gold digger?" He paused. "Have dinner with me tonight."

Rayne was stunned by the invitation. "Dinner? After what you just said to me? Are you insane?"

"After what I just said? I paid you a compliment."

"A compliment?" Her voice was peppered with outrage. "My God, you are delusional."

He uncrossed his thick arms and walked over to Bob's side. Lifting the flap on the English saddle, he undid the girth strap and placed it over the seat. "Go and cool your horse down. I'll pick you up at seven tonight and you can rip into me at length over sushi and sake." His eyes veered to her. "You do like sushi, don't you?"

"Yes, I like sushi," Rayne jumped in, shaking her head. "But I'm not having dinner with you."

"Why not? You eat dinner, don't you?"

"I don't want to have dinner with a man who first thinks I'm a gold digger, and then insults me when he discovers I'm not."

"I didn't insult you," he chuckled.

"Yes, you did."

He shook his head, grinning. "Fine...if it makes you feel better, I insulted you. You can give me directions to your house before you leave."

"Did you hear me? I am not having dinner with you!"

He stood over her. "Please?"

"What?" she almost screamed with frustration.

"Please have dinner with me."

She stepped back from him. "Why?"

"Because I will be hungry tonight, and I want to spend some time getting to know you."

She stood for a moment gaping at him, not sure of what to do or say next.

"Is that a yes?" he pestered.

"No, it's not."

"Does that mean you're still thinking about it?"

"I'm not thinking about having dinner with you at all, Trent."

"Then that means yes."

"What is wrong with you?"

"Look, Rayne, you're having dinner with me. I won't take no for an answer."

Rayne knew she should refuse, but a mysterious tingle in her gut told her to accept his invitation. There was just something about the man that…intrigued her. Maybe this was what Rebecca had meant by being "open to new possibilities." She needed to trust her instinct and take a chance. "Okay, I'll have dinner with you, Trent. But only if I can meet you at the restaurant."

"I insist on picking you up. It is the gentlemanly thing to do."

"Gentleman? You?" She refrained from laughing. When that determined fire in his eyes failed to dim, Rayne uttered an exasperated sigh. "Why do you want to have dinner with me?"

He slowly came forward. When he was inches away from her face, he whispered, "I thought that was obvious."

She took in the wrinkles carved around his eyes, his tanned skin, and the thin, almost cruel line of his lips. "Somehow I get the impression nothing is obvious with you."

He patted Bob's neck. "Take care of Bob. We'll talk later."

"Maybe I shouldn't have dinner with you." She clenched the reins in her hand. "You're technically my boss."

His lips stretched into a mischievous grin. "It won't be the first time you've dated your boss, will it?"

Rayne should have been rattled by his comment, but surprisingly she was not. If anything, his sinful smile was eliciting a more confusing emotion that had nothing to do with anger and everything to do with desire. Desperate to get away, Rayne turned and led Bob along the shaded shed row.

"Rayne," Trent spoke out.

She showed him her profile.

"Just so you know, I never once suspected you were like Selene. From the moment I met you, I knew you were different."

"Different? You have no idea." She started back down the aisle with Bob, wondering, *What have I gotten myself into?*

But as Rayne came to her red tack room door, her apprehension gave way to excitement…something she had not felt since Foster Greer had first invited her to have coffee. But Rayne was no longer a twenty-three-year-old girl enamored with a much older man. Her painful past had made her wiser in the wicked ways of men, and Trent Newbury was one man she knew could never be trusted.

Alexandrea Weis

Chapter 3

Checking her baggy gray slacks and loose-fitting pale blue top in her bathroom mirror, Rayne groaned out loud.

"I look like a hooker." She ran her fingers through her unruly, honey-blonde hair. "God, I hate my hair."

Leaving her frizzy hair curled about her shoulders, she applied an extra coating of black mascara and black eyeliner to make the flecks of gold in her hazel eyes stand out. But on viewing her reflection, she worried the warm blush and lava red lipstick she had selected contrasted sharply against her creamy skin. Reaching for a tissue on her vanity counter, she tried to blot away the extra makeup from her eyelids, lips, and cheeks. When she reappraised her appearance, she flinched.

"Great, now I look like a hooker on crack."

The chime from her doorbell cut through the air.

Grabbing the lava red lipstick, she hurriedly reapplied it to her full lips, and swept the warm blush back on to her cheeks. By the time she bolted from her master bathroom and into her light gray bedroom, a flurry of barking resonated from the living room.

"Frank!" she yelled, scrambling down a short hallway toward her living room.

Sprinting across the burgundy carpet on her living room floor and past the stone and birch fireplace that rose all the way up to the ceiling, she reached the beige and white entryway that led to her front door. Nearly tripping over a large, dark brown mound of fur lying right in front of the door, Rayne silently cursed as she grasped the fancy brass doorknob she had installed with the help of a kind Home Depot associate.

"Hi," she greeted, catching her breath after she opened the door.

The scent of Trent's citrusy cologne teased her nostrils. His gray eyes shimmered beneath the porch light as they glided up and down her trim figure, taking in the curve of her gray slacks and the swell of her breasts beneath her silk top.

"Is that what you're wearing?"

Her throat tightened. "What's wrong with it?"

"You look like you're trying to hide behind it." He took the two short steps into the doorway and stood beside her. "Maybe you should change into something that makes you look less…terrified."

She cleared her throat and stepped back from the door. "Do you usually criticize a woman's outfit?"

"I wasn't criticizing. I was commenting." He spied the dark brown furry dog sitting up by the door. The animal's thick tail was beating rhythmically on the white-tiled floor. "Who's that?" Trent pointed to the dog.

Rayne waved at the panting creature. "Frank."

"Frank?" Trent arched an eyebrow at her. "A horse named Bob and a dog named Frank. What is it with you and names?"

"I like simple names," Rayne professed, shutting the door.

Trent held out his hand to the dog, testing if he was safe to pet, and then gently stroked behind his fluffy ears. "What kind of mix is he?"

"Great Pyrenees and chocolate lab, I think. I got him at the pound when I bought my house last year. I'd hoped for a guard dog, but instead I got a big cuddle ball." She was enchanted at the way Trent and her "guard dog" were getting along.

Leaving Frank, he turned to living room beyond the entryway. "Why don't you go and change into something else?"

"You really don't like my outfit?" She winced, thinking she sounded like an insecure teenager.

"I love your outfit, but you don't. I could tell when I walked in the door you weren't happy with it. Perhaps try something you're comfortable in."

"I don't think I can wear sweats to the restaurant."

His harmonic laugh bounced about the walls of the short hallway, stirring the disquiet in Rayne's belly. "No, but maybe some jeans; I have a feeling you would be much more comfortable in that."

She motioned to his black slacks and white button-down shirt. "But you're not in jeans."

"But I'm comfortable." He waved into the living room. "Go on."

She was about to walk past him when she murmured, "I don't think I'll ever be comfortable with you."

Trent rested his hand on her forearm. "I'm hoping to change that. I think you're the kind of woman who needs to be gentled into a man."

The close proximity of him made her knees wobble. "Gentled into a man? You make me sound like an unbroken horse." Rayne struggled to focus on his words and not his lips.

"Not unbroken, just...skittish." He let go of her arm, making her momentarily waver on her feet.

Trent proceeded into the open living room and perused the white leather sofa and matching armchairs before the grand hearth, then he raised his eyes to the assorted framed travel posters Rayne had purchased to cover her eggshell-painted walls.

As he assessed her home, Rayne scrutinized his sharp profile; the way his slightly crooked nose sloped down to his lips, and how his square jaw accentuated the hint of authority in his features. Even the curl of his long black lashes fascinated her, and when Rayne caught herself staring, she swerved her eyes to her bedroom hallway.

"I'll just...ah, go and change."

"Frank and I will be waiting," Trent assured her.

After darting into her bedroom, Rayne began pulling off her clothes while her heart flitted about in her chest. When she went to the bathroom mirror to do a quick check of her makeup, she was appalled to see her beet red face staring back at her.

"I must be crazy for doing this." She clapped her hands over her cheeks. "This guy is so...what is the word?" As Rayne tried to find the words to describe Trent, she knew one thing was for certain; he was unlike any man she had been with, including Foster.

Her ex-husband had been attentive in the beginning and always generous with his wealth, but he had never been...intense. That was the word she felt that best described Trent. He had an unusual intensity that made her feel as if she were being constantly analyzed.

Shaking off her misgivings, Rayne opened her compact powder and began blotting out the redness on her face. Once satisfied with her reflection, she went into her bedroom and shimmied into her favorite blue jeans and buttoned up the creamy pink dress shirt she had always loved. Finishing her outfit off with a pair of dark leather pumps, she took in a relieved breath. Trent had been right; she did feel better. Grabbing a leather clutch that matched the color of her low-heeled shoes, Rayne confidently strode to the door.

"All right, Mr. Newbury, now I'm ready to take you on."

***

Mt. Fuji Restaurant was not far from Rayne's Highland Village home. A few customers were sitting in the black vinyl booths that packed the dining area, enjoying the variety of Asian fusion and hibachi dishes. Bright neon lights of blue, pink, and gold complemented the Mexican tile covering the walls. In the center of the restaurant, a flaming hibachi infused a fantastical flare to the eclectic atmosphere.

"Intriguing décor," Rayne commented as she slid into a booth in the corner of the restaurant.

"Unusual for a Japanese restaurant, but the food is good." Trent took a seat on the bench across the table from her.

An almond-eyed waitress, with sleek black hair hanging loosely down her slender back, came up to their table carrying two clear vinyl menus. With a slight bow, she placed the menus on the table.

"I'll be back to take your order." She turned her eyes to Rayne. "Would you like a cocktail?"

"Hana Raspberry Sake," Trent told her. "For two." He smiled at Rayne. "I hope you like sake?"

"In small amounts."

Trent returned to the waiflike waitress. "We'll have that to start. Then, two glasses of your sauvignon blanc with our meal."

"Very good." She bowed once more, backed away from the table, and then scurried to a silver kitchen door across the room.

Trent snapped up his menu. "May I make a recommendation?"

Rayne placed her hand over her menu, which was still on the table, and nodded.

"The eel and avocado sushi roll is excellent here."

"Eel?" Rayne grimaced. "You eat eel?"

He smirked at her distaste. "Then no eel. How do you feel about salmon?"

"More palatable than eel, definitely."

"All right, a salmon and avocado roll to start, and then shrimp tempura for the main course. How does that sound?"

Rayne could not help but smile as she eyed the handsome face of the man sitting across from her. It had been a long time since she had been made to feel special in the presence of a member of the opposite sex. It was the little things that had delighted her so far. Opening the door of his 550i BMW for her, taking her elbow as they entered the restaurant, and even locking her front door had all been touches that had thrilled her.

"When Rebecca first told me about you, she indicated that you were her best instructor." Trent sat back in his seat, putting his menu to the side. "I'm glad to see she wasn't exaggerating."

She ran her fingers over the walnut-stained table between them. "How would you know what kind of instructor I am? You haven't seen me teach a class yet."

"I, ah, hate to admit it, but I sneaked a peak at your first class this morning."

"But how?" Rayne furrowed her brow. "I never saw you, and there aren't a lot of places to hide in the front ring."

"No, but there were some parents watching, and I kind of blended in with them."

Annoyed, Rayne folded her arms over her chest. "You blended in, or eavesdropped?"

"Both," he admitted with a slight nod. "The best way to find out what kind of instructor you are is to listen to the parents of those you teach. If they are happy with you, then their kids are happy with you."

She could not decide if she should be enraged or inspired by his method.

"All the parents there gave you glowing recommendations. They all agreed that you were firm, patient, encouraging, and had a way with children."

Rayne shook her head. "I know I should be mad at you for pulling such a stunt, but somehow I'm relieved, like I passed some kind of test."

"Who said you passed?"

She stared at him, trying to decipher exactly what was going on behind his captivating gray eyes. "Well, I assume if I had not passed, we wouldn't be here, having dinner together."

"Why we are having dinner together has nothing to do with your skill as a riding instructor. I want to get to know you outside of the stables, but that doesn't mean I won't ride your ass if you're screwing up with your students."

She smirked at him. "Gee, and I was just beginning to like you, Mr. Newbury."

His rumbling chuckle made a few of the other diners look their way.

Bothered by the extra attention, Rayne leaned in closer to the table. "Why are we having dinner together? I thought this was about the stables."

"Really? And I thought my intentions for you were pretty obvious."

Her face fell and she shifted uneasily on her bench.

Trent rested his arms on the table, intently observing her. "Why do you always look so scared as soon as I even hint at any intimacy between us?"

Rayne's eyes flew to his and she pushed down the rise of panic in her throat. "I wish you wouldn't use that word."

"What word?"

"Intimacy. It sounds so…personal."

He broke out in a fit of loud laughter, making Rayne squirm even more.

"Are you always this uncomfortable with men?" Trent probed after his laughter had abated. "You act like you've never been with a man."

"I've been with a man," she obstinately defended. "I just don't like…discussing such things."

"By 'things' do you mean sex?" His grin widened.

Rayne ran her hands up and down her bare arms, remaining quiet.

Trent paused, taking in her obvious discomfort. "Rayne, I want to ask you something, and I don't want you to get offended or upset, all right?"

She hesitated, leery about his intentions. "What is it?"

"What was your marriage like?"

"My marriage?"

"Yes." His eyes stayed locked on her. "How was it? How did Foster treat you?"

She sighed as she mulled over the question. "Okay, I guess. I mean, Foster worked a great deal, and when we did have time together it was usually attending those parties or benefits I told you about. In the beginning, I was kind of disappointed there wasn't more time for us; after a while, I began to enjoy my time apart from him."

"Why did you enjoy your time apart?"

She placed her hands on the table. "After the first three years, Foster changed. Nothing big, but it was the little things I began to notice. We didn't talk as much, he spent more time at home on the phone or watching television, and was always distracted with business. He still bought me anything I wanted, but the personal attention was less. Does that make any sense?"

Trent eased back on his bench. "And the sex?"

Rayne was dumbfounded by the question. Her eyes darted about the restaurant as she tried to come up with some kind of answer.

"Was the sex the same or worse?" he pressed.

"I...I really don't think that is something...I hardly know you and I—"

"Was it better or worse? That's all you have to say, Rayne. Usually when a marriage begins to fall apart, the sex is the first thing to go."

"And how would you know that? Rebecca told me you've never been married." Instantly regretting her words, Rayne closed her eyes as her dread rose.

"That you were discussing my marital status with Rebecca gives me hope that beneath that cool exterior, there is a part of you that finds me attractive."

Rayne opened her mouth to say something when their diminutive server returned to the table carrying a black tray with two flat white cups, and a blue and white ceramic flask.

"Your raspberry sake." The dark-eyed woman slid the tray onto the table. "Shall I serve?"

Trent smiled warmly for her. "I will do it, thank you."

"Are you ready to order?"

He gave the shy woman their dinner order, and after she had made a few notes on a small pad, she backed away from the table.

Trent scooped up the flask of sake. "You get very emotional when you talk about sex, did you know that?"

"I don't get…why are we even discussing this? It's none of your business how or why my marriage ended, and what happened between me and Foster in the privacy of our bedroom is…over."

Trent carefully poured a cup of the pink-colored sake. "So was Foster your first lover?" He put the cup in front of her.

"Jesus!" Rayne almost shouted. Taking in the other patrons, she dropped her voice and added, "What is it with you?"

Trent frowned, appearing perplexed as he filled the other cup with sake. "I'm just trying to understand what happened to your marriage."

"How can you sit there and pass judgment on me when you've never been married?"

He put the flask down on the table with a thud. "That's the second time you've made a comment about me passing judgment on you. Is that what you think I'm doing?" He raised the cup of sake to his lips. "I'm simply trying to find out what makes you tick, Rayne." He took a sip of his drink. "So why did you ask Rebecca about me?"

Completely befuddled, she seized her drink. "I didn't ask anything. She volunteered the information and wanted to know what…." At a loss for words, Rayne hastily took a drink of the sake. The strong alcohol burned her mouth and she tried desperately not to choke.

He put his cup down on the table. "Is that why you came to watch me with my class yesterday?"

She gulped down the sake, wishing she had spit it out instead. While her eyes watered and her stomach lurched, Rayne fought to keep any hint of her discomfort from Trent.

"I...ah." She swallowed hard again as she set her cup on the table. "I wanted to see you in action. I was curious."

Trent tapped his finger against his white, saucer-like cup. "And what did you think?"

She sucked in a breath, hoping to alleviate the horrid aftertaste the sake had left in her mouth. "You were...very good."

"Nothing else?"

Rayne shifted in her seat. "What else were you expecting?"

"Forget it." He shook his head. "Are you always this nervous on a date?"

"Is this a date or an inquisition?" she snapped.

Studying her, he stroked the rim of his sake cup with his long finger. "All right. Why don't you ask me some questions?"

Rayne's hand shook as she picked up her sake, deliberating on how to pose the one question that had been eating away at her.

"Why haven't you ever married?" she eventually got out, and then took a small sip from her cup, relieved to discover that the sake tasted better the second time around.

"It's not for lack of trying, I assure you. I've lived with two women; the last one moved out about a year ago. We had talked about marriage, but...." He pushed his sake cup away. "Don't get me wrong, I want to get married, but I've had a hard time finding the right woman."

She deposited her cup on the table. "Who's to say if any of us ever meets the right person? Maybe it's more about finding someone who fills a void, or fulfills a need." The welcomed warmth of the alcohol began to flow through her system.

"What kind of void did Foster fill for you?"

Easing back in her seat, she recalled the first time she had met Foster Greer. "He made me feel…happy. Like I was part of something important, kind of like a family." She rubbed her hands along the thighs of her jeans. "When my father and sister died, I lost that sense of family."

"What about your mother? Is she still alive?"

Rayne cringed. "Yeah, Estelle is still with me."

"You almost look like that is a bad thing."

"If you knew my mother, you would understand." Wanting to gloss over the topic of her mother, she quickly asked, "What about your family?"

"We're kind of spread out all over the place." He shrugged his wide shoulders. "My father passed away a few years ago. He was an analyst for a big insurance company in Dallas. My mother relocated to Florida after he died to be with her sister. I have two younger sisters. They're both married; one lives in Tennessee, the other in Dallas. We get together around the holidays."

She settled her elbows on the table, transfixed by the warmth in his eyes as he spoke of his family. "Any nieces or nephews?"

"Two nieces and one very spoiled nephew named Cohen. He's just like my old man, driven as hell. You name it, he becomes perfect at it."

"Any of them want to ride horses like their uncle?"

"My niece, Heather, rode for a while in Tennessee, but then she discovered ballet. Cohen doesn't like horses. I think he prefers sports that involve hitting or kicking the hell out of your opponent."

The alcohol helped to quell Rayne's jittery nerves. Leaning toward Trent, she fondled her cup of sake. "How did you get into riding?"

"Summer camp, when I was seven," he answered, watching her fingers play with her cup. "They took us to this stable outside of Dallas every day to ride horses. I fell in love with it and begged my father for lessons, but he believed it wasn't manly enough. My mother eventually won him over. The first state championship I won, he finally agreed that it was a tough sport."

"When Rebecca first talked about you, I guessed you were gay."

"I get that a lot." His gray eyes flickered with merriment. "But most women eventually figure it out."

As his eyes swept over the contours of her face, her feet fidgeted underneath the table and Rayne yearned for another sip of sake to calm her, but then decided against it.

"How did you get into riding?" Trent inquired.

"I was—"

"Here is your salmon and avocado roll," their bashful server cut in as she stood next to their table, balancing a wide black tray.

The petite woman set plates, chopsticks, silverware, and dipping bowls of soy sauce and wasabi on their table. Finally, she put a plate of seaweed-wrapped rolls in the center. Then, she lifted the jug of sake. "Would you like more sake?"

Trent gestured to Rayne. "Do you want more sake?"

Rayne held up her hand. "No, thank you. But could I have a glass of water?"

"Of course," the dark-eyed waitress replied, and then scampered away.

"Sake not to your liking?" Trent reached for the small bowl of wasabi.

Rayne split her chopsticks apart. "Just trying to keep my wits about me."

"Why? Think I'll try something later?"

"No," she lied, avoiding his leering gaze. "I just don't like to drink that much."

"No, you just don't like to lose control." Collecting the plate of rolls from the table, he pushed a few onto her plate with his chopsticks. "I don't think you like to let anyone see the real you."

She stabbed at one of her rolls with her chopsticks. "This is the real me."

"No, it's not." He scooted two rolls onto his plate. "You keep people at a distance, but I'm hoping I can break you of that habit."

"I'm not a horse, Trent. I don't need to be broken or gentled or anything else." She dropped the seaweed-covered roll back on her plate, her appetite suddenly usurped by her aggravation.

"On the contrary," Trent argued. "People are very much like horses, and horses are very much like people." He pointed a chopstick at her. "You remind me of the mare I just sold. She was always guarded, hesitant of every new adventure, and resisted me at every turn. If I rode her too hard, I would frighten her, and if I was too gentle, I would lose her interest. Took me a while, but I won her over." He angled closer to her. "And I plan on doing the exact same thing with you."

Rayne grabbed for her sake, needing the alcohol to squash the lust pulsing through her. Unexpected images of Trent's muscular body riding her naked from behind kept popping into her head.

"You all right?" Trent queried, cutting into her fantasies. "You look flushed." He plucked the cup of sake from her hand. "I think you've had enough of this."

Rayne poked at the sushi rolls on her plate with her chopstick. What was happening to her? It was as if her best intentions were being usurped by an intense carnal desire, the likes of which she had never experienced. Rayne just hoped that when their evening ended her disturbing feelings would go away. But in the back of her mind she wondered if that was possible. As long as Trent Newbury was in her life, Rayne had a sneaking suspicion that her lust for the man would continue to haunt her, and could make the coming days and weeks at the stables very…uncomfortable.

Chapter 4

After dinner, Trent drove Rayne home, keeping the conversation focused on her riding, Bob, and her students. Rayne had been thankful for the reprieve from his previous line of questioning. But when they strolled down the dimly lit walkway toward the white door of her red-bricked bungalow, Rayne's anxiety returned.

Pretending to fumble for the keys in her purse, her mind flew through a plethora of excuses to avoid letting Trent inside.

"Give me your keys," he directed as they climbed the three bricked steps to her front porch. "I'll get your door."

Unable to come up with a reasonable reason not to, Rayne handed over her keys. After he had opened her door, he waited for her to go inside.

Rayne stood in her entryway, hoping he would give her back her keys and insist he should be on his way. But instead of handing her the keys, he shut her front door and walked through to the open living room. Rayne sighed as she placed her purse on a round, intricately carved wooden table to the side of the entryway.

"Where's Frank?" he called from the living room.

Rayne stepped through the arched living room entrance and motioned to a hallway to her right. "Probably in my bed. He sleeps with me at night."

Trent turned to her, but said nothing. He didn't have to…his intentions were written over every inch of his devious smile. He tossed the keys in his hand to her kidney-shaped glass coffee table.

Eager to find something else to do, Rayne went to her kitchen. Stepping behind the beige granite breakfast counter that divided the living room from the kitchen, she dashed to an oak cabinet above the sink and stretched for two old-fashioned glasses.

"Do you want something to drink?"

"No." Trent came up behind her. "I'm not thirsty."

Rayne replaced one of the glasses in the cabinet. "Well, after all that soy sauce with dinner, I sure am. Didn't know that—"

Trent pried the glass from her hand and put it on the countertop. "You're not thirsty, Rayne."

When she faced him, he slipped one arm around her and tilted closer until her lips were inches from his.

"This isn't a good idea, Trent. You and I have to work together, and if…." Her resistance was fading along with her voice.

"I really don't give a damn about our working together at this very moment." He slid his other arm behind her. "And neither do you."

"You're wrong about that." She trembled, afraid of what was about to happen. "I do care."

But the intoxicating aroma of him, the heat of his skin, and the liquid color of his eyes quickly snuffed out any defiance Rayne had left in her.

"Why are you shaking? I'm not going to hurt you."

"It's just been so long...I'm not very good at this."

"Do you want me to stop, Rayne?"

She bobbed her head.

His lips veered closer. "I don't believe you."

She was about to open her mouth and protest when he kissed her. The instant his lips touched hers, she wanted to push him away and retreat to her bedroom, but then something happened. Rayne began to return his kiss. She ran her hands up his back, and as she crushed her breasts to his chest, her lips parted.

His kisses were electric, eliciting feelings she had never known. She felt as if she was on a roller coaster, terrified and thrilled all at once. The air grew thin, her heart raced, and her legs felt weak. Then, a powerful longing shot up from somewhere deep inside her. It was like a sudden wave of pure desire creeping into every facet of her being. Foster had never done this to her. No man had.

He broke away, breathing heavily against her cheek. "Christ, you feel good."

Rayne struggled to stay upright. "Ah, you don't feel so bad yourself." She tried to back out of his arms but was blocked by the kitchen counter.

Trent ran his finger along the outline of her jaw. "You're adorable." He took her hand and led her from the kitchen.

Her heart thudded as he walked into the living room. When he spied the hallway that led to her bedroom, Rayne trembled once more. Trent must have sensed her fear, because instead of leading her to the bedroom, he guided her toward the front door.

In her entryway, he let go of her hand. "I'd better get out of here before I do something...stupid." He took a breath while contemplating her eyes. "I'll be busy with a job in Dallas all week, but I will see you next Saturday at the stables.

Saturday night you can come over to my house, and I'll cook you dinner."

Rayne nodded in agreement.

"Do you like Italian?"

She nodded again.

He wrapped an arm about her waist. "Get some sleep."

When he kissed her again, Rayne felt that overwhelming yearning rising up once more. But before she could respond, Trent withdrew, putting his hand on her fancy brass doorknob.

"Good night, Rayne." He gave her one last smile, stepped outside, and then quietly shut her door.

Rayne stood in her beige and white entryway and touched her fingers to her lips. "Damn."

Still reliving his kiss, she went about the house, locking doors and turning out the lights. By the time she entered her bedroom, Rayne was fretting about their next meeting. When she saw him again, how should she act, what would she say?

"Stop acting like a sixteen-year-old girl," she loudly chided, making a brown, furry face look up at her from the bed. Frank was lying sprawled out over her gray and white comforter on her queen-sized brass bed.

"What do you think I should do? See him again, or nip this in the bud now?"

Frank plopped his head back down on the bed and closed his eyes.

"Yeah, I feel the same way."

Walking into her bathroom, Rayne determined that it would be in her best interest to call the whole thing off with Trent before it interfered with her life at the stables. She could not afford to have her students, along with Selene, whispering behind her back. And when the relationship ended—Rayne was thoroughly convinced that it would—she would be left embarrassed and insecure at the one place she had considered a sanctuary.

"Next weekend, I'll talk to him." She stood before her beige vanity, plotting her strategy. "I'll very calmly explain that we can't be more than friends. It isn't professional. It isn't wise, and it certainly isn't healthy, at least not for me."

But you know you want to see him again. That kiss....

Rayne shook off the notion. "No, this is for the best. I'm better off without a man." And then her body slouched against the beige countertop. "Damn it, who am I kidding? That was the best kiss ever."

***

The next morning, Rayne rose from her bed feeling more confident that she could push Trent Newbury away. Sure it had been a great kiss, but she was convinced that it was just a kiss and not the basis for a relationship.

"He's just not worth the bother," she told her reflection in the mirror as she applied her makeup for work.

In the kitchen, she was enjoying a few moments with her morning cup of coffee as Frank ate his breakfast when a jazzy ringtone blared from the entranceway. She hurried to her purse on the table by the front door and retrieved her cell phone.

"Hello?"

"Did you sleep well?"

Rayne came to a standstill in her entryway when she heard that seductive voice. "Trent? How did you get my number?"

"From Rebecca. I always keep the phone numbers of all my instructors on file."

"Oh, ah...I...," she stumbled. "Yes, I did sleep well. How did you sleep?"

"I didn't," he sighed into the phone. "I kept thinking about you."

Shaking her head, she shot back, "Please, you expect me to buy that line?"

"You're cranky in the morning." His exuberant chuckle rolled around inside the hollows of her heart. "Admit it. You spent the night thinking about me."

She walked back to her kitchen. "You would love to hear me say that, wouldn't you?"

"You think about me, Rayne, but you'll never admit it to me. I have at least learned that much about you."

"Yeah, well, there's a lot you don't know about me, Trent."

"Yes, but I am willing to dedicate hours of study, going over every detail of you."

"That sounds dangerous," she admitted with a twinge of alarm in her voice.

"Having doubts about us already?"

Swiping her coffee from the kitchen countertop, she grumbled, "One kiss hardly makes an 'us.'"

"Hell of a kiss though."

Rayne racked her mind looking for a cute comeback, but came up blank.

"I'll take your silence to mean I was right about the kiss," Trent smugly returned. "Don't be so fast to look for excuses to get rid of me, Rayne. You haven't tried my spaghetti sauce yet."

She stared into her black coffee as her reservations about Trent intensified. "I think this is a mistake. We have to work together at the stables and there might be a lot—"

"I had a hunch that you would be talking yourself out of seeing me again. That's why I called."

"Well, now you know how I really feel about this…situation."

"That's not what your kiss told me last night."

Rayne's grip tightened on her iPhone when she thought of his kiss.

"You have a good day, Rayne. I'll call again." He hung up before she could get in a smart reply.

"Damn it!" She tossed her cell phone to the kitchen counter. "Just when I had put him out of my mind, he calls and it starts all over again."

Fed up, she dumped her mug of lukewarm coffee in the sink, grabbed her cell phone and dark blue backpack from the kitchen counter, then trudged to the back door.

The best way to get her mind off the man was by spending a long day at work. Being buried beneath a pile of pending blood samples and running a flurry of tests was the best medicine she knew to forget about that goddamned kiss.

***

The square gray office building of Reynolds Medicine Group was home to four internal medicine physicians and two nurse practitioners who cared for patients with a host of conditions.

Rayne parked her gunmetal gray Toyota Highlander in her usual spot by the corner of the lot, next to a wide oak tree that provided enough shade to keep her car cool beneath the hot Texas sun. Glancing down the street to the sprawling Medical Center of Lewisville, Rayne was glad she had stayed out of the hospital setting when she returned to work after her divorce. It was hectic enough being pulled in every direction in a busy clinic, but the demands of a big hospital would have been too stressful for her. She liked being the only lab technician for Reynolds Medicine Group; in fact, she preferred working alone. For Rayne, people were difficult; horses were easy.

While rushing toward the glass entrance with her backpack slung over her shoulder, Rayne found it odd how she could recall the name of every horse she had ever ridden for Rebecca, but could not remember any of the individuals she had worked side-by-side with at Greer Laboratories.

"Hey, Rayne." A heavyset secretary whose name always eluded Rayne waved from the front desk as she hurried through the pastel blue reception area.

Walking past the double doors that led to the patient exam rooms, Rayne made her way to the end of a narrow white corridor. The last door on the right had a large red sign with Employees Only in bold red letters. She eased the door open and stepped inside.

"There she is, right on time as usual," an attractive blonde greeted from a round table in the middle of the employee break room. She was wearing white scrubs with pink teddy bears embossed on her top. Her wavy blonde hair was mashed into a messy ponytail, and her delicate, almost childlike features were scrunched into a condescending scowl. In her hands was a paperback book with a bare-chested man on the cover holding a scantily clad woman in his arms.

"Hey, Lindsey. Which one is that?" Rayne went to a short refrigerator set into a wall of white cabinets.

"*Bound By Love.*" Lindsey held up the book. "Sex and a whole lot more by my favorite author, Monique Delome."

"You and your romance books." Rayne's eyes scanned a wall covered with mandatory employee posters from OSHA touting the benefits of washing hands, proper techniques for the disposal of blood products, and a few other regulations that everyone usually ignored.

"Hey, don't knock romance books." Lindsey flourished the book in her hand. "The only sex I get is in these books." She flipped the book down on the faux wood table. "See what ten years of marriage has driven me to?"

Rayne placed her backpack on the white Formica countertop next to the refrigerator and unzipped the top. "You're lucky to have Casey. He's a great guy."

"I know." Lindsey picked up the mug of coffee on the table before her. "But I would be happy to rent him out to you for a nominal fee."

Rayne chuckled and placed her brown bag lunch inside the refrigerator. She then went to a desktop computer in the corner and typed in her employee ID code.

"What did you do this weekend?" Lindsey inquired. "No, wait. Let me guess. You rode that horse of yours."

After Rayne finished clocking in, she turned back to the waiflike blonde with the alluring blue eyes. "I also taught my lessons."

"Wow." Lindsey plunked her coffee mug down on the table. "Rayne, I love you to death, you know that, but you have got to start having some fun."

Rayne stepped over to the coffeemaker set up on a silver cart next to the computer. "I have fun. I ride."

"You know what I'm talking about. The kind of fun you have with a member of the opposite sex of our species."

Rayne snatched up white mug from the cart. "What is it with everyone wanting to set me up? First, Rebecca at the barn wanted to hook me up with the new riding master, and now you—"

"What new riding master?" Lindsey interrupted.

Rayne filled her mug with coffee. "His name is Trent Newbury, and Rebecca hired him to oversee all the instructors at the stables."

"Cute?"

Rayne glowered at her friend. "Obnoxious."

Lindsey sat back in her green plastic chair, dissecting Rayne's expression. "You like this guy. You wouldn't have noticed if he was obnoxious or even a serial killer if you weren't interested."

Rayne glanced down at her black coffee. "Actually, we had dinner last night. That's how I know he's obnoxious."

Lindsey jumped from her chair. "You had dinner with him?" She went to Rayne's side and nudged her back to the table. "Sit." She pulled out a green chair for her. "I want details."

"There are no details to tell." Rayne sat down and put her coffee on the table. "We went to dinner at this sushi place. He wanted to order eel, can you believe that? So we had this—"

"Rayne, I could care less about what you ate. What happened on the date? Did he kiss you, or was there more to it than that? Please tell me there was more to it."

"Lindsey, you've been reading way too many romance novels. It was nothing like what you're implying. This was a dinner to talk about…the stables, you know, business." A warm flush cascaded through Rayne as she remember Trent's kiss.

"Bullshit!" Lindsey pointed at Rayne's face. "You're red, and you only get red when you're really embarrassed about something. And knowing you, the only thing that would get you that way is sex. So spill it. What happened?"

Rayne fingered the rim of her mug, wanting desperately to keep what happened with Trent private, but then again also needing a friend to help sort out her tangle of emotions.

"Lindsey, how much…I mean, have you ever…?" She struggled to find the right words.

Lindsey waited patiently with her arms folded over her chest, tapping her white tennis shoe on the dull gray linoleum floor.

"Aw, hell...he kissed me," Rayne finally blurted out. "There, satisfied?"

Lindsey tossed up her hand. "That's it?"

Rayne raised her coffee. "Trust me, it was enough."

Lindsey was quiet for several agonizing seconds. Rayne was about to explode with curiosity when she finally spoke up.

"What kind of kiss?"

"Kind of kiss?" Rayne lowered her mug, not comprehending the question. "It was a kiss, Lindsey."

"There are all kinds of kisses, Rayne. Friendly, passionate, family kisses, and then there are—"

"It was passionate, all right?" Rayne flopped back in her seat

One side of Lindsey's tiny pink mouth rose ever so slightly. "That good, huh?"

Rayne slowly nodded her head. "I've never been kissed like that. Even after eight years of marriage, I—"

"Foster Greer was a selfish old man more interested in having a trophy wife than keeping you happy," Lindsey cut in.

"But I don't think Trent can make me happy, either, Lindsey. He's technically my boss at the stables."

"Stop," Lindsey cried out, raising her hand. "You're making excuses like you always do when you're afraid."

"I'm not afraid," Rayne balked.

Lindsey looked her friend over, sporting a dubious frown. "Rayne, by the expression on your face, you're terrified that this guy could be someone special."

"He's not special. He's just like all the rest," Rayne protested with a smirk.

"What did his kiss tell you?" Lindsey had a seat next to her at the table. "You can tell a lot about a man from a kiss; his intentions, his desires, and his sincerity. If he really wants you — and I'm not talking about sex — if he wants all of you, you can tell by his kiss. That's how I knew my Casey was the one for me."

Rayne mulled over her words. "His kiss was…it really took me by surprise. It was so…intense." Rayne shook her head. "Everything about the guy is intense."

Lindsey sat back in her chair, grinning. "Then you need to pursue this."

"I think that is a mistake."

"So what? Hell of a fun way to make a mistake if you ask me." Retrieving her book, Lindsey shrugged. "Besides, there are no mistakes in dating. Every man you're with teaches you more about what you want and don't want in a guy."

"I'd hoped I was done with dating after I married Foster."

"Get to know the man, Rayne." Lindsey closed her book, tucking it under her arm. "You're too pretty and too smart to be alone." She stood from her chair and collected her coffee mug. "Time for me to get out there and tackle Dr. Moffet's bad breath."

"Didn't you buy him a jar of breath mints?" Rayne wrapped her hands about her white mug.

"I did." Lindsey left her mug in the sink. "But instead of using them, he gave them to the secretaries in reception."

"Why not just tell him he has bad breath?"

"You know how old man Moffett is…I have to be careful so I keep my job." Lindsey went to the break room entrance. "I'll never find another nursing job that pays as well as this one." She opened the door. "Keep me posted on the guy from your barn. You know how much I love a juicy romance." She winked at Rayne and then darted into the hall.

Rayne took two quick sips of her coffee, eager to feel the rush of caffeine. As the warm liquid eased down her throat, she recalled Trent's conversation over the phone with her earlier that morning. Perhaps Lindsey was right; she needed to give the assertive man a chance. She peered into her black coffee and the same old trepidation about the opposite sex returned to her gut. She had never been an avid dater before her husband, and after the pain of her divorce, her dating nerves were shot. But now another opportunity for happiness was before her, and Rayne only prayed she could muster the courage to put the past behind her and try again with the charismatic riding master.

Chapter 5

A warm evening breeze greeted Rayne as she stepped from her garage and progressed across the short stone-covered path to her back door. The blue jeans she had changed into after work reeked of Bob. Her black riding boots were dusty, and her frizzy blonde hair was matted down by the riding helmet she had worn while working Bob over some fences.

As she fumbled with the lock on her back door, her cell phone ringtone sounded. Quickly opening the door, she rummaged through the work clothes in her backpack for her phone. While punching the alarm code into her keypad just inside her back door, Frank came trotting up to her. Barking with exuberance at her return, she was trying to calm him down when she answered the call from an unknown number.

"Hello?"

"Where are you?" a smooth voice demanded.

She sighed as she heard his velvety tone. "Hi, Trent." She turned to Frank. "Hush up."

"Was that my friend, Frank, barking?"

"Yeah, he gets excited when I get home." She patted Frank's head.

"You're just getting home from work? It's almost seven, Rayne."

"I went to the stables after work to exercise Bob. Why are you calling me?" She shut her back door.

"I just wanted to make sure you got home safely."

"I'm fine." She set the deadbolt on her door. "Just like I was fine coming home late from the stables before I met you."

"But that was before I met that overgrown floor mop that you have for protection."

She stepped around Frank and into her kitchen. "I also have an alarm system to back up the floor mop."

"That doesn't make me feel any better, Rayne."

She heaved her backpack onto the beige granite breakfast bar. "Well, it's the best I can do."

"Have you ever considered buying a gun?"

Rayne went to her refrigerator. "Only if I get to use it on you."

Trent's deep chuckle made her insides quiver. Removing a carton of orange juice from the refrigerator, she took a few quick sips.

"Now what are you doing?" His voice was strained with curiosity.

She thumped the carton down on the kitchen countertop. "What is it with you and questions?"

"I just want to know how you spend your time when you're not working."

"Why?" she challenged, sounding aggravated.

"Rayne, I'm making an effort here. The least you could do is talk to me."

She silently berated her shortness with the man. If she wanted to make a go of it with him, Rayne knew she needed to open up. "What do you want to know, Trent?"

"How do you spend your evenings at home?"

Rayne spied the open living room that connected to her kitchen and tried to think of something interesting to say. "Sometimes I watch television, other nights I go online, and three nights a week I do yoga."

"Yoga?" The surprise in his voice made her smile.

"Yes, yoga. It's good for the joints, and helps to condition me for riding. You should try it."

"I prefer running five miles a day."

She pictured his toned and tanned body and her smile got a lot bigger. "Yeah, I can see that is working out just fine for you."

"So glad you noticed." The husky quality in his voice soothed her.

But when the conversation stalled, Rayne searched in vain for something to say, reviving her anxiety. "Well, I should go," she mumbled.

"No, don't go," Trent seductively begged through the phone speaker. "Talk to me, Rayne. Tell me about your job."

"Trent, I don't understand why you want to—"

"Just talk to me."

She took a moment thinking of something to tell him. "My job. Okay. I work as a lab technician for this group of physicians in Lewisville. I've been there for about a year and I really like it."

"That's good." Trent's silky voice skipped about her kitchen. "Go on."

Rayne did go on. She took a seat on a wooden stool by her kitchen breakfast bar and began to tell Trent about her job and the people she worked with. Rayne explained what she did in her small lab, the kinds of tests she ran, and how she liked working with the staff there. She even told him about Lindsey.

Rayne was still in her dirty jeans and boots, and Frank was lying patiently at the foot of her stool when she caught sight of the clock on her microwave oven.

"Oh, my God. It's after eight. I've been talking to you for over an hour." She ran her hand over her flushed face. "Why didn't you tell me to stop?"

"I like listening to you. You open up to me over the phone, unlike when you're alone with me. You always seem so nervous."

"I do not," she argued.

"Afraid it's true, Rayne."

She heard a muffled rustling in the background. "What's that?"

"Paperwork. I'm still sitting at my desk."

She imagined him working in a high rise office building. "Where do you work?"

His boisterous laugh rang out from her phone speaker. "No, I think I'll save that for our discussion tomorrow night."

"Tomorrow night?" she skeptically returned.

"Yes, we should make this a nightly thing. I'll call you, you can tell me about your day, and I'll tell you about mine. So by the time we have dinner this weekend, you will know all about me, and hopefully won't be so nervous."

"I don't think that—"

"I'm just trying to gentle you into me, Rayne." He uttered a long sigh and then she heard the sound of more rustling papers. "I need to get back to my paperwork, and you need to get to your yoga," he added.

"Actually, I need to feed Frank." She eyed the dog sleeping next to her.

"Give my best to the beast, and I'll talk to you again tomorrow night."

She was going to tell him not to call, but something stopped her. There was a part of her that wanted to speak to him again.

"All right, Trent."

"No protests, no begging me not to call? Can it be that I'm making headway with you?"

Rayne smiled and envisioned his lively gray eyes. "Don't get your hopes up, Mr. Newbury."

"Too late." He hung up before she could bid him good night.

She eyed the iPhone in her hand, grinning at his childlike exuberance. Perhaps he was right; he was "making headway." She had always been so reluctant to let new people in her life. And even when someone did manage to squeak by her rigid defenses, she was still wary about trusting their intentions.

Developing friendships had never been easy for Rayne. Not long after settling with her mother in Dallas, she had made the fateful decision that hers would be a life of acquaintances, and no friends. Acquaintances were easier to forget and it was a lot less painful when someone suddenly disappeared, or worse…died.

That was the real crux of it for her. Recalling the terrible day when her father and sister had been killed, Rayne had been home alone when the police had knocked on her door. She had been the one to break the news to her mother. After being told, her mother had curled into a ball on the living room floor, sobbing like a child. At seventeen, Rayne had become the adult, spending her time caring for a parent who was no longer emotionally capable of making any decisions.

Shaking off her memories, she stood from her stool. Those days were long behind her, and even though every now and then the heartache still stung her eyes with tears, Rayne was convinced she was over it.

"Maybe, this is a new chapter for me." She rested her black iPhone on the countertop.

The sound of a tail thumping on the floor made her glance down at Frank's eager face.

"Come on, monster. Let's get something to eat."

***

The following evening, while whipping torrents of rain poured from the black skies above, Rayne ducked in her back door. After checking on Bob, she had returned home disappointed she was unable to take her horse out for a trail ride. Just as she was locking her back door, her cell phone began belting out its musical ringtone. Eagerly grabbing for the phone in her backpack, Rayne was anxious to hear his voice on the other end. All day long she had been looking forward to the call.

"Hi, Trent." She punched in her alarm code.

"Are you home yet?"

"Just walked in the door from the stables." She looked out the window in her back door. "But it's pouring down, so I couldn't ride."

"Raining here, too."

"Where are you?" She headed down the short rear hall to her kitchen.

His frustrated sigh poured through her phone speaker. "I'm sitting at a desk on the thirtieth floor of some nondescript office building in downtown Dallas. The rain is smacking against my window, and as I look out I can see flashes of lightning in the dark sky."

"Is that where you work?" She entered her kitchen and patted Frank's head as he came loping up to her.

"I'm doing a consulting job for an oil and gas firm I work for every now and then, Propel Oil and Gas. The CEO, Tyler Moore, is a good friend. He hires me to do QA for him."

"What does that entail?" She slung her backpack on the breakfast bar countertop and went to the refrigerator.

"Safety protocols mostly. I assess whether or not industry safety standards are being maintained on gas and oil wells."

"Is that what you do? Safety inspections?" She took the orange juice carton out of the refrigerator.

"I'm a safety engineer who specializes in the petroleum industry. I mostly do consulting work for big oil companies. Tell them what they are doing right and wrong, so they can keep the feds off their backs."

Rayne swallowed a few quick mouthfuls of the orange juice. "Do you like what you do?"

"Why do I hear slurping?" Trent's voice rumbled through the speaker.

"I was drinking orange juice. I always drink orange juice when I get home from the stables."

"Out of the carton or in a glass?"

Rayne giggled, feeling flirty. "What does that have to do with anything?"

"It tells me a little something about you."

She replaced the orange juice in the refrigerator. "What? That I'm a slob because I drink it out of the carton?"

"No, that's the way I drink it, too. See there? We have something in common."

"Hardly a reason to pick out china," she ribbed, shutting the refrigerator door.

"Well, at least we won't have to worry about the glassware."

Rayne's unexpected laughter surprised her. It was the first time she could remember laughing, really laughing with happiness in a long while. She stood by her kitchen sink, a little mystified that Trent had done that for her.

"I like the sound of that," Trent remarked. "You've got a great laugh. You should do it more often."

Rayne traced her fingers over her smooth, beige granite counter. "Haven't had a lot of reasons to laugh lately."

"I promise that is going to change."

Rayne shook her head, not sure she wanted to get bogged down in his promises. "Tell me more about what you do." She headed to her bedroom to change.

Trent described the ins and outs of his job as she wiggled out of her jeans and slipped into her favorite sweat suit.

"I hear grunting. What are you doing?"

She tugged her sweatshirt over her head. "I was changing."

"Changing into what?"

"Sweat suit." She reached for her iPhone on her bed. "I like to get comfortable when I get home."

"What else do you like to do when you get home besides drink orange juice and put on a smelly sweat suit?"

"It's not smelly. I just washed it," she defended.

"I'll let you know what I think the next time I come over."

Emboldened by the way he made her feel, she playfully posed, "What makes you think you are coming over again?"

There was a lapse of silence, then Trent whispered, "Tell me what else you like to do when you come home."

Rayne smiled and began to tell him of her nightly routine. How she collected her mail from the floor of her entranceway where it fell from the slot in her door, what she fed Frank....

Trent was still listening to her as she popped a frozen dinner in the microwave.

"That's not healthy," he insisted.

"I don't like to cook."

"Lucky for you, I love to cook."

He listened as she munched on her hearty chicken and potato dinner, asked her to describe the flavor, and then went into a long explanation about what kind of wine she should have with her meal. That conversation led to a lesson on how to choose the best wine at restaurants.

They had talked of favorite foods, favorite movies and television shows, and had even touched on the best place to get ice cream.

"Braum's Ice Cream in Lewisville, hands down," he had related. "No place like it."

"Best flavor?"

"Mocha chocolate chip. I like ice cream with a kick. What's yours?"

"I've always been a straight up chocolate fan," she had replied. "But that mocha flavor sounds intriguing."

By the time Rayne glanced up at her microwave clock, she could not believe she had been on the phone with the man for over two hours.

"Trent, it's almost nine o'clock. Don't you need to get back to your safety audits?"

"Probably," he said, sounding downhearted. "But I prefer talking to you. I have all night to do my paperwork."

"Then I'll be responsible for keeping you up all night, and I can't have that. You'd better get back to work."

"What are you going to do?"

Rayne glimpsed Frank asleep beside her stool. "Let Frank out in the yard, watch some television, and go to bed."

"No yoga?"

She smiled, glad he had remembered. "No, not tonight. Too tired."

"Then get to bed early, and I will call you tomorrow."

"You don't have to keep doing this, you know. You don't have to call me every night."

"I like talking to you. Get some sleep." Again, he hung up before she could get in a comment.

As she put her black cell phone down next to her backpack, she realized she enjoyed talking to him, too. It had been so long since Rayne had just talked with anyone about all the small trivialities of life. Not since she had been a carefree student in high school back in New Orleans had she spent hours on the phone chatting about nothing in particular. In a way, that was how Trent made her feel…like an innocent girl, before all the pain of loss had beaten down her belief in hope. That warm, jubilant glow attributed to the unmarred magic of adolescence was returning, making Rayne feel completely alive for the first time in years.

Leaning against the breakfast bar, she wiped her hands over her face, concentrating on the reality of her situation. She was a thirty-two-year-old divorcée, and the lure of romance was something better suited to the young and impressionable.

"No!" She beat her fist on the beige granite countertop. "Don't let him do this to you. If you let him in, he'll hurt you. They always do."

Feeling her determination return, Rayne reasoned that all the phone calls in the world would never make her comfortable with the inquisitive man. Anyway, how could a man like the alluring Trent Newbury be interested in her?

She went to the living room and flopped down on her comfy, white leather sofa. As her gaze drifted to the kitchen where he had pinned her against the counter, she mulled over that kiss. Closing her eyes, Rayne lingered over the memory of his lips, the feel of his firm body, and as she reveled in the image of him naked in her bed, Frank jumped onto the sofa and nestled his furry muzzle in her lap.

Stroking the dog's soft head, her eyes closed again and she slipped further into her fantasy of being with Trent. Rayne's skin flushed, her breathing quickened, and her loins ached with lust. The urge to have him touch her, to run her hands along the curves of his wide chest and round, tight ass, made her heave with longing. Just when her racy daydream started getting a little too graphic, her eyes flew open.

A new dilemma seized Rayne. She might not have wanted to hand her heart over to Trent, but she sure did want to give him her body, and that was a feeling Rayne had never had with any man. Maybe she had been too hasty in wanting to end it. Perhaps she should just give in to her desire for the handsome man and see what developed.

Chapter 6

All the next day at work, Rayne was distracted. She kept dropping vials of specimens in her lab, and asking people to repeat information on the phone. Obsessed with Trent's impending phone call, she had found room for little else in her mind. Even Lindsey noticed the change in her when they shared a mid-morning cup of coffee in the break room.

"You've got it bad."

Rayne shook off her preoccupation and turned to her friend. "What?"

"You." Lindsey lifted the coffee mug in her hand and grinned at Rayne over the rim. "You've been sitting there for five minutes staring off into space. I've seen you distracted before, but this takes the cake." She took a sip from her coffee. "Is this about that horse guy?"

Rayne kept her eyes on her mug of coffee, sitting untouched on the round table before her. "He's been calling every evening when I get home. We talk a lot, about all sorts of things, but I'm still not sure about the man."

Lindsey's eager blue eyes deepened with worry. "Why? He's calling you all the time, that's a good sign. If he only wanted sex, he would come over and try to sleep with you. Over the phone means he wants to get to know you. Unless of course you have phone sex, then I guess you could say he was after you only for sex, but it's not the same...I think."

"Phone sex?" Rayne's tinkling laughter permeated the break room. "No, that hasn't happened. We talk about silly things really. Movies, food, wine, you know, the casual stuff."

"Ever try phone sex with him?"

"No." Rayne shifted uneasily in her chair.

"Ever want to?"

"Eww! No."

Lindsey settled her coffee on the table, sat back in her chair, and folded her arms over the front of her pink teddy bear-clad scrub top. "Have you ever had phone sex with a man?"

Rayne reached for her coffee. "Of course not." She quickly sipped from her mug.

Lindsey smirked, shaking her head. "Yeah, Foster never struck me as that type, but this guy...you should do it."

Rayne almost choked on her coffee. "What?"

"See what he's like on the phone. It will give you a good idea of what he will be like in bed." Lindsey ran a finger through a strand of blonde hair that had fallen from her ponytail. "Me and Casey used to do it all the time when he was working offshore."

Rayne plopped her mug on the table. "Lindsey, I'm trying to get rid of the man, not have sex with him over the phone."

"Get rid of him? What on earth for? You've got a guy you're crazy for who wants to be with you. Why would you want to push him away?"

"I'm not crazy for him," Rayne declared.

"Do you think about what he would be like in bed?"

Rayne shocked eyes dropped to the table.

"Rayne, you have got to loosen up," Lindsey giggled. "You only live once, and you've seen enough sorrow in life to know that you have to grab every chance you're given for happiness." She patted Rayne's hand. "Besides, I've got a feeling about him."

"A feeling?" Rayne knew she needed more than Lindsey's feelings to believe in Trent. "What kind of feeling?"

Lindsey let go of her hand and clasped her white mug. "I can tell when two people are going to make it or just go up in flames. You and this guy are going to make it."

Rayne sat back in her chair, amazed at her friend's confidence. "Ever think you could be wrong?"

"I'm never wrong." Lindsey put her mug to her lips.

Lindsey's profound confidence swayed Rayne. Maybe she needed to stop thinking and start making a concerted effort with Trent. But where to begin? She turned to Lindsey as an idea percolated.

"So how exactly do you have…phone sex?"

Lindsey put her coffee down. "Are you interested in trying it out with your riding instructor?"

"Technically he's a riding master at our stables. The person in charge of all the other—"

"Rayne," Lindsey roared. "I could care less if you call him your scout master and let him tie you up in his pup tent. What I want to know is…does this guy turn you on?"

Rayne already knew the answer to that question. She had been thinking about his luscious body ever since the first day she had laid eyes on him.

"Don't laugh, but…." She nodded her head. "Yeah, he really does. I don't know how to describe it."

Lindsey's evil grin betrayed her angelic features. "That's good. Now we're getting somewhere." Her plastic office chair squeaked on the linoleum floor as she jerked it closer to

Rayne. "If you want to get him to have phone sex with you, you have to start out by letting him know you're interested in trying it," she began.

"How do I do that? Just ask him?"

"No, you have to be subtle about it," Lindsey suggested, with an insistent shrug of her shoulders.

"Subtle? About phone sex?" Rayne snickered, sitting back in her chair.

"I usually start out by telling Casey about how much I miss him and how lonely I am without him." Lindsey playfully leered. "That really gets him going."

"But I can't stay that. I hardly know Trent."

"So use another approach. Flirt with him."

Rayne's dark eyebrows rose up. "Flirt?"

"You do remember how to flirt, don't you?"

Biting her lower lip, Rayne clutched her coffee mug. "I think it should come back to me, eventually."

***

Driving back from the stables after a quick work out with Bob, Rayne stared at the iPhone on the car seat next to her, waiting for it to ring. Ever since her tutorial with Lindsey earlier that morning on the finer points of phone sex, she had been a complete wreck. Sex had always been awkward enough for her, but now having to describe it over the phone to someone was more than a little intimidating. But Lindsey had promised that it was a sure fire way to find out how interested Trent was in their relationship.

As she pulled into her driveway and hit the remote on her garage door, her anxiety increased, knowing his call could come at any minute. After flying in the back door, petting Frank, and then banging her backpack down on the beige kitchen countertop, she went to her refrigerator and lugged out the carton of orange juice. As she chugged the sweet liquid, she yearned for something with a bit more substance. Remembering the bottle of amaretto she kept in the cabinet below the sink, she put the carton of juice down on the counter and went to retrieve the liquor.

With a tall iced tea glass of orange juice and amaretto, and her cell phone in the back pocket of her blue jeans, she made her way to her bedroom door. Just as she was putting the glass down on her dark pine dresser, she heard her jazzy ringtone.

"Hey, Trent."

"Hello, Rayne." He sounded worn out and his voice lacked the smoothness she had grown addicted to.

"You okay? You sound tired." She took her drink and had a seat on her brass bed.

"I spent the day in meetings with a few of the staff around here. I guess I'm talked out."

"Then why don't we make this a short call and you can get some rest?" Rayne sipped from her glass.

"No," he insisted in a firm tone. "I've been looking forward to this all day."

Her heart beat a little faster at his disclosure. "You have?"

"Now why do you sound surprised?" He sighed heavily into the phone speaker. "If you don't know how I feel about you by now...."

She took another bolstering gulp from her drink. "I think I can guess."

"I promise after this weekend, you won't have to guess anymore," he asserted in his sexy, husky voice.

His determined tone made Rayne tremble with anticipation. She pictured his hands roaming over her body as his words repeated in her mind. Instantly, Lindsey's advice from earlier that day popped into her head.

"But what exactly do you plan on doing to me this weekend? I mean, to show me how you feel?" She hoped she sounded flirty enough for him to get the hint.

He was very quiet on the other end of the line, making Rayne wonder if she had gone too far.

"Where are you?" His voice was darker and edged with insistence.

"Sitting on my bed. Why?"

Another moment of silence from him tore at her nerves, and then he whispered, "What are you wearing?"

Unhinged by the lust in his voice, Rayne took a swig from her drink. "I'm in my riding jeans," she answered.

"Are you going to put on your sweats?"

She put her drink down on the dark pine nightstand by her bed. "I was."

"I have an idea."

Rayne's hand gripped the phone. The captivating change in his voice was alluring as hell. He was not the friendly Trent she had spent the past few nights talking to; he was different.

"I'm listening." She focused on keeping calm.

"I want you to…undress for me."

When she heard the sensual throatiness of his voice, she began to panic. What Lindsey had described sounded fun at the time, but with Trent…she was not sure she could go through with it.

"Rayne? Do you want me to go on?"

Spurred on by the sound of his voice, she murmured, "Yes, Trent. I want you to go on."

"Unzip your jeans and slide them down your thighs."

Rayne placed the phone by her jeans so he could listen as she slowly lowered the metal zipper down the track. Then, she scooted back on the bed, put the phone to the side, and inched the jeans down around her thighs and all the way to her ankles.

"I'm on the bed and my jeans are off." She kept her voice soft and breathless, just like Lindsey had told her.

"Tell me you want me to go on, Rayne."

His voice was killing her. She took a breath, and then turned to the phone on the bed next to her. "Go on, Trent. Tell me what you want me to do."

"Take your hand and run it lightly up and down your stomach, and then across your breasts. Tease your skin with your touch."

She closed her eyes and tried to relax as her hands scraped across the outside of her T-shirt.

"Imagine it's me doing this to you," he suggested over the speaker.

"I wish...."

"What do you wish, Rayne? Tell me."

"I...I wish it was you." She slapped her hand over her mouth, completely embarrassed that she had even mentioned such a thing.

"Soon, Rayne, soon." He paused. "Take off your shirt and bra."

She fumbled with her clothes as he waited patiently on the phone.

"All right, they're off," she told him, reclining back on the bed.

"Now slide your underwear down and drop them along with your jeans to the floor. I want you naked on the bed. Then, I want you to listen to the sound of my voice and do exactly as I say. Do you understand?"

"Yes, Trent." She kicked off her jeans and tossed her beige silk panties to the floor. As she lay naked on the bed, the burning desire coursing up from her groin began to take over her senses.

"I'm naked. What do you want me to do?"

Nothing. There were no words, no sounds from him. The absence of any noise from the phone speaker went on for what felt like an eternity to Rayne; then, very softly, he ordered, "Open your legs, reach down, and touch yourself."

Gulping back her disbelief at what she was about to do, she slowly lowered her hand to the valley between her legs. When her fingers touched her moist flesh, she sighed.

"Do you like the way it feels?" His voice was like a drug.

"Yes," she moaned into the phone.

"Run your fingers up and down. Think of me as you do it. I want you to think only of me, Rayne."

She imagined Trent beside her in the bed, his muscular chest, tanned arms, and supple hands rubbing against her. She tried to taste his kiss on her lips, the way he had kissed her in the kitchen, and then a jolt of electricity zipped through her.

"What do you feel, Rayne?"

She yanked her hand away. "What do I feel?" she echoed, becoming nervous. "I'm not sure what you—"

"Relax. It's not a test. I just want to know how this makes you feel."

"Silly," she confessed into the phone. "I've never done this before, and I'm beginning to understand why."

"It's just like when you do it alone, but this time I get to listen in. Now tell me how you feel. Are you turned on?"

She let out a long breath. "You have to ask?"

"What you are feeling? Describe it to me."

"I feel warm and tingly all over."

"Close your eyes and picture me there, lying beside you. What would you want me to do to you?"

She closed her eyes, and her mind was consumed with images of him. "I would want you to touch me...there."

"Put your hand where you would want mine to be."

She slowly moved her hand back between her legs.

"Think of me and do what you would want me to do," he went on. "Your hands are my hands."

The sound of his voice over the phone speaker was mesmerizing. She worked her fingers up and down her folds as she imagined Trent touching her in the exact same way. The urgency in her groin rose as her fingers moved faster.

"Rayne, I want to hear you say my name."

"Trent," she gasped.

"Do you like how this feels?"

"Oh God," she moaned as her approaching orgasm crept up her belly.

"Do you want me inside of you?"

"Yes," she cried out.

"Are you going to come for me?"

She ached for release as she stroked her sensitive nub. Rayne could feel the tension bending her like a taut bow. "Yes, yes, I can feel it...." She groaned as her body flexed.

"That's it," Trent calmly encouraged. "Let go, baby."

Rayne threw her head back and cried out as a burst of white heat tore through her.

When she settled on the bed, breathing hard and feeling a light film of sweat covering her brow, she forgot for a moment about the man listening on the other end of her phone.

"I wish I could hold you in my arms." Trent's voice was like velvet.

She opened her eyes, and as if realizing what she had just done, her glow of satisfaction quickly turned into a flush of shame.

"God, did I really just…? I can't believe I—"

"Hey, don't do that," he cut in. "It was wonderful, Rayne. You brought you and me pleasure, and there is nothing wrong with that."

She clapped her hand over her eyes. "I feel so cheap."

Trent's warm laughter made her smile. "Just think about this weekend, and when I have you all alone, I will do everything you just did and so much more. I promise you that."

Biting back her returning desire, she picked up the phone on the bed next to her, cradling it in her hands. "I was going to tell you to go to hell the other night. I was going to say we could only be friends, and nothing more."

"But you don't feel that way about me anymore, do you?"

She hesitated before she answered. "No, not after…what we just did."

"That's good, because I would never have let you just give up on me like that. I can be pretty determined, Rayne."

She blew out a long breath, stretching out on the bed. "Yeah, I've noticed."

"Next time you feel the urge to run, talk to me. I want you to come to me whenever you're nervous or scared. All right?"

"Sure, Trent."

"Promise me, Rayne."

She nodded her head. "I promise."

"Good girl."

"I can't wait to see what we do tomorrow night." She giggled and wiped her hand over her face. "Might be hard to top this."

"I'm afraid I'm going to be tied up in meetings for the next two nights. I have a dinner party to attend tomorrow night at Tyler Moore's house in Dallas. He's the CEO who hired me for this job, and he wants to introduce me to a few of his friends in the oil business."

"A dinner party at an oil tycoon's fancy mansion? Poor you." An image of him rubbing elbows with the rich and powerful fueled Rayne's doubts about why he was pursuing her.

"It will be all about business," Trent's low voice broke into her thoughts. "Then I have the wrap-up meeting Friday night with Tyler's department heads to discuss my findings. So we won't have a chance to speak again until Saturday at the stables."

A trickle of disappointment tightened her throat. "I understand. You have a job to do," she said, sounding upbeat.

"I'll be thinking of you the entire time, trust me."

"Trust you?" She took a breath, leaving him hanging, and then added, "I'm not there yet, Trent."

"But you will be, Rayne. One day you will trust me."

"We'll see." She sat up in the bed. "But in the meantime, you should get back to work, and I need to feed Frank."

"How is fluff face?"

Rayne spotted Frank waiting at her bedroom door. "Looking hungry?"

"Better see to him while I get back to my reports. With the way I'm going, I'll be pulling another all nighter to get everything finished in time for my meetings."

"Don't work too hard," she offered, feeling a little sad he had to go.

"Not to worry. I have thoughts of you and this weekend to keep me going."

Rayne's insides ignited with his words. "Do you want to hear something funny?"

"Absolutely," he cooed.

"I think I'm nervous about seeing you again."

"Don't be nervous, Rayne. Tonight was only a prelude of what is to come. Pleasant dreams." Then Trent hung up, leaving a mystified Rayne staring at her cell phone and wondering how she had let things progress so far.

"I must be crazy." She tossed her iPhone to the bed.

Jumping up, she went to her favorite sweat suit laid out on a flower print high back chair by her bedroom door. After slipping on the gray sweat pants and sweater top, she clapped her hands at Frank.

"Come on, buddy. Let's eat."

With a happy Frank at her side, she made her way down the short beige hallway to her living room. As she crossed the plush burgundy carpet to her kitchen, the reality of what she had done with Trent hit her and the heat rose in her cheeks.

"I don't think I'll ever be able to look him in the face again." She spotted Frank dancing beside her, anxious for his dinner. "Maybe if you had chewed his face off that first night he came here, I wouldn't be in this situation."

Frank let out a loud "woof."

She nodded her head. "Yeah, I know. I like him, too."

Chapter 7

Existing. That was how Rayne saw her life evolving over the next two days. It was if she were going through withdrawal by knowing she was not going to hear from Trent. She was anxious, jumped every time a cell phone rang, and found her mind continuously drifting back to their night of intimacy over the phone.

What struck her as odd was that she had grown comforted by his phone calls. When she returned home that Thursday night from a long afternoon with Bob, Rayne had been sad knowing that she would not hear from him. She had occupied her time by paying bills and doing yoga, but as her bedtime hour came and went, she was unable to sleep.

Visions of Trent's dinner party slowly turned from the business dinner he had professed to an orgy with prostitutes and horny businessmen running amuck. Rayne knew her overzealous imagination was getting the better of her, but she questioned if there was more to Trent Newbury than the simple life he described. After all, what did she really know about the man?

By the time Friday afternoon rolled around, her casual second-guessing about Trent's lurid life away from the stables had morphed into something akin to a porn movie. As she envisioned him with a boatload of girlfriends, having affairs with wealthy, married women, and living a lifestyle even a gigolo would envy, she would talk herself out of seeing him again.

"He could be toying with me," she told Frank that evening as she sat at her breakfast bar and picked at her frozen dinner of rice pilaf with chicken tenders marinated in a white wine sauce. "Maybe I'm just a distraction until something better comes along."

Frank tipped his ears forward, but seemed more interested in her microwave dinner than what she was saying.

"I knew I should never have listened to Lindsey. That's what you get for letting a girlfriend talk you into—"

Her cell phone ringtone reverberated inside her backpack on the counter next to her. She bolted from her stool and grabbed at her backpack. When she spied the number on her phone, her heart sputtered. With a slight shake of her head, Rayne flipped her thumb across the iPhone screen and took the call.

"Hello, Estelle."

"You would think you'd be over that adolescent phase you've been in for twenty years and start calling me Mom," a raspy voice drenched in a Texas twang came over the speaker of her phone.

"How many scotches have you had tonight, 'Mom'?" Rayne returned to her stool and eyed her half-eaten dinner.

"Why didn't you come and see me today?"

Rayne jabbed at her rice pilaf with her fork. "What makes you think I was coming to see you today?"

"It's Saturday. You always come to visit on Saturday."

"It's Friday, Estelle, not Saturday. And I stopped coming to visit on Saturday's when I started teaching my riding classes last year, remember?"

"Oh, yeah." A crackling sound came over the speaker. "Well, why don't you come and see me tomorrow after your class?"

Rayne listened as the crackling sound continued. "What is that noise?"

"It's a candy wrapper."

"Is that what you're having for dinner, Mother, candy?"

"I'm not hungry," Estelle huffed, sounding like a ten-year-old.

Rayne rolled her eyes at the prospect of listening to another one of her mother's childish tantrums. "What did you eat today?"

"Do you care? I could starve to death in this big old house and no one would find me," Estelle whined.

"Don't start, Mother. I've told you to get rid of that monstrosity."

"It's home, Raynie," Estelle insisted, her voice wavering with emotion. "I can't part with it."

Disgusted, Rayne dropped her fork on her plastic plate. "Look, I'm busy. Why are you calling me?"

"What do you mean, 'why am I calling'?" Estelle barked. "I want to see you." More wrapper noises continued in the background.

"We both know that's not true," Rayne objected, raising her voice. "What do you want?"

"What makes you think I want something?"

"Mother, please."

A hush over the line ate away at Rayne's patience.

"Well," Estelle finally began. "You know how I hate to ask, but I got another letter from the city today, demanding the overdue taxes. If I could just send them a little something to get them off my back for a while, I'm sure I can get the money later."

Rayne mouthed a silent scream while squeezing her phone. "I don't have anything to send you. I've told you before that since the divorce things are tight."

"Oh, I see," Estelle shouted. "You can spend money on that horse of yours, but not on your mother?" She feigned a whimper.

Rayne knew the sound was just a tactic to get sympathy. Estelle had been using the same manipulations for years, but Rayne was now immune.

"You know Foster pays for Bob. He pays all the feed bills, the vet bills, and his boarding fees. It was part of the settlement agreement in the divorce. I declined alimony in exchange for his keeping up with payments so I could hold on to Bob."

"You should sell that nag, and use the money to help me. I need help, Raynie. If your father was still—"

"Dad and Jaime have been dead for fifteen years, so stop using them as an excuse for everything." Rayne pushed her plate away.

"You don't need to remind me that they're gone. I think about it every day. I think about my good daughter who died, leaving me with you. Jaime was always better than you. Your father adored her, and he only let you take those stupid riding lessons because Jaime pleaded with him."

Rayne ran her hand over her forehead. "Does it make you feel better telling me that story over and over again?"

"You need to know the truth." Her mother's voice was as cold as her words.

"Your truth, Mother. You've spent every day since Dad and Jaime died blaming me. But Dad wouldn't have been picking Jaime up from school if you hadn't forgotten her in the first place. You always forgot about us."

"I never forgot," Estelle's voice howled over the phone speaker. "I was just busy maintaining the house for all of you. You have no idea how hard it was for me."

"Hard?" Rayne snorted with contempt. "You had a maid, a gardener, and a cook to take care of everything. Dad was the one who worked sixty hours a week at his law practice."

"I could have worked, but your father wanted me to stay home. You know how much he liked being the man of the house. He needed to take care of me, so I let him."

"And after Dad died, you had Grandpa John and Grandma Rose to take care of you. They paid for you to go to therapy, sent you to all those fancy rehab programs, and even left you that expensive house when they died. Never once did you work or help pay for anything after we left New Orleans. So don't tell me how hard your life has been, okay?" Rayne fought the urge to throw her cell phone across the kitchen. Every time her mother called she got sucked into the same argument.

"You married Mr. Moneybags, and never once…once…did you offer to have me come over, or stay in that fancy house of yours. You never paid for any—"

"Foster paid for everything you ever wanted, so don't even go there, Mother." Rayne's rage was reaching a boiling point. "And you know why he never wanted you living with us. He could never abide your drinking."

"I drink because it helps me cope with—"

A musical tone from her phone cut in, alerting her to a text.

Thinking of you. Until tomorrow night….

Rayne's heart sped up when she read the text from Trent. All the insane fantasies she had been having about his other life disappeared as she stared at the brief message.

"Are you listening to me, Rayne Elena Masterson?" her mother's voice squawked.

She scowled at her cell phone. "I have to go, Mother."

"Where do you got to run off to?" Estelle screeched. "You don't have a husband to cater to, or friends you have to meet. Why can't you talk to your mother?"

"Because it's always the same old conversation with you. I have other things to do."

"Ah, I get it," Estelle voiced, sounding smug. "You've got a new man." Her mother chuckled, a sickly sounding laugh that reminded Rayne of a cat coughing up a hairball.

Rayne was unnerved by her mother's uncanny perception. "What makes you think I have a new man?"

"Because whenever there's a man in your life, you don't want to talk to me."

"I never want to talk to you, Mother."

"Who is he, Raynie? Is he rich?" The hope in Estelle's voice was nauseating.

"Drop it, Mother."

"No, I want to hear about him." Rayne could almost see her mother's sarcastic smile. "God knows, I've watched you chase away more men than a whore in a white dress at a Sunday social."

"I never chased away any men."

"Then why did you find Foster in bed with that other woman?" The biting barb dug into Rayne's flesh. "Maybe you drove him into the arms of that girl, you ever consider that?"

Rayne struck her hand down on her breakfast bar. "I'm not doing this again with you. Good-bye." Rayne hung up and clicked over to Trent's text message.

After the infuriating phone call with her mother, her reservations about Trent seemed almost inconsequential. Here was a man who at least was making an effort to win her affection. After a lifetime of Estelle Masterson's conditional love, manipulation, and tantrums, it was a wonder Rayne's tenuous self-esteem had not run the man off completely. Perhaps she should give Trent a little encouragement.

Looking forward to tomorrow night, she texted back.

"See, Mother. I'm not chasing this one away," she muttered.

There were times when she pondered if the weight of her mother's influence had helped contribute to the failure of her marriage. Rayne's distrusting nature had made her uncomfortable with the long line of conceited, social bigwigs Foster constantly pursued. When she began to spend more time at the stables than attending parties, Foster had pulled away. Soon his days at the office grew into late nights, and instead of confronting her husband, she had buried her emotions in the world of horses.

The musical tone of an incoming text brought her back from her painful memories.

What are you doing?

"What am I doing?" She scanned her kitchen, looking for inspiration. When Frank let out a loud snore from the floor beside her stool, she grinned.

Watching the furry mop snoring next to me, she texted back.

Are you in bed?

Rayne laughed at the suggestion, knowing what he was thinking. All the embittered resentment stirred by her mother's phone call retreated to the depths from which it had been summoned.

Sorry, I'm in the kitchen. How is your meeting going? she typed into her phone.

On a break, but going well. Hoping to get on the road for home soon. Tired of sleeping in a hotel.

Miss your bed, huh? she teased.

Very funny. I'll make you pay for that.

Promise?

Several seconds passed before he texted back, *Must go before I need a cold shower. Sleep well and dream of me.*

Standing from her stool, she read over his last text once more and smiled, satisfied that he was sufficiently encouraged. After turning off her phone, she eyed Frank still snoring on the floor.

"I think if there was a dog Olympics for sleep, Frank, you would get the gold medal."

One brown eye opened and looked up at her, but the dog's body never budged.

After getting a slow moving Frank outside to do his business, she turned out the lights, set the alarm, and checked the locks on the doors before retreating to her bedroom.

In the confines of her soft gray bedroom, Rayne changed into her favorite nightshirt, waited until Frank got comfortable on her gray and white comforter, and then slipped between the sheets of her brass bed. Her mind wandered ahead to her coming day at the stables, her lessons, and her meeting with Trent.

All the time they had spent together on the phone had strengthened her connection to him. She was less apprehensive, but despite their intimate interlude, she worried exactly what would happen when she was alone with him.

Slinking down in her bed as Frank's snoring started up, she mulled over the idea of sex with Trent. It had been so long since she had been motivated to think about sex, and she recalled all of those girlish notions she had entertained before marrying Foster. What would it be like to be held in the arms of a man who was passionate, experienced, and interested in only pleasing her? Her mind raced with images of Trent's firm ass in her hands, his thin lips on her neck, and his naked body rubbing against hers. As the pictures in her head grew even more erotic, her body began responding. Giggling at her arousal, Rayne rolled onto her side.

"What in the hell is wrong with me?"

Closing her eyes and willing sleep to take her until morning, Rayne already knew what her problem was. She only hoped the handsome Trent Newbury was the solution.

ALEXANDRA — THE RIDING MASTER 2014 (312)
WEIS
(IN HER 30's) — 6 MOS. DIVORCED — "MILLIONAIRE"
~~RAYNE GREER 31 EX-HUSBAND FOSTER CREER~~
~~REBECCA — 3 EX HSBANDS (SHE OWNS STABLE)~~
~~+ INTRODUCES HER TO NEW RIDING MASTER~~
~34 & NEVER BEEN MARRIED (9) OIL & GAS CONSULTANT
~~TRENT NEWBURY~~ — THE NEW RIDING MASTER
SHE IS LAB TECH ... TEACHES HORSE BACK RIDING
ON WEEKENDS (SHE WAS MARRIED 8 YRS)
TRENT IS HER NEW BOSS AT STABLES. (51)
SHE WAS M. 8YRS (selfish old man)
SHE TALKS 2 HIM ON PHONE — I AM A LAB TECH (66)
HE 17 — HER DAD & SISTER KILLED / HE'S A
HE IS CONSULTANT 4 OIL & GAS FIRM (SAFETY ENGINEER)
SHE DOESN'T LIKE 2 COOK (frozen dinner) HE DOES
HE WILL CALL EVERY NITE "I LIKE TALKING 2 U (72)
83 — THEY HAVE PHONE SEX + SHE COMES 4 HIM!
HER MOM — ALCOHOLIC. MANIPULATOR & TANTRUMS
"98" SHE (from DISTANCE) WATCHES HIM (RING MASTER)
HIS FRIEND ASKED IF I WAS SEEING ANYONE I SAID "U!
U INTRIGUE & EXCITE ME (101) 102 (WHEN WILL U SUBMIT
2 ME? (104) HE TAKES HER C HIS FINGERS
SHE BLUSHES, I'VE NEVER DONE THAT BEFORE, C HIM SHE
SAYS "I'M COMFORTABLE (105) 118 SHE GOES 2 HIS HOUSE
THAT HE DESIGNED & 5 BEDROOMS (HIS SISTERS VISIT
HER MOM ALCOHOLIC) U CAN TELL ME ANYTHING HE SAYS
HIS HOUSE 5 BEDROOM (124) 129 NITE WITH TRENT
(RAYNE) ON HIS COUCH 113 "MAKE LUV 2 ME TRENT"
~~HE GOES~~ HER TO ALCOHOLIC MOM IN HOSPITAL + CALLED
HER BY 4 HELP! SHE TURNS UP TRENT IS CISSO
HIS MOM LIVES ALONE IN MANSION SHE WON'T
GIVE UP (152) HASN'T PAID TAXES 2 YRS 2000 $$ HOUSE
MOTHER WON'T GIVE UP HOUSE. SHE SOLD ALL THE FURNITURE
RAYNE & TRENT — HE SAYS (174) YOUR X STILL HAS FEELINGS 4 U
PROVE U WANT 2 BE C ME (176) TAKE OFF YOUR CLOTHES 179 + 180 — SEX 6X
P 178 — I'M A L WOMAN MAN. 198 HE SAYS "I U DAT U IN HORSE
SHOW (196) 208/209 THEY HAVE SEX + TALK OF HAVING A
CHILD 212) 217 — HIS FRIEND TY LOR ASKED THEM 2 HER
HOUSE PARTY (217) 238 THEY GO 2 HOUSE PARTY X HER EX —
FOSTER IS THERE. + SO IS HIS EX LISA (239) TRENT SAYS "LET'S
GET THE HELL OUT OF HERE (241) 245 THAT NITE HE GIVES HER
THE KEYS 2 HIS HOUSE + TAKES HER IN HIS BED 2 (6
P. 260 LISA TURNS UP NAKED IN HIS POOL, HE THROWS HER OUT
+ GET KEY BACK RAYNE SEES P 262 — GIVES HIM KEY BACK +
SAYS "WE'RE DONE" + GOES TO HORSE BOB AT STABLE 263
267 — SHE HIDES FROM HIM ALL WEEK + 270 HER MOM
CALLS HER ON 17" WHEN I LOOK AT TRENT, I SEE
YOUR FATHER 270/271 272 — DR. TELLS MOM, NO MORE
DRINK (BAD LIVER. DOCTOR IS "UNCLE CHARLIE" (273)
SO MOM SAYS (274) I'M SELLING HOUSE." REBECCA TELLS HER
"HE HASN'T GIVEN UP ON U (279) HE'S JUST GIVING U SPACE
SO IF U SPLIT UP C TRENT, ROSIE R SAYS MAYBE YOU'LL GO OUT
C ME CHE IS EX HUSBAND) 286 298 APPLAUDS 4 HER HORSE
THEY GO THRU JUMPS — TRENT HAS BROTHER MOM 2 SEE
291

Managing Print Jobs

Chapter 8

Rayne arrived at the stables soon after sunrise, eager to take Bob out for an early trail ride before her classes. She was also anxious to see Trent, and decided a morning workout with her horse might help settle her restless nerves.

As she took Bob through his paces on the trail, she practiced things she would say to Trent when she first saw him, trying to come up with opening lines that sounded seductive, sexy, and yet not too desperate.

"Hey, did you have a productive meeting?" she mumbled while Bob's ears swerved back, listening to the sound of her voice. "No, that's terrible. A productive meeting sounds something like a productive cough. Ugh."

She loosened Bob's reins as she rode along a narrow path toward the stables. "How about...hello, Trent. It's really, really good to see you." She shrunk down in her saddle. "Now I sound desperate. Who am I kidding? I am desperate."

Taking in the thick trees on either side of her, she admired the changing color of the leaves and how the gold and red on the branches gave way to waves of green. The dirt path below Bob's hooves kicked up a wave of dust as a light breeze brushed past her face.

"What do you think?" she asked the horse. "Should I be assertive or more laid back? You know, let him come to me?" She shook her head at memories of having the same conversation with her tall palomino, Jasper, when she had a crush on a boy from a neighboring school.

"Here I am a grown woman and I still don't know how to act around boys." She observed how Bob's ears jockeyed back and forth, attentively listening to her every word. "You ever have problems talking to women?" Rayne chuckled. "Yeah, I bet they're all over you, huh, Bob?" She patted his sleek neck. "You're the best looking guy in the barn."

As they came over a slight rise in the trail, she spotted the white jumping ring at the rear of the barn, and in the ring she saw the massive black gelding named Titan that belonged to Selene Kendrick. Over eighteen hands in height and with a temper to match his size, whenever Titan's hooves pounded the ground, every nearby building shook.

The black horse moved in and out of the particular gaits and intricate footwork required in dressage, but when Rayne saw a tall man emerge from the early morning shadows on the side of the ring, her interest perked up. She recognized Trent's long legs and determined stride as he walked up to Titan and patted Selene's shiny black boots as she sat atop the thick Morgan horse.

"Son of a...." Rayne's eyes stayed glued on the ring as she gently tapped Bob's sides, urging him down the path. When the dirt trail meandered behind a thick clump of trees, blocking Rayne's view, she kicked a little more eagerly, wanting Bob to move faster.

After getting around the high trees, she finally got an unencumbered view of the ring, and then urged Bob to slow down. She watched as Trent motioned about the ring and then waved his hand at Selene. Titan returned to the rail, and Selene put him through another series of difficult drills.

Getting closer to the ring, Rayne could hear Trent's deep voice calling to Selene, but could not quite make out the words. Selene's flirty, girlish giggle responded to Trent's comments, and Rayne debated whether or not she should approach the ring. But as Selene's playful twittering continued, and then Trent's harmonious chuckle joined in, Rayne's decision to interrupt them turned into a gut-wrenching retreat. Wishing she had not seen the two of them, she quickened Bob's pace for the stables.

Beneath the protective shadows of the barn's tin roof, she quickly took Bob to her red tack room door and secured his reins to a nearby hitching post. As she undid the buckles of his girth, the sound of Selene's laughter rang in her ears.

"I should have known."

She hoisted the English saddle and white fleece pad from Bob's back and carried them into her tack room. After flipping on the single light bulb hanging by a cord above, she whisked the pad from beneath the saddle and placed it to the side. Grunting slightly, she lifted the saddle onto a wooden rack on the wall.

Rayne was shaking out the fleece pad and placing it on a hook to dry out when a shadow crossed her open tack room door. Thinking it was just Bob shimmying around his hitching post, she never bothered to turn to check on him. That was until she heard the distinct sound of boots entering her tack room, and then the thump of the thick red door closing.

When she spun around, Trent was standing in the doorway. His long-sleeved, white button-down shirt hugged his thick arms, and the few buttons he had left undone afforded a view of his smooth, tanned chest. His wavy black hair was slightly windblown, and his blue jeans were covered in dust. But when she caught sight of his winsome grin and the sparkle in his gray eyes, Rayne was done for.

"I saw you coming back from the trails." He shifted closer to her. "I was hoping to see you before you set out on your ride, but I just missed you."

She gave him a cool look of indifference. "Yes, I wanted to take an early morning ride before my classes."

He angled closer still, making Rayne take a step back. "I would have come after you on one of the schooling horses, but I got held up with an instructor."

"You mean you got held up with Selene. I saw you two in the back ring when I came in from the trails."

His grin grew wider. "You saw me and didn't stop by to say hello?"

She took another step back. "You were…busy."

"Busy?" He came up to her and stared diligently into her eyes. "Is that what you really thought?"

She turned to a wooden shelf on her right with an assortment of brushes and currycombs on it. Picking up a soft white brush, she avoided looking into his face. "I need to see to Bob."

Trent never budged, blocking her path. "Bob can wait."

She kept her eyes on the brush in her hand, and ran her fingers over the soft white bristles. "How was your dinner party?"

"It was a dinner party. Tyler was gracious, and his wife, Monique, was very kind. She's a writer. I told her about you, and she wants to meet you."

Rayne raised her eyes to him. "You told her about me? Why?"

"Because she wanted to know if I was seeing anyone, and I told her I was seeing you."

"Seeing me?" She shook her head. "You're hardly seeing me, Trent. One dinner and a few phone calls are—"

He took the brush from her hands and put it back on the shelf. "What is it? You're distant again. You weren't like this the other night."

"I'm not sure the other night was such a good idea." She circled around him to the tack room door, but he held her arm.

"It was a very good idea. You opened up to me and you promised to talk to me whenever something was upsetting you."

Rayne struggled to remember the little bits of information she knew about the man. "Are you sure you want to be with me?" She wrenched her arm away from his grip. "Or maybe there's someone else you find more appealing."

"Ah, I think I get it. This is about Selene and me in the ring. She's not my type, Rayne." His gaze drifted over her curves.

"Your type?" She folded her arms over her bosom and jutted out her chin, trying to appear impervious to his charm. "What exactly is your type, Trent? I guess I'm just beginning to wonder if I would be your first choice in a line up with other women…or your last." She scooted to the door of the tight-fitting tack room, but he barred her way by placing a thick arm before her.

"I only want a woman who intrigues me, excites me, and makes me want her. And that woman, is you…only you, Rayne."

"A skittish horse excites you? That's what you called me. So once you have broken me, Mr. Newbury, then what?"

He moved right up to her, lowering his head to her face. "You know that a horse is never truly broken, it just agrees to submit to your pleasure for a little while. So maybe the question you should be asking is…when are you going to submit to me?"

Her pulse raced as she stared into his hypnotic gray eyes. He smelled of sweat, dust, and a hint of his sexy cologne. Rayne's body began to ache with longing.

He let his lips hover over hers. "All week I have been able to think of nothing else but you, and the first time we see each other, you're jealous of a woman I cannot stand." He smiled and placed his hands about her face. "You are a wonder."

"You really can't stand Selene?"

"Her laugh is as fake as the rest of her body. Forget about her." Trent contemplated her lips. "Now what do you say to a proper hello?"

He kissed her and Rayne instantly surrendered to him. His arms wrapped around her, pulling her so close that she feared she would not be able to draw a breath. His mouth teased her, encouraged her, and when she parted her lips, his tongue darted in and out, driving her mad.

As his lips worked their way down her neck, his hand skimmed her right breast and then roamed over her abdomen until it curled into the crotch of her beige jodhpurs. "You know what I want to do to you right now?"

Rayne giggled. "Yeah, I know."

"Turn around."

Rayne's eyes flew open. "Here?"

He kissed the tip of her nose. "Just do it."

With a pensive pout on her lips, she faced the racks of saddles on the wall.

His hands came around her hips to the zipper on the side of her riding pants. "Ever since the other night on the phone, I've wanted to touch you." He pushed the clingy fabric down her thighs.

"Trent?" She wiggled in his hands.

He crashed into her, shoving Rayne into the saddle before her. Grabbing at the saddle to steady herself, she tried to fight against him. "We can't," she protested.

"Relax," he murmured, placing his mouth against her ear as his hand slid along the elastic band of her beige panties. "You told me the other night you wished I could touch you. Well, I'm here now." He lowered her hand from the saddle in front of her. He kissed the back of her neck and then lightly nipped at her skin, just as he took her hand in his and slid them both inside her underwear.

Rayne trembled when he encouraged her fingers to caress her folds.

His teeth grazed her earlobe. "Show me what you like."

"I...I'm not—"

"Rayne, show me what you did the other night," he demanded.

With his hand on top of hers, urging her onward, she slowly began to stroke her wet flesh. His body pushed into her back as she closed her eyes and felt that burning hunger roar upward. Trent's hot breath caressed her cheek and his hand became more insistent, forcing her to move faster.

"Christ, Trent."

Rayne held on to the saddle before her as he took over her hand. She bent over as the need in her caused her gut to clamp down hard. Her orgasm spiraled up her back, tensing every inch of her being with the hope of release.

"God, yes," she moaned.

"That's it, baby. I want to hear you." He shoved her fingers hard into her folds.

When her body shuddered and her hips rocked against her hand, she bit down on her lower lip, trying not to scream. But just as she threw her head back, he shoved her hand out of the way and drove his fingers up into her, causing her climax to explode.

Grunting loudly, she bucked as he slid his fingers ruthlessly in and out of her. Just when the pulsations of pleasure eased, he fondled her again, even more aggressively than before.

She gripped the saddle in front of her with both hands, fighting to stay upright. "Trent, please," she begged in a ragged voice.

"We're going to do this again, Rayne. But this time, I'm gonna make you scream."

His fingers were merciless as they pinched her tender nub and rammed up into her. She was defenseless against his assault, and when the second orgasm overtook her, she fought like hell to contain her reaction. But just as the shockwaves of electricity blasted through her, Trent bit down hard into the back of her neck, causing her to lose control and utter a savage scream.

Seconds later, Rayne was clinging to the saddle with the last vestiges of strength she possessed as she tried to catch her breath.

Trent gently eased her underwear and pants up her hips, and then turned her to face him. Rayne could not look him in the eyes; she was too embarrassed.

He lifted her chin. "You're blushing."

"I…I've never done that before."

He tilted his head to the side, still watching her reaction. "You've never fooled around in a tack room?"

"No, I've never had a…with a man before."

He stared into her eyes for several seconds, knitting his brow. "But you were married?"

"Yeah, well, Foster never really asked if I ever did…you know. I guess he just assumed I did."

"You never told him?"

"When we were first together, I figured it was me." She shook her head. "Maybe I was doing something wrong...I didn't know. I only had one lover before my husband and that was," she grimaced, "really uncomfortable."

"You should have told him. You need to tell a man what you want. From now on, if I do something you don't like, tell me. I want to please you, Rayne."

She rested her forehead against his wide chest. "You just pleased me, very much."

He hugged her. "There's a lot more of that to come."

With her body satisfied, and her heart beginning to open up to the possibility of Trent Newbury, Rayne felt an unusual sense of comfort. All the novels she had read as a young girl had described lurid details of sexual encounters between the hero and heroine. But the reality of her experience with Trent was nothing like what she had read about; it was better.

She backed out of his embrace and zipped up her jodhpurs. "You'd better get out of here, before someone wonders what we're up to."

He kept his arms loosely about her sides. "Let them wonder."

"Aren't you worried people will find out about us?"

"No. Let them find out. I know Rebecca could care less."

"And what about Selene?" Rayne stepped out of his arms. "I know how that woman's mind works, and I'm sure she will be pretty pissed to hear about us."

He studied her face, trying to discern her thoughts. "Why is what Selene thinks so important to you? I know you two don't like each other, but is there something I'm missing?"

She tucked her T-shirt into her riding pants. "I've been on the receiving end of Selene's threats and gossip before. She loves to ruin lives, especially the lives of people she thinks are interfering with her plans."

"What happened, Rayne?"

She sighed and frowned at him. "A few years after I married Foster, there was this pathologist who came to work with Greer Laboratories…his name was Aiden Hudson. He was divorced but closer to Foster's age than mine. Whenever we would meet he was always very friendly with me, but it never occurred to me that…." Rayne was unsure how to go on.

"He was interested in you?" Trent surmised.

She nodded. "One night Foster invited Aiden to the house without telling me. We were supposed to attend a party for one of the numerous charities Foster supported, but he decided at the last minute not to go, and told me Aiden was taking me. I argued I didn't want to go, but Foster insisted. He really insisted on it." She ran her hands up and down her bare arms. "I remember thinking at the time it was odd how he pushed us together, but I went to the party with Aiden anyway. We were having a pretty good time until Selene arrived. When she saw Aiden, she was all over him. I told her to go back to her husband and leave Aiden alone because he was with me. She got mad, created a scene, and started calling me a whore in the middle of the party, and claimed I was having an affair with Aiden. It got so bad we had to leave."

"What did Foster say?"

Rayne vacillated, apprehensive about telling Trent the truth. "He was furious," she revealed in a tremulous voice. "Rumors flew about town that I was sleeping around, probably started by Selene. Things were never the same between Foster and me after that. I wonder sometimes if it wasn't some kind of test. Foster was always asking me if I was faithful. A week after that party, he fired Aiden. A month later I heard Aiden had to transfer his medical license to another state because no one would hire him in Texas. Foster knows everyone in the medical field, and I'm sure he used his influence to destroy Aiden."

Trent was quiet for a moment. "Sounds like you were married to a real piece of shit, Rayne," he finally commented.

"Just be careful with Selene, Trent. She and Foster are cut out of the same mold. They both have a habit of destroying people."

"Don't worry about me. I've tangled with Selene's kind before."

"She has a bone to pick with me, and you could get caught in the middle."

He slid his arms about her. "I won't."

She balled her hand up and tapped it against his chest. "You sure you want to get involved with me?"

"Most definitely." He then smacked her behind. "Now get out there and see to your horse. You have a lesson in thirty minutes."

She stepped back and sarcastically saluted. "Yes, sir."

"I'll see you later." He kissed her quickly on the mouth and then headed for her tack room door. After he opened the door, a gust of cool air enveloped her. Trent gave her one last devastating smile and walked out of the tack room.

Rayne went to the shelf with her horse brushes and once again picked up the soft white-bristled brush. While running her fingers over the bristles, snapshots of their brief interlude rolled through her mind.

"Don't lose your head. Just keep it together."

As Rayne exited her tack room, she desperately prayed she could stick to those words. The last thing she needed was another Foster Greer in her life. One was about all she could handle.

Chapter 9

Later that morning, after she had finished with her last riding class, Rayne was making her way back to the stables from the schooling ring as two of her students rode alongside her, asking a flurry of questions.

"How old where you when you first showed?" a tiny redhead with glasses interrogated as she sat astride her dapple gray pony. "My dad said I can't show until I'm thirteen, but that is two whole years away and I think I'm ready to show now. What do you think, Ms. Greer?"

"I think you should discuss it with your father, Kimberly," Rayne advised. "He is your father and wants only what is best for you."

"Yeah, right." Kimberly rolled her big green eyes beneath her thick-rimmed glasses. "He also told me I couldn't date until I was thirty, and my mom called him an idiot."

"At least you can date," a gangly, blue-eyed blonde, mounted on a slender brown mare, griped beside Rayne. "Mine told me I couldn't date until after I got married. Now how's that gonna happen?"

"Don't worry girls. Your fathers will come around, eventually," Rayne told them as she noticed Selene sashaying their way.

Selene's black riding breeches appeared unusually snug and her long black hair was down, flowing in the soft breeze. As she came closer, Rayne spied the liberal application of makeup on her face and suspected the additional touches were for Trent's benefit.

"Oh, it's her," Kimberly groaned next to Rayne. "My mom says she's a real slut. Is she a slut, Ms. Greer?"

"Girls," Rayne patted Kimberly's black boot next to her, "why don't you two go on ahead and take care of your horses? I'll see you back at the stables."

"Okay, Ms. Greer," the two girls spoke almost in unison, and walked ahead on their mounts.

Rayne waited patiently as Selene approached, smiling cordially at the girls as they rode past.

"You got a minute, Rayne?" Selene sounded way too friendly, immediately making Rayne suspicious.

"What do you want, Selene?"

Selene gazed about the open field around them before returning her black eyes to Rayne. "I wanted to talk to you about Trent."

Oh, this should be good, Rayne mused. "What about Trent?" she inquired, playing dumb.

Selene superficial giggle grated against Rayne's nerves. "Aw, come on Rayne. Girl-to-girl, is it serious between you two?"

Rayne folded her arms over her chest and glared at Selene. "Is that really any of your business? I seem to recall the last time you believed I was 'interested' in someone, it damn near ruined my marriage."

Selene showed her pearly white fangs. "We both know you and the good doctor had a thing for each other. It was so obvious to everyone. But I don't blame you. Pity Aiden had to leave town so quickly."

"Selene, you really have got...." But instead of getting angry, Rayne decided to go in for the kill. "Trent and I are seeing each other. In fact, we have another date tonight."

A fleeting look of surprise registered on her face, and then Selene regained her sinister composure. "But, Rayne, what do you really know about the man?"

"What's your point Selene, or do you even have one?"

"Did Trent happen to mention why he left Shelby Stables?" Selene cocked a black eyebrow at her.

"Does it matter?"

With a crafty grin on her red-painted lips, Selene kicked the dirt with her shiny black boot. "He and Lisa Shelby were well-known around Shelby Stables as being real into each other, if you know what I mean."

Rayne weighed Selene's disclosure. "How did you hear about this?"

"A girlfriend teaches over at Shelby. Apparently, it was common knowledge about the two of them. Then one day, Trent up and quits. No explanation, not even a good-bye to his instructors."

"I already know about Lisa Shelby." Rayne spun around and was about to walk away when Selene's irritating voice caught her.

"And did Trent tell you why he walked out on her?"

"Selene, that's none of my concern. It's his past."

Selene came slowly up to her, smirking. "I'd make it my concern, if I were you. You don't want to make another mistake like you did with Foster."

Having had enough of Selene's conniving, Rayne stomped toward the stables. Once beneath the shaded shed row, an infuriated Rayne marched straight to Rebecca's office. After arriving at a door painted with the black silhouette of a horse jumping a fence, Rayne knocked.

"Enter," Rebecca bellowed.

Pushing the door open, Rayne hurried inside and a cool blast of air-conditioning chilled her skin. Spotting Rebecca at her old wooden desk, with a pile of receipts and bills sitting on top, Rayne stood by the door, hyperventilating.

"Should I call 911?" Rebecca questioned, looking over the top of her reading glasses at Rayne.

While catching her breath, Rayne let her eyes take a turn of the numerous show ribbons on display on the white walls. "Can we talk?" she finally got out.

"Sure." Rebecca sat back in her worn chair and frowned up at her. "What is it?" She dragged her reading glasses further down her nose.

Rayne waved to the office door. "Selene just told me something and I need...I need to know if it's true."

Rebecca tossed the reading glasses to her desk. "You do know that Selene is a lying bitch, right?"

"I know," Rayne conceded. "But what she told me—"

"Let me guess." Rebecca held up her hand, silencing her. "It was about my new riding master."

Rayne walked over to a row of shelves, cluttered with a selection of family photos and reference books on horses.

"I think I understand what this is about." Rebecca's throaty chuckle saturated the air. "She's jealous of you and Trent."

Rayne stepped over to Rebecca. "You know about us?"

"Your tack room is only three doors down from my office. So yeah, I know. I heard you two this morning."

Rayne blushed and covered her face with her hands. "Dammit!" She raised her head. "Do you think anybody else heard us?"

"Perhaps not anyone east of the Mississippi," Rebecca ribbed with a cocky grin.

"Rebecca!"

"Well, sweetie, you spooked quite a few of the horses with all of that commotion. But I think that was what your man intended. Me and two other people watched him deliberately walk into your tack room and shut the door. If you ask me, he wanted us to see him. I think it was his way of telling everyone what you were up to."

An idea occurred to Rayne. "Do you think Selene heard us?"

"She was one of the two people I mentioned."

"Son of a bitch." Rayne punched the air. "So that's why she told me that bullshit about Trent having an affair with Lisa Shelby."

"Well, that's not surprising. Lisa Shelby likes them good-looking and loaded. She's a real gold digger."

Rayne's heart sputtered at the prospect, and then she remembered Trent's comments about dating such women. "So it's true."

"So what if it is?" Rebecca shrugged. "Lisa never let on to me that anything happened. In fact, she gave him a glowing recommendation."

Rayne twisted her hands together as doubts about Trent's intentions gnawed at her. "But if it is true...what do I do?"

"Nothing. Just be thankful you found a man who knows how to give a woman a great orgasm."

"Christ, Rebecca." Rayne rubbed her hand against her brow as her cheeks turned red.

"What? We can say orgasm these days, can't we? Or is it no longer PC? What do the college kids call them now...refreshers?"

"What?" Rayne half-laughed more out of embarrassment than surprise. "Where in the hell did you hear that?"

"I picked it up from my youngest daughter. She's into all the new slang."

Rayne went to the desk and slid into a wooden chair to the side. "I don't think I'm cut out for this dating crap."

Rebecca waved off her comment with her pudgy hand. "It's only just beginning for you two. When you've been with him a while and settled into the couple mode, all of this newbie stuff will fade. You'll see." She picked up her glasses from her desk.

"And what if we don't make it that far?"

Easing back in her chair, Rebecca fiddled with the glasses in her hand. "Kid, you've gotta have faith. I know you have been kicked in the heart like most of us, but that's the trick with love. You can't push it away when it's offered; otherwise you'll never truly know how wonderful it can be. Love is a lot like believing in something, God, Allah, whatever. You have to believe before you can find faith, just in the same way you have to believe before you can find love. Don't become like Selene. She's a woman who is dead on the inside because she has given up on love. You know your heart; she lost touch with hers a long time ago."

"Since the divorce, I've felt a lot like one of those heartless women. But with Trent...." Rayne let out a long sigh. "It's like I'm sixteen again, thrilled that the quarterback from the football team has noticed me. But love?" Rayne grimaced. "I don't know if we will ever get there."

"We'll see." Rebecca slipped on her glasses. "Just make sure next time you two do it in a car in the parking lot away from the horses. I don't want to have to lie to another ten-year-old."

Rayne stood from her chair. "What are you talking about?"

"The other person who heard you scream was Kit Watson's daughter. You know Kit, she owns that big red thoroughbred. Well, her daughter was standing right outside your tack room door looking very confused. She asked me what the two of you were doing in there, so I had to come up with something on the fly."

Rayne thought of the shocked little girl and felt mortified. "What did you tell her?"

"That he was helping you pull off your boots."

Rayne stared at Rebecca, her hazel eyes round with astonishment.

"I don't lie well under pressure." Rebecca reviewed one of the bills on her desk. "So just take it somewhere else when you two get the urge. I'm not running a brothel."

"Not for people, anyway," Rayne joked under her breath.

"Yeah well, horses don't scream when they have their refreshers."

Rayne narrowed her eyes on the round, middle-aged woman with the bleached blonde hair. "You're really scary sometimes, Rebecca, you know that?"

"My second husband used to say the same thing, but that was usually after we made love."

Shaking her head, Rayne went to the office door. "I did not need to hear that."

"And don't worry about Selene," Rebecca offered. "Her bark is worse than her bite."

Rayne paused at the door, considering her past with Selene. "You don't think she will try something?"

"Nah." Rebecca looked up from her bill. "Just worry about keeping that man of yours happy…very happy, if you know what I mean."

Worry twisted in Rayne's gut. "Rebecca, do you think I can keep him happy? I didn't keep Foster happy."

"He's not Foster, Rayne." Rebecca lowered her glasses over her nose. "Foster could never be happy with a woman, because he was never happy with himself. Trent is very different. He's a better man."

Exiting the office, Rebecca's comparison between the two men stuck with Rayne. Was Trent the "better man," or would she be repeating her past mistakes and setting herself up for even more heartache? She knew Trent was no Foster, but the more Rayne learned of his past, the more she began to doubt their future.

"I just wish I knew if I could trust him," she muttered, walking back to her tack room. "For once I would like to meet a man who keeps his promises."

Chapter 10

After donning a casual blue cotton summer dress and pulling her frizzy blonde hair back with a fashionable clip, Rayne got into her gray Highlander and made the short drive to Trent's house in Lewisville. The upper end subdivision had spacious two and three acre lots with massive, modern-looking mansions. As Rayne maneuvered her car along the winding streets with Victorian lampposts, picturesque babbling brooks, and colorful white, pink, and red crape myrtle trees, she was reminded of something out of a children's storybook. All that was missing were fairy huts, pixie dust scintillating in the twilight, and gatherings of wispy-winged creatures.

When she found 1722 Hoffsmill Road, as written on the directions he had given her earlier, Rayne parked in front of the sprawling contemporary home and let out a low whistle.

Built on a natural rise, the irregularly shaped, one-story structure had a square entrance with natural wood beams above and on each side of carved double wooden doors. Oversized windows were positioned along the façade in an irregular pattern. Built of thick timber and natural stone, the house blended with the long gardens of small green trees and landscaped shrubbery in front. Rising from the street, a brown-bricked staircase was carved into the bedrock, with glowing lights above each step.

Standing on the recessed porch, Rayne pushed the silver doorbell to the side. Chimes could be heard echoing throughout the home, and as she heard hurried footsteps approach, Rayne held her white clutch bag to her chest and tried to remember to breathe.

"You made it." Trent opened the front doors. "Did you have any trouble finding it?"

"No, your directions were fine."

Dressed in blue jeans, a pale yellow button-down shirt, and loafers, his dark hair was still damp and he smelled wonderfully citrusy. After he kissed her cheek, Trent guided her through the doorway.

"Dinner is in the oven, so come in and I'll give you a tour."

In a short entrance hall with an elevated ceiling done in alternating shades of chocolate brown and beige, Trent took her purse and put it on a dark Shaker table by the door. Placing his hand behind her back, he escorted her through the hall and into the living room.

"Wow," Rayne mouthed as surveyed the grand room.

Open in design with the living area, kitchen, and dining section all merging together, the room was made up of walls done in white with a main wall housing a massive stone hearth. Above the hearth was a painting of a herd of horses running across a green field. Scattered about the other walls were smaller paintings, also of horses in various settings. The floors were bamboo, and the furniture simple, modern, and a combination of wood and leather. Wide patio doors along the far wall opened on to a deck with an outdoor fire pit, grill, and black iron furniture. Behind the deck, a five-tiered, step fountain drained into a rectangular pond that was also made of natural stone.

"This is magnificent, Trent."

"Thanks, I designed it myself. I wanted to be an architect, but changed my major in college when I discovered I could make more in the oil and gas business."

"You designed this place?" She turned to him. "I have to say I'm more than a little impressed."

He walked to the open kitchen and settled behind a breakfast bar of stone and cedar. Shiny stainless appliances glistened in the recessed lighting above as he went to a built-in refrigerator and collected a bottle of wine.

"This is the Frascati I told you about. It's a nice Italian wine that will go great with the chicken Parmesan I'm preparing for dinner." He then acquired two wineglasses from a rack beneath the natural wood cabinets behind him.

"Where did you learn so much about wine?" Rayne remarked as he placed the glasses in front of her.

"My college sweetheart, Claudia West." He retrieved a wine opener from a nearby drawer. "Her father owned a vineyard in Hill Country outside of Austin. Clark West taught me all about wine; how to choose the best, and how to pair wine with foods. He was a wizard with wine." He jabbed the opener in the cork and began twisting it into the bottle.

Rayne took a seat on a wood and leather stool in front of the bar. "Your college sweetheart?"

He popped the cork from the bottle. "We dated from freshman year to our senior year at UT Austin. Then, I met Louise Lyndale. She was an older woman—two years older—beautiful, very smart, and a graduate student in the engineering program. We met in the library and started studying together; one thing led to another, and...." He poured the wine into the glasses. "Anyway, I soon learned Claudia had been seeing someone else, too."

"What happened to Louise?"

"Louise turned into Mary Lynn; Mary Lynn became Lydia; Lydia became Beth. Beth introduced me to…." He handed her a glass of wine. "I should stop before you make a run for the door."

"You've been with a lot of women. I get it." She knocked back a quick shot of wine.

"Not something I set out to do, Rayne." He examined the wine in his glass. "I'd always hoped I would be married and settled by now. It just never worked out that way."

She took another long sip from her glass, imbibing the courage to ask a question that had been bugging her all afternoon. "What about Lisa Shelby? What happened with her?" Rayne watched him over the rim of her drink.

A hint of surprise registered on his face. "How did you know about me and Lisa?"

"The riding community is pretty tight-knit. I've heard rumors."

He put his glass down on the bar. "Nothing much to say. We had some fun, but neither one of us were looking for anything permanent."

"And is she why you left Shelby Stables?" Rayne could hear the uncertainty in her voice.

"No, I left because I did all I could there. I was ready for a new challenge." He ran his long fingers along the countertop as if debating his next course of action. "Don't believe all the gossip you hear, Rayne. If you ever have questions about me, ask. I have nothing to hide."

"I'll keep that in mind." She downed another swallow of wine, almost finishing her glass.

He came around the bar and took her wineglass. "You don't trust me. That's obvious." He put the glass down on the bar. "But I want you to trust me. I'm not out to hurt you."

"I know that, Trent, but I guess I'm still smarting from my divorce."

He placed his arms about her and lifted her from the stool. "What can I do to prove I'm worth your trust?"

Rayne's hands slid up his thick arms and around his neck. "I'm sure we can come up with something."

"Yes, I'm sure we can."

Trent kissed her lips, and instantly her body responded to him. His arms tightened around her as she opened her mouth, tempting him with her tongue. His hands explored her back, and when he grabbed her butt, lifting her from the floor, a thunderbolt of panic seared through her.

"Perhaps we should...eat, first."

He put her feet down. "Are you nervous?"

"No." She tried to sound confident. "I just think we should eat before we get...distracted."

"Distracted? I'm already distracted." He let her go. "You know we don't have to sleep together tonight, Rayne. We can wait, if that would make you more comfortable."

She took a step back from him, rubbing her hands together. "I don't know if I'll ever be comfortable, Trent. Sex has always been...challenging for me."

"That will change with me, I promise." He took her hand. "Let's not talk anymore about it. I want you to relax and enjoy yourself."

He led her from the kitchen to the open patio doors. When they stepped outside, the crisp scent of evergreen bushes planted in a garden along the side of the deck hung in the air. The sound of water cascading down the steps of the fountain and into the narrow pond helped to calm Rayne's nerves; or perhaps it had been the wine she had quickly downed…she wasn't sure.

"I still can't believe you designed this house," she commented, gaping at the varied levels of the deck as they sloped down to a bright blue oval-shaped pool just beyond the rear of the home.

"I was always fascinated with contemporary designs. I had drawn and redrawn this place for years. It took me a while to make enough to build it, but I knew when I did it would be perfect." He motioned to the house. "It's got five bedrooms, four full baths, and a three car garage along the back."

"Why five bedrooms? Seems like a lot for one person."

"Sometimes my sisters come to stay and bring my nieces and nephew." He shrugged his wide shoulders. "I hoped one day I might fill the place with my children."

"You want kids?"

He nodded. "Someday. You?"

Her eyes drifted over the dimly lit gardens about the deck containing juniper and assorted dwarf shrubbery. "Yeah, eventually."

"Did Foster want children?"

"No." She breathed in the evening air, remembering her ex. "His first wife, Melissa, miscarried three times. He said that was enough pain for him, and he had no intention of going through it again."

"Did you ever tell him you wanted kids?"

She shook her head. "I was twenty-three when we married. I had no idea what I wanted. When I hit thirty, I realized I did want children, but by that point in our marriage I knew what I wanted didn't matter to Foster."

"Sounds like you should have left long before you did, Rayne."

"I know, but I was afraid to leave him," she admitted. "I didn't want the kind of life I had before we were married, and I couldn't go back to living with my mother. So, I stayed."

"What kind of life did you have with your mother? It had to be better than your marriage."

"My mother is not the easiest person to deal with. Ever since my father died...no, that's not right." She ran her hand over the back of her neck. "Ever since I was old enough to understand, I knew my mother was...difficult." Rayne took a few steps closer to the stone pond next to the deck. "Mom was always very fond of...scotch. Most of my years growing up were spent covering for her drinking. It wasn't bad when Jaime, my sister, and I were younger, but once adolescence came around and we didn't need her as much...well, she started drinking a lot more. She would forget to do things, like pick us up at school, cook dinner, and buy groceries. Jaime was always trying to pick up the slack for her; cooking, cleaning, shopping...whatever Mom needed. I spent my time at the stables, and stayed away from her."

"Where is your mother now?"

Rayne faced him. "She lives in the house my grandparents left her in Highland Park. Most of the social security money she gets she drinks away, and when there's nothing left to pay the electric bill or buy groceries, she calls me. She used to call a lot more when I was married to Foster. He always sent her money, but since the divorce I can't afford to, and she gets...angry."

Trent eased up to her, his stern face half-lit by the outdoor spotlight. "Have you tried to get her help?"

"Yeah, plenty of times." Rayne's sarcastic titter hung in the air. "Estelle's been to just about every rehab program in Dallas, but none of them got her sober for long. She doesn't want to quit. One day I figure I'll get that phone call from the police saying she's hurt or worse. Then I guess I'll have to put her somewhere."

"I'm sorry." Trent placed his arm about her shoulders. "I know that must be hard."

She stiffened next to him, ashamed that she had burdened him with her problems. "I'm sorry. I'm ruining this nice evening by talking about my mother. I shouldn't have unloaded all of that on you."

"You can tell me anything, Rayne." He pulled her into his arms. "There would be no evening without you."

His hands rubbed up and down her back, chasing away all of her unhappiness. But his touch also awoke a hunger in Rayne, and as flashes of their earlier encounter in her tack room roared to mind, she took a wary step away from him, waving back to the house.

"I would very much like to see the rest of your place."

He took her hand. "And I would very much like to show it to you."

***

After viewing all five bedrooms, including his master suite with skylights above the king-sized bed, and a shower stall wide enough for three people in his white marble master bath, they settled down at a rustic oak dining table. Once sliced homemade rosemary bread, a fresh green salad topped with a white wine vinaigrette dressing, and a platter of chicken Parmesan over spaghetti had been placed on the table, Rayne stared at Trent with renewed appreciation.

"Where did you learn to cook like this?"

"I worked as a waiter in a few restaurants to help pay for my riding growing up. I hung out in the kitchens, talked to the chefs, and learned a few things." Trent loaded a portion of the chicken smothered in red sauce on her square dinner plate. "The first woman I lived with, Erin, hated to cook. I think that was when I got good at it. Had to, otherwise we would have starved."

Rayne adjusted the white linen napkin in her lap. "How long did you two live together?"

"Four years." He put a slice of rosemary bread on her side plate. "I met her when I was working for Shell right out of college. She was a geologist."

Rayne swiped a pat of butter from a dish in the center of the table. "What happened?"

"Erin got a job with BP and transferred back to her native Scotland."

She buttered her slice of bread. "Did you want her to go?"

"We both knew the relationship was pretty much over." He seized a pair of silver tongs in the glass bowl loaded with salad greens. "At the time, I was trying to get into consulting work and was gone a lot. I think the last few months we were together we spent more time apart than actually under the same roof." He added some salad to the bowl by her dinner plate.

"You mentioned you lived with someone else," she hinted, attempting to sound casual as she reached for her fork.

"Natasha." He put the salad aside. "She only lived with me for about a year."

"What did Natasha do?"

"She was a physician at Baylor University Hospital." Trent grinned. "Very smart, very pretty, and never home."

Rayne cleaved off a piece of the chicken in red sauce. "She was always working?"

"I knew what I was getting into when we started seeing each other." Trent shrugged. "She was a cardiothoracic surgeon who got called away at all hours of the night."

"But you wanted more?"

"I wanted her here. After a few months together, it became obvious it wasn't going to work." He nodded to her plate. "Try my chicken."

She placed the chicken in her mouth and was surprised by the spicy taste. "Very good."

He watched her cut off another piece of chicken and curl some spaghetti around it. "You mentioned this morning that you had only one lover before Foster. Who was he?"

Rayne finished chewing on her food and put her fork down. "His name was Devon and we met at a nightclub when I was in college."

"Was he a student?"

"No." She snapped up her wineglass. "He was a bartender."

Intrigued, Trent sat back in his chair. "How long did it last?"

Rayne took a big swallow of wine. "One night." She thumped the glass back down on the table. "He was a cute bartender at this nightclub I went to with some people after a late class. I was twenty-two, a virgin, and dying to know what all the fuss was about, so...." She hurriedly put her wine to her lips.

"So your first time was with a stranger from a bar."

Rayne gulped more of the sweet wine. "I know that sounds terrible, and trust me, it was. After...well, I swore I was never going to do it again until I was married."

Trent took the wineglass from her hand. "Why was it terrible?"

She waited as he placed her glass on the table beside him. "I was brought up Catholic and felt guilty as hell after."

"But how did it feel with the bartender?"

Nervously running her hand over her brow, she sighed. "I don't understand. How did what feel?"

"Did he hurt you? Did you enjoy it? Most people place a lot of importance on the first time they have sex."

Rayne flopped back in her chair, wondering where this was going. "Did you enjoy the first time you did it?"

"This isn't about my first time, it's about yours. How was it?"

She stared into his eyes, trying to figure out why he was so interested.

"Why do you want to know?"

"It will help me to know more about you. How a person views sex is usually the result of their experiences. So tell me, what did you think?"

Appeased by his explanation, Rayne pondered the question. "I guess I found it...surprising. I had never been so intimate with anyone before."

Trent rested his arms on the edge of the table. "Did you sleep with Foster before you married him?"

"I wanted to, but when I told him about my experience with Devon, he insisted we wait."

"And was it better with your husband?" he entreated, leaning in a little closer.

"No. I'd hoped there would be more to it once I was married, but...there wasn't. I sometimes think I should have slept around before I got married, like all my friends did." She snatched up her fork from her plate, amazed at how he had gotten her to open up. "What about your first time? What was it like for you? Did you think it was a big deal...or not?" she blabbered, desperate to shift the focus away from her sex life.

He cocked his head to the side as Rayne fidgeted before him. "Actually, my first time wasn't bad. Her name was Beverly, and she was a waitress at one of the restaurants where I worked. I was sixteen, she was twenty-eight."

"You started young, didn't you?" Rayne picked at her salad. "Was it only the one time?"

"No, not quite." Trent raised his fork. "It happened a few times. I came to find out later that I wasn't the only one. She had a thing for all the young boys working at the restaurant."

"So you weren't in love with her?" She stuffed the salad into her mouth.

"Hardly. I was sixteen and getting laid was more important than love." He took a bite of chicken.

After swallowing her salad she asked, "Do you still feel the same way?"

"I'm not sixteen anymore, Rayne."

"Only on the outside, Trent. You could still be that boy on the inside."

He lowered his fork. "If I were, I would have taken what I wanted from you this morning and walked away; but here we are."

She smiled, heartened by his words. "Yes, here we are."

***

After dinner, Rayne insisted on helping clear the dining room table. Once the dishes had been loaded into the stainless Bosch dishwasher, and leftovers put away in the refrigerator, Trent poured the last of the Frascati into their wineglasses and escorted Rayne out the wide patio doors to the deck.

"You get a great view of the stars at night." He walked over to a pair of cedar chaise lounge chairs beside the rectangular pond.

Rayne sipped from her wine and eyed the heavens. "You like the stars?"

"Not particularly. But with the way you've been chugging that wine, I figured you could use some fresh air."

Rayne modestly lowered her glass. "You noticed."

"I'd have to be blind not to see how nervous you've been all night." He came up to her and took the wine from her hand, and motioned to the chaise lounge next to them. "Have a seat."

Trent placed her wineglass and his on a wooden table between the two lounge chairs. After Rayne sat down, he took a seat behind her.

"You need to relax." He rested his hands on her shoulders and gently kneaded the muscles beneath. "You're very tight."

She tensed as his hands worked into her tender flesh. "You're killing me."

"That's because you're fighting me. Loosen up your shoulders."

She let out a long breath and her shoulders fell forward.

"That's it. Now close your eyes and let me work out some of these knots."

As his hands expertly squeezed into her flesh, Rayne relaxed and began to enjoy the sensation. She rolled her neck around, feeling all the wine in her system.

"And where did you learn to do this?"

He chuckled lightly. "Years of competitive riding have left me with more than a few dings and dents. I get massaged at least twice a month to combat the stiffness and pain of my injuries."

"I know what you mean. I've cracked my ribs, had two concussions, dislocated my shoulder, and have broken numerous fingers."

His hands worked into her neck. "Broken wrist, clavicle, busted two ribs and an ankle when a rebellious stallion fell on me, and I've lost count of the number of concussions I've had."

"And still we ride."

He wrapped his arms about her, lowering her into the chair next to him. "Yep, gluttons for punishment."

"When I had to give it up in college, I missed it, a lot. The only time in my life when I feel right with the world is on the back of a horse."

"Me, too," he agreed.

Resting her head against his chest, Rayne closed her eyes and listened to the steady beat of his heart. Content, and slightly tipsy, she let her mind drift off as visions of riding Bob beneath the open blue sky warmed the furthest reaches of her soul.

Chapter 11

Slits of bright sunlight burrowed into Rayne's closed eyes, making her slap her hand over her face. Cringing against the horrible dryness in her mouth and the sudden throbbing in her temples, she sat up and opened her eyes. At first, she was disoriented, gazing about the white room with its clean-cut lines, paintings of horses, massive hearth, and leather and wood furniture.

As flashes of the night before started to creep back, she crumpled back against the brown leather sofa she was sitting on. A green blanket had been placed over her, and a fluffy white pillow beneath her. Shaking her head, she remembered closing her eyes as she had nestled against Trent on the deck.

"Damn it."

"Good morning." His smoky voice came from the open kitchen on the other side of the wide living room. "You want some coffee?"

Willing her blurry vision to come into focus, Rayne directed her gaze toward the kitchen. Behind the breakfast bar, a clean-shaven Trent was dressed in a casual pair of jeans, blue T-shirt, and pouring out coffee into two white cups.

Pushing the blanket aside, she stood from the sofa. "Tell me I didn't pass out on you." She rubbed her hand over her face, imagining how bad she must have looked.

"Pass out, not quite. You fell asleep, so I carried you in here and put you on the sofa."

She stumbled toward the counter. "Why didn't you wake me?"

He pushed a cup of coffee toward her. "You want that black?"

"Definitely." Her hands eagerly embraced the cup.

"You drank three glasses of wine and barely touched the dinner I prepared. Waking you was not an option."

She took two long sips from the coffee and felt her stuffy head begin to clear. "So much for our date."

He lifted his white cup. "I don't know. You can learn a lot by watching someone sleep."

She rolled her eyes. "Please tell me I didn't do anything I will live to regret, like snore or talk in my sleep."

The open kitchen reverberated with his heartwarming chuckle. "No. And even if you did, I wouldn't embarrass you like that."

"Why doesn't that make me feel better?"

"Drink your coffee and relax. I can post my naked pictures of you on Facebook later."

"Cute." She put her cup down. "No, I'd better get home and check on Frank. He's probably destroyed my house by now."

"I'll drive you."

"No, Trent. I can drive home."

He came around the breakfast bar, carrying his coffee. "Stop fighting me. I'll take you back to your place, you can shower and change, then we will get some breakfast and head over to the stables."

"What about my car?"

He took a sip of coffee. "You can get it when we come back here later this evening."

"Most guys would be anxious to get rid of me."

He walked up to her and kissed her forehead. "I'm not 'most guys.'"

"Yeah, I've noticed."

He peered down into his coffee. "After your lessons today, I want you and I to work with Bob. We have a lot to do to get him ready for that show."

Feeling energized by more than the caffeine, Rayne actually found that she was looking forward to working with Trent. Never before had she met a man who inspired her to reach for her dreams, and was willing to help her attain them. "It's a date. Mr. Newbury," she happily chirped.

He put his coffee down on the bar. "I'll get my shoes, and then we'll go."

Rayne's stomach did a few excited tumbles as Trent walked toward a hallway that led to the master bedroom. Someone up above must have been smiling down on her, because Rayne had a funny feeling her bad luck with men was about to change.

***

Before his 550i BMW had even come to a stop in front of her simple red-bricked bungalow, Rayne was already pulling her keys from her purse, anxious to get inside.

At her front door, picturing a house torn apart by a frustrated Frank, she placed her key in the lock. "Frank's never been alone all night before, so be prepared."

"Maybe he'll surprise you." Trent gave her shoulder a confident squeeze.

She worked the lock as her feeling of dread rose. "Yeah, I'm sure he's left surprises all over the living room for me."

When they entered the door, a resounding "woof" greeted them, followed by the cacophony of four feet zooming across the living room floor. Frank came barreling up to the door before they were both inside. The large furry dog ran up to Rayne and put his front feet on her blue dress.

"Hey, buddy." She rubbed his face and scratched his back. "I know. I was a bad mommy."

Immediately, Frank went running from her to the back door by the kitchen that led to the large fenced yard.

"I'd better let him out." Rayne put her purse down on the table by the door and jogged down the entrance hallway.

Doing a quick scan of the living room as she flew through it, she was surprised to discover a lot less destruction than she had expected. Short of some sofa cushions on the floor, and an imprint on her white leather sofa, nothing else was out of place.

After Frank had run out the back door, she returned to the living room to find Trent gathering the cushions from the floor.

"I think you lucked out." He tossed the cushions on the sofa.

"Yeah, well, I haven't checked my bedroom yet."

He came up to her side. "Better get it over with."

They went down the hallway to her open bedroom door, and when Rayne peeked inside, she discovered where Frank had spent the night. Her gray and white comforter was twisted into a ball on her brass bed, and several of Frank's stuffed toys were spread out next to it.

"I think his secret is out," Trent joked.

Rayne walked up to the bed and then became distracted by a white wisp of paper on the gray carpet. She spotted what appeared to be toilet paper and her eyes followed the trail of shredded paper to the bathroom.

"Oh, no." She trotted to the bathroom door and then came to a grinding halt. "Son of a bitch."

When Trent came up to her side, his sudden fit of laughter only sharpened her anger.

The entire bathroom was covered with toilet paper. It was stuck on the walls, and covered the vanity, the bathtub, and was even up on the shelves located to the side of the shower stall.

"How in the hell did he do that?" she shouted, waving into the bathroom.

Trent was leaning over at this point, grabbing at his side.

"It's not funny, Trent!"

"Oh, God," he chuckled, sounding short of breath. "Yes, it is, Rayne." He waved his hand about her master bathroom. "Where did he get all of that toilet paper?"

"I keep a few extra rolls on the back of the toilet."

Trent leaned his shoulder on the doorframe, shaking his head and sighing as his laughter ebbed. "God, you should have seen your face."

"I can't believe I have to clean up this mess."

He patted her shoulder. "I'll help."

She headed out of the bathroom. "No, you don't have to do that. I'll just take a shower in the guest bathroom and deal with it when I get home tonight."

"God, you're stubborn." He followed her into the bedroom. "I said I would help, so let me help."

At the bed, she scooped up Frank's stuffed toys. "It's my problem."

He reached for her hands. "You're not alone anymore, Rayne."

When he turned her to him, a flutter of anticipation rocked her. Instead of pushing Trent away and carrying the dog toys out of the room, she was transfixed by him. She was not sure if it was the aftereffects of the wine, but his eyes were strangely intoxicating, and his hands felt profoundly sensual.

"What will it take to convince you that I'm not going anywhere?" he pleaded, moving closer.

"You can't keep that kind of promise, Trent. Time is the enemy of all promises."

"I don't abandon people I care about." He lowered his mouth to hers. "And I care about you."

When Trent kissed her, Rayne let the toys in her arms fall to the floor. She wanted to believe in him, and as his kiss grew more ardent, Rayne's apprehension slowly receded. Then, that inexplicable longing to have Trent naked next to her took control.

Wrapping her arms about his shoulders, she moved against him, pressing into him, enticing him with her curves. Rayne's fingers groped his muscular back, teased his chest, and eventually landed on his tight, round ass. When she squeezed his cheeks, Trent promptly deposited her on the bed.

"You're driving me crazy."

Pushing the comforter off the bed, Rayne scooted back on the sheets. "What are you going to do about it?" she demanded, emboldened by her desire.

"What do you want me to do?" He kneeled on the bed and crept toward her. "You have to tell me what you want, Rayne."

She hooked the collar of his blue T-shirt, tugging him closer. "I want you."

Trent covered her body with his. "You've already got me." He nuzzled her cheek, "Now tell me what you want me to do with you."

"Do with me? Why do I have to say it?"

He touched his forehead to hers. "I want you to be comfortable with me; comfortable enough to tell me exactly what you want me to do to you."

She was afraid to say the words; afraid at how he would react. Rayne had never been any good at telling a man what she wanted. "Make love to me, Trent," she finally whispered.

His arms lovingly enveloped her. "There, was that so hard?"

She yanked his T-shirt over his head. "No."

Once she had tossed his shirt to the floor, her hands avidly caressed his smooth chest and his ripped abdominal muscles. When Rayne pushed her hands beneath the waist band of his blue jeans, eager to feel his round butt, he laughed into her neck and then unzipped his pants.

"I like it when you're hungry for me." He plucked his wallet from his back pocket.

"What are you doing?"

"Protection," he told her, pulling out a yellow condom packet from his wallet.

"I, ah, forgot…about that." Rayne's cheeks flushed, rattled that she had not suggested a condom.

"Just relax. I've got it covered." Trent tossed the packet and wallet to the side of the bed. "Now where were we?" He kissed her again and soon Rayne felt her inhibitions slip away.

He bit into her neck as she helped him wriggle out of his pants and briefs. "I've been daydreaming about having you naked next to me since the day we met," she breathlessly confessed.

"So that is what you were thinking behind those lovely hazel eyes. I've always wondered."

When he was naked on top of her, she slid her hands around to his erection and gently stroked him. "That first day

I saw you in the ring, teaching your riding class, I was attracted to you."

Aroused by her touch, Trent hiked her blue cotton dress up her hips. "Why didn't you just admit that to me?" He pressed his hand into the valley between her legs.

She kicked her head back. "Because I thought you were an asshole."

He rubbed his hand up and down the crotch of her underwear, making her moan against him. "Do you still feel that way?"

"Of course not."

Smiling up at her, he slowly lowered her panties to her ankles. "Are you sure?" He then dramatically dropped her underwear to the floor.

"I'm positive," she giggled.

"Good, now turn over."

Trent eased the zipper down her back and peeled the dress from her body. Then, he unhooked her bra and threw it to the floor.

Rayne was about to flip back over when he held her. "No, stay this way." He pushed her knees beneath her, raising her hips from the bed. "I've dreamed of riding you from behind," he murmured, tracing his fingers along her wet folds.

His fingers dipped ever so gently into her and she backed her hips into his hand, wanting him to go deeper. Slowly, he withdrew and then pushed inside her, driving apart her flesh. With his thumb flicking her nub, and his fingers stimulating her from the inside, Trent began to slowly, rhythmically bring her to climax.

Rayne groaned as her loins exploded with heat. She rocked against his hand as her coming orgasm pooled in her gut. Waves of excitement shut off her mind from everything around her. She swore she heard Frank barking, could make out Trent's rapid breathing, but all noises sounded so far away. When the need of her release began to consume her, Rayne pushed harder against Trent's hand.

"Yes," she cried out.

"That's it, baby, let go."

Just as he spoke the words, an unrelenting surge of energy burst forth from her groin and her entire being shuddered. When the last traces of her orgasm were dying away, Trent flipped her over on her back.

"God, I want you." He climbed on top of her. Snatching up the condom package, he eagerly ripped it open.

Catching her breath, Rayne watched with interest as he slipped on the condom, fascinated at how quickly he did it.

Trent laughed at her expression. "Haven't you ever watched a man put on a condom before?"

She looked up at him, wide-eyed. "No. You're my first."

He kneeled between her legs. "Next time you can do it for me."

Lifting her hips to him, Trent spread her folds wide apart. Rayne wrapped her legs about his waist, entreating him to enter her. Trent leaned over, kissed her lips, and then slowly drove all the way into her with one forceful thrust. When he pulled out, he groaned against her cheek before diving back into her moist flesh.

Rayne held on to his shoulders as he rammed into her again, then a tendril of disappointment snaked through her when her body did not respond. There was no dizzying sensations, no urgent need. Perhaps there was something wrong with her. Maybe she was one of those women not able to orgasm during sex. As the sounds of his exertions filled the bedroom, Rayne waited for him to climax. But just as she hoped he was almost done, Trent stopped.

"You're not enjoying this, are you?"

"No. I am."

He sat up slightly. "Rayne, you need to tell me if this isn't working for you."

"I told you, I'm one of those women who just aren't any good at sex."

He placed her on her side. "We'll try it another way."

"Trent, it's all right."

Spooning against her, he gently caressed her back. "Do you trust me?"

She nodded her head.

"Then we will do it in every position until we find one that excites you."

He tucked her knees into her chest. "There is nothing wrong with you. We just have to experiment a little."

He kneeled behind her, and when he entered her, Rayne instantly felt something very different. A tantalizing tingle began in her lower body, and when he pushed into her once more, the tingle turned into a consuming ache.

"Is this better?" he mumbled in her ear.

She dug her claws into his hips.

He kissed her ear. "I'll take that as a yes."

His thrusting became more insistent. The faster he pushed into her, the more desperate she became.

"Harder, Trent, do it harder."

Balling up the sheets in her hands, her body vibrated as his hips slapped loudly against her. Rayne grabbed the pillow in front of her as the fire in her gut spread throughout her limbs. She moaned, overcome with desire, desperately wanting him to drive harder into her. Her muscles twitched as she lost all sense of her surroundings. Rayne lowered her head into the pillow, bit down hard, and when she could not stand it any longer, she screamed.

Trent was grunting behind her when she bucked against him. He held her close as he drove into her one more time, and then he cried out her name before he went still.

Curled into her back, she could feel the rapid rise and fall of his chest. She could not believe what they had just shared.

So that's what everyone keeps raving about.

He kissed her back. "I think you're getting the hang of this."

She rolled over to him. "It was so much better the other way."

"We just had to find what worked for you. Foster never wanted to try different positions?"

The mention of her ex-husband's name made her snort with resentment. "With Foster there was only one position for sex, and that was only after he had downed a few drinks. It was never good with him."

"Sex is supposed to be fun and bring you pleasure, Rayne. I want you to enjoy being with me."

She marveled at his practical approach to something she had always seen as mysterious and forbidden. All during her marriage, Rayne had grown used to sex being what she was supposed to do and not something she enjoyed. Now here was a man showing her a whole new world, where the joy in her heart matched the intensity of the physical relationship.

As her mind jumped ahead to Trent's expertise in bed, she began to speculate about his other lovers. How many had there been? And where did she stack up? Carefully considering how to broach the subject, she leaned back from him, intent on learning more.

"I guess I must seem pretty inexperienced compared to the other women you've been with."

He stretched out next to her. "What makes you think that?"

"You just know so much." She hesitated before asking, "Have you had a lot of lovers?"

He sat up and removed the condom. "Would it matter if I have?"

"No, but it makes me wonder what you could possibly see in me?"

He dropped the condom to the floor. "You need to start seeing your assets, Rayne. You're a very unique and—"

The ringing of her house phone interrupted him.

"Do you need to get that?"

She pointed to an answering machine on her dresser. "The machine will get it." As the machine answered the call, she turned back to him. "You were saying something about my assets?"

"Rayne? Are you home?" a thundering voice rang out from the machine.

Rayne bolted up in the bed. "Oh, shit!"

"What?" Trent implored.

"I'm at the hospital with Estelle," the man on the answering machine went on. "She phoned me last night, claiming she couldn't find you. She fell and hit her head. Rayne, you need to come to Texas Health Presbyterian in Dallas on Walnut Hill Lane. We're in the emergency room. I hope you get this. I'm going to call Southland Stables and see if you're there. I've got my cell. Call me."

Rayne sat motionless in the bed as the message came to an end and the machine clicked off.

Trent clasped her arm. "Rayne, what is it?"

She kicked her legs over the side of her brass bed. "It's my mother. I have to go to the hospital." She stood from the bed and went to the bathroom door.

"But who was that on your machine?"

"That was my ex-husband." She gestured to the mess Frank had left in the bathroom. "Shit, I need to shower in the other bathroom."

Trent came up to her. "Take a shower and I will clean up Frank's mess." He grabbed a blue fuzzy robe hanging on a hook just inside the bathroom door. Wiping a few shards of toilet paper from the robe, he draped it about her shoulders. "Go on. We need to get to your mother."

She fastened the robe around her waist. "We?"

"I'm going with you," he stated, moving back into the bedroom.

"Presbyterian Hospital is almost an hour away, and you have to get to the stables, and…this isn't your problem, Trent."

"It is my problem, Rayne. I told you I'm not going anywhere." He collected his jeans and briefs from the floor. "You'd better go get ready."

As Trent was pulling on his pants, she went up to his side and kissed his cheek. "Thank you." Before he could reply, she dashed through the door and down the hall to the guest bathroom.

When she closed the bathroom door, she leaned back against it and wiped a tear from her cheek. For the first time in years, Rayne no longer felt alone.

Chapter 12

Trent careened his dark blue BMW through the scant early morning Sunday traffic on I-35 toward the hospital. When his car entered the road to the mammoth complex that made up Texas Health Presbyterian, Rayne's stomach started to churn.

She flashed back to her previous hospital visits with her mother and how uncomfortable they had been. Estelle had often been drugged, her speech had sometimes been slurred, but the worst was when she had witnessed her mother suffering through the delirium of alcohol withdrawal. Estelle's screams, curses, and cries for her sister, Jaime, still haunted Rayne.

"You all right?" Trent pulled into a parking spot outside of the emergency room.

"I've just gone through this with her so many times before that I…."

"This time it will be different."

She turned to him. "How?"

He switched off the ignition. "Because I'm here."

Leaning over in her seat, she kissed his cheek. "In case I get too pissed off later, thank you for coming with me."

He reached for his car door. "We'd better get in there."

Entering a double set of glass doors, they found a round reception desk located in the center of a modest-sized waiting area decorated with peaceful ocean prints, comfy chairs, and a coffee and tea service to the side of the room.

After a brief conversation with the reception staff, Rayne and Trent were escorted by an aide dressed in blue scrubs through the two white doors marked Exam Area. A short walk down a white-tiled hall brought them to the door of Exam Room 6.

Queasy and feeling drained, Rayne stepped inside. The first thing that hit her was the antiseptic smelling air, and then she heard her mother's grating voice.

"Who in the hell is it now? They've already drained all the goddamned blood I got. How much more do they need?"

"Just calm down, Estelle," a man impatiently pleaded.

Rayne quickly spotted the owner of that voice, adding to her discomfort.

The attractive older man was standing by the foot of the hospital bed with his arms folded over his chest, looking grim, as usual. His thick gray hair was gently tossed about his head, and his angular face, pointed chin, and smooth brow were exactly the same as she remembered. Rayne had hoped in the few months since they had last seen each other that he would have aged, but Foster Greer could never afford to grow older. He had always maintained an active lifestyle, adhered to a healthy diet, and avoided all alcohol and drugs—probably to keep up with his younger wives. She eyed his pressed blue slacks, starched white dress shirt, and polished black leather shoes, and recalled his propensity for always looking his best. Despite any emergency, Foster would take the time to make sure his clothes were just right before heading out the door. When he turned his blue, dictatorial eyes to Rayne, a deluge of unhappy memories engulfed her.

"Rayne." Foster approached her side and cordially kissed her cheek.

When he saw Trent, Foster stiffened with surprise. He held out his hand to Trent. "I'm Foster Greer."

Trent took his hand. "Trent Newbury."

"Are you Rayne's boyfriend?"

"He's just a friend, Foster," Rayne jumped in. "We ride together at the stables."

Foster's blue eyes contracted into two discerning slits as they appraised Trent. "Just asking, Rayne."

She ignored him. "Why did she call you? She knows my—"

"Is that her?" Estelle croaked from the hospital bed.

Rayne veered her eyes to the corner of the exam room. Next to a large window covered with green and white-checked curtains was a raised hospital bed, and lying in the bed, the white sheets tossed about her tiny figure, was her mother.

It always shocked Rayne whenever she saw Estelle. She was instantly reminded of her sister. Jaime had inherited their mother's blue eyes, petite figure, and creamy white skin, whereas Rayne had always favored her father in looks and eye color. The only thing she had gotten from their mother was her frizzy, honey-blonde hair. As Estelle's heart-shaped mouth turned downward, Rayne was reminded of how the woman's delicate, almost fragile features had stirred the protective instincts of every man she had ever known. As far back as Rayne could remember, Estelle Masterson had used her exquisite beauty to get exactly what she wanted from the opposite sex.

"Where in the hell have you been?" Estelle pointed a bony finger at her daughter. "I called your cell phone a dozen times. I even tried your house and that damn stable you love so much."

"I was out last night and turned off my phone," Rayne asserted, standing a few feet away from the bed.

A white bandage was covering her mother's right forehead, making her steely blue eyes appear even colder. Despite her condition, Rayne noticed that her mother still had found time to apply lipstick, rouge, mascara, and carefully style her short, curly blonde hair. Her aquamarine silk dress had not a drop of blood on it, while her black low-heeled pumps were sitting neatly on the floor next to her bed.

"Why did you turn off your phone? I had no way to get you. Thank God Foster was home. I'd be dead without him."

"Estelle, don't be so dramatic," Foster chided as he came up to Rayne's side and gave her shoulder an encouraging pat. "You only bumped your head…you weren't dying." He looked over at Rayne. "I phoned Brian Rancor, the administrator here. You remember Brian."

Rayne nodded. "Yes, Brian from your Saturday golf game."

"He contacted the ER and had her seen right away. I left you a message as soon as we got here."

Uncomfortable with his touch, Rayne edged away from Foster's hand. "Mother, what happened?"

"I tripped on those stupid slippers you bought for me last Christmas." Estelle played with the bandage on her forehead. "I told you they were too big!"

"Estelle, please," Foster begged, gesturing for her to lower her voice. "You don't have to shout."

Rayne pleadingly cast her eyes to her ex-husband. "What really happened?"

Foster grudgingly shrugged. "Do you need to ask?"

Rayne sighed and shifted her gaze to her mother. "How much did you have to drink, Mother?"

"Oh, so you think I did this because I was drunk," Estelle's aggravating, raspy voice echoed about the exam room. "It was those damned slippers, I told you."

"I need to go." Foster took Rayne's elbow. "Walk me out," he whispered.

"Mother, I'm going to have a word with Foster."

"You two are going to talk about me behind my back. I get it." Spotting Trent close to the room door, Estelle paused and then stared at him. "Who's he?"

Rayne gave Trent a beseeching glance.

"Trent Newbury." Trent smiled radiantly as he neared the hospital bed. "I ride horses with Rayne at Southland Stables."

Estelle regarded him with a speck of skepticism in her blue eyes. "Are you gay?"

Rayne spun around. "Mother!"

"What?" Estelle shrugged her thin shoulders. "Aren't all men who ride horses gay? You told me so, Raynie."

"Well, I'm not gay," Trent assured her, his smile still intact.

Estelle did not appear convinced. "What are you doing with my daughter?"

Foster turned Rayne toward the door. "Let's leave them."

"What happened?" she questioned as soon as they were in the ER hallway.

Foster's eyes glided over Rayne's snug jeans, white T-shirt, and damp hair. "It was a little after three in the morning when she phoned the house, frantic because she was bleeding all over the place and didn't remember falling. By the time I got to her, she was still pretty drunk, and I knew she was going to need to be seen by someone."

Rayne gripped the white railing along the hallway wall, choking back her shame. "Thank you for bringing her here. I'm just sorry you had to deal with her."

"Your mother always did drive me nuts, Rayne, but I knew if she was calling me, it had to be pretty bad." He pointed to the exam room door. "Were you with him last night?"

A swift kick of suspicion hit Rayne's gut. "Does that matter?"

He shook his head, appearing frustrated. "I know things didn't end on a high note with us, but don't shut me out completely. I'm still here for you."

Rayne forced a half-smile across her lips, wanting to appease him. She had no desire to remain cordial, but she did need him to continue paying for Bob and his upkeep.

"I appreciate that, Foster."

He glanced about the bustling ER hallway. "Look, the ER doctor wants to keep her, but I told him she won't stay. There's something wrong with her blood work. I didn't get the whole story, but they wanted to wait to talk to you."

Rayne rested her shoulder on the wall. "It's probably the drinking catching up with her. The last time she was in rehab they told her to quit or she would start having problems."

"Yeah, I remember. It was right around our eighth anniversary."

She browsed his stern blue eyes, wondering what she had found so damned attractive about the man all those years ago. Sure he was good-looking, with his strong, angular features and well-toned body, but now his looks seemed so generic, like all the other polished and presentable businessmen she had encountered over the years. There was nothing alluring about him anymore. His stoic features held none of the fascination that had captivated her when they first met.

"You doing okay, Rayne?"

She defensively folded her arms over her chest, not wanting to buy into his concern. She knew better. "Yeah, I'm good."

"You need any money? You know I always told you if you needed anything to come to me. I'll take care of you."

She shook her head. "No, I'm doing all right."

"How's Bob?"

This time her smile was genuine, happy that he had at least remembered her horse's name. "Trent is the new riding master at the stables, and he wants me to get him ready for a show in another month. Looks like I'm going to start showing sooner than I expected."

His eyes grew a little colder. "Is Trent good to you? Does he take care of you? You need to be taken care of, Rayne. You know you were never any good at being on your own."

She fidgeted slightly, tucking her hands in the back pockets of her jeans. The condescending tone of his voice was more than she could bear. Rayne could not remember a time when he did not speak to her in such a manner. "I've been on my own for a year, Foster. And Trent is…a good friend, that's all." She curled her hands into fists inside the pockets of her jeans. "How's Connie?" she posed, eager to change the subject.

He rolled his eyes. "She wants to redecorate the entire house."

Rayne gently laughed. "You hate redecorating."

"Yeah, I know. But everything I think of as comfortable, she calls old-fashioned." He searched the hallway, his lips drawn together in a contemplative frown. "I think the problem is I may be a little too old-fashioned for Connie."

"I thought you two were happy," she offered, not sure what else to say.

"So did I, for a while." His eyes returned to her. "Nowadays I find myself missing how comfortable we were together. You always understood me."

Rayne pushed away from the wall and held up her head, knowing what Foster was doing. An expert at manipulation, he had for years made her believe that she was the only one for him. But experience had taught her to distrust his words and actions. "I'm beginning to think I never understood you at all," she admitted, and turned toward the door.

"I'm still the same man you knew. Nothing has changed."

She put her hand on the silver door handle of her mother's exam room and thought of Trent. "Everything has changed, Foster. I'm different. I...I should get back to Mother."

"You look good, Rayne."

A pang of past regret raked across her heart. "Good-bye, Foster," she uttered and rushed in the door.

Rayne halted just inside the room, pushing down all the unwanted memories of Foster welling up in her mind. This meeting had been easier than the ones before, but still difficult for her. She debated if it would ever get better.

Trent's seductive laughter tore her away from her troubles, and recollections of their time together earlier that morning soothed her frazzled nerves.

"Raynie, where did you get this one?" Estelle happily called to her. "I like him."

Rayne moved toward the bed, curiously noting her mother's flirtatious smile.

"I was just telling your mother about some of the people at the stables," Trent explained, winking at her.

"He's funny." Estelle's blue eyes flashed with approval, something Rayne had never seen before. "He's not too bad on the eyes, either. He's the one you mentioned on the phone the other night, isn't he? Are you two sleeping together yet?"

There it was, Rayne silently admonished. Just when she let her guard down, Estelle found a way to humiliate her. "Mother, please. We're not sleeping together. We're friends."

"You told your mother about me?" The hope was evident in Trent's voice.

"So you are sleeping with him." Estelle sat up in the bed, grinning excitedly. "How long has this been going on?"

"That's none of—" Not wanting to give Estelle any more ammunition, Rayne hastily muttered, "Never mind. Tell me what happened last night."

Estelle lowered her eyes to the bed sheets and then twisted a small section in her fingers. "I fell, that's all."

"After how many drinks, Estelle?" Rayne loudly interrogated.

Trent took a step back from the bed. "I'll wait outside while you two talk." He shot Rayne a reproachful look, and then turned for the door.

After he had left the exam room, Rayne stared at her mother's frail figure in the bed. The dark circles beneath her eyes made the blue inside them stand out, and for a split second Rayne saw Jaime; the adorable little sister that everyone had pampered and treated like a china doll because she was so small and fragile.

"You embarrassed him, Raynie. You shouldn't have done that. He seems like a nice guy."

With no more need for restraint, Rayne's anger came pouring out of her. "Why on earth did you call Foster,

Mother?" She threw her hands up. "Do you know what it's like to come to the hospital and find my ex here with you?"

"I couldn't get you, and the only other number I had was his," Estelle whined. "I knew you two stayed friendly, so I gave him a call."

"What about 911?" Rayne hollered.

"I wasn't serious enough for that," Estelle balked with a wave of her hand.

"But you felt it was serious enough to call my ex-husband!"

Estelle punched her fist into the bed. "Don't you dare shout at me."

"Why not?" Rayne stormed up her mother's side. "The only time you listen to me is when I shout, Estelle!"

A knock at the door made Rayne wheel around in time to see a very tall man with thinning gray hair and thick glasses entering the room. Wearing a long white coat, blue tie, and gray slacks, he appeared to be the epitome of a doctor, even down to the sunken look of fatigue in his small brown eyes. Lumbering into the room with a friendly smile, he carried a blue binder under his arm.

"Are you Mrs. Masterson's daughter?"

Rayne stepped forward. "I'm Rayne Greer."

He extended a thick hand to Rayne. "Dr. Clifton. I'm the ER physician attendin' to your mother," he announced in a deep Texas drawl.

"He's the one who wants to do more tests on me," Estelle griped from the bed.

"Well, Mrs. Masterson, your liver enzymes are worrisome, along with your blood counts and recent weight loss," Dr. Clifton defended. "We need to find out what's goin' on with you."

"Weight loss?" Rayne stared at her mother. "What weight loss?"

Dr. Clifton opened his blue binder. "Your mother reported that she's lost ten pounds over the past few weeks."

"It's because I don't have any money for food," Estelle bellyached.

"You have money, Mother. You just spend it on scotch."

Dr. Clifton cleared his throat as he gleaned the paperwork in the binder. "She's also pretty anemic, her liver functions aren't too good, and her other blood levels are pretty troublin'."

"It's all because of the drinking, right? She drinks too much."

"So she told me." Dr. Clifton closed his binder. "I think we should see how extensive the damage is first. I've ordered a consult with an internist on the staff here. He can run some more tests and give you a more definitive diagnosis. I think she should make an appointment as soon as possible."

Estelle sulked in her bed. "I don't need another doctor. I like Dr. Emerit."

Rayne's eyes veered from her pouting mother to the doctor. "That's her internist. She's been with him for years. I can call him and schedule an appointment."

Dr. Clifton's dark eyes registered with understanding. "If I can have a word with you outside, Ms. Greer." He walked to the room door and opened it, waiting for Rayne to join him.

Estelle folded her arms and sulked in her bed like a spoiled child. "I'm the patient here. Shouldn't someone talk to me?"

"Enough, Mother." Rayne went to the door. "I'll be right back."

After Rayne and Dr. Clifton were safely in the hallway, he turned to her, looking grave.

"Ms. Greer, I don't need to tell you that the drinkin' has done extensive damage to her liver. How advanced the cirrhosis is needs to be determined to decide what course of treatment to take, but whether your mother will be compliant with that treatment…well, I've got my doubts."

Rayne saw Trent coming down the hall. "She won't be compliant. That is pretty much guaranteed."

Dr. Clifton hugged the binder to his chest. "She can be medicated to avoid any profound problems, but I think you've got no other options right now. She needs to get into a rehab program."

"She's been in several, Dr. Clifton. None have helped."

"I understand, Ms. Greer, but please consider it. I would be remiss in my duties if I didn't strongly advise that she get some kind of help for her drinkin'."

"I'll see what I can do," Rayne avowed. "She might listen to Dr. Emerit. She always listens to him, for a little while anyway."

Trent walked up to her, carrying a white paper cup of coffee. "I'm sure you can probably use this."

Rayne motioned to Dr. Clifton. "Trent, this is Dr. Clifton."

They two men exchanged nods.

Trent examined Rayne's somber face. "So what's the verdict?"

Rayne took the coffee cup from his hand. "Dr. Clifton wants her to get some more tests. I'll set up an appointment with her internist on Monday and go from there."

"Is she ready to go home?" Trent asked, moving to Rayne's side.

"Just let me finish up the paperwork." Dr. Clifton lowered the binder from his chest, gripping it in one hand. "I'll have the nurse come in and give you directions for keepin' her wound clean, and then you can take her on home."

Rayne took a sip from the coffee. "Should someone stay with her tonight?"

"That's up to you, Ms. Greer," Dr. Clifton replied in his thick accent. "The injury was just a slight cut that didn't require stitches. I think she was scared more than hurt because she didn't remember fallin' down. But the amnesia was a result of the alcohol in her system, and not the head injury. Her alcohol levels were still pretty high when we drew her blood."

Rayne sucked in a breath, quieting her outrage. "Thank you, Dr. Clifton."

Dr. Clifton patted her shoulder. "Good luck to you, Ms. Greer."

While silently cursing her mother for putting her in this situation yet again, Rayne watched the long legs of Dr. Clifton stroll away.

Trent rested a reassuring arm about her waist. "How are you doing?"

"I'm fine. I've been here many times before."

"Is there anything I can do?"

Rayne stared into his warm gray eyes and then gave him an encouraging smile. "Thank you for just being here. I know this is a lot to take in with my ex and my mother, but I—"

"Rayne, I don't care about your ex-husband or your mother; I care about you. Now tell me what can I do to help you?"

She tenderly kissed his cheek, touched by his offer. It had been a long time since she had shared her burdens with anyone. "You've already helped."

He looked to the exam room door. "I'll wait out here until you are ready to take her home."

"Perhaps you should just bring us back to my house. I can get my car from your place and then take her home."

"No way." Trent dismissed the suggestion with a stern glare. "We'll take her home. I can leave you at her place, then go to the stables. When you're ready, I'll pick you up."

"Trent, my mother lives in Highland Park. That's an hour away from the stables. I can't ask you to drive back and—"

"Rayne, stop arguing with me," he insisted, cutting her off. "We'll take her home."

"You really are a glutton for punishment, aren't you?"

He kissed her cheek and took the coffee from her hand. "It all depends on your vantage point, baby."

She sighed and eyed the watch on his wrist. "I should call Rebecca. I've got a lesson in a little over an hour."

"I'll take care of it." He set the coffee cup on a nearby medicine cart. "After I drop you off at your mother's, I can go to the stables and take over your lessons for you."

"That's just perfect. My students are never going to forgive me. You're the Marquis De Sade of riding instructors." She swerved to the exam room door.

He put his hands on her shoulders and gently turned her to him. "You don't have to be brave with me, Rayne. I know this is killing you."

"I hate to disappoint you, but I'm not being brave." She patted his thick chest, relishing the firm muscles beneath his T-shirt. "Estelle and I have never had a great relationship, so when she has setbacks like this…." She shook her head and dropped her hand from his chest. "Setbacks? Who am I kidding? Her entire life has been one big setback. She's been drinking for so long…she'll never give it up."

"Do you have any idea why she drinks?"

Rayne took in the busy ER hallway around them. Everywhere people were going in and out of exam rooms, phones were ringing, voices were humming in the background, and occasionally the sounds of papers shuffling, or a mechanical beeping would float by.

"I think she drinks to forget her past." Rayne wrapped her arms about her body. "She was once the darling of Dallas society. My grandfather owned two meatpacking houses and was keen on marrying her off to a man who could help continue the family business. But my mother met my father at a college fraternity party, and after that…all my grandfather's plans went out the window. They eloped and settled in New Orleans, where my dad started a law practice. Mother used to say she gave up everything for my father, but I think it was the other way around. Dad worshipped the ground she walked on until the day he died."

"Is that why you two don't get along? Because of your father?"

"That list of reasons is way too long and too sordid to get into." Rayne dropped her arms to her sides. "Suffice it to say, when I was growing up my mother stayed out of my life, and I've always tried to stay out of hers."

Trent knitted his dark brows. "But what about your riding? All the horse shows you competed in? Surely she—"

"She never attended any of my shows," Rayne interrupted. "Not a single one. My mother believed my riding was…foolish. No matter how successful I was in the show ring, she was always disappointed in me. Still is."

"I can't believe Estelle is disappointed in you, Rayne. I think maybe she's just too stubborn to admit how she feels. Kind of like you." Trent gripped her shoulders. "But there's always a chance to fix things between the two of you."

"There's nothing to fix." Rayne's back stiffened. "We're so broken that even God couldn't fix us."

"No one is beyond hope. Not people, horses…or mothers."

She opened the exam room door, hardening her resolve against his encouragement. "Don't even go there, Trent. I gave up on hoping for any kind of relationship with my mother a long time ago."

"But it's never too late to try again. Sometimes if you just give someone a chance, they might surprise you."

Rayne gazed into his keen eyes and knew he was talking about more than just her mother. She longed to give him that chance, but past heartbreaks had taught her that looking to another for strength only led to deeper torment. Wanting to spare him further insights into her warped psyche, she rested her hand on his forearm and forced a pretty smile on her face…the kind men always preferred.

"I appreciate that. Perhaps someday I might heed your advice…but not today."

She turned away and slipped inside the door. The past was done, and she had more pressing matters to attend to. For Rayne, looking ahead in some ways was just as painful as looking back. Sometimes she did not know what was worse; the regret over past mistakes, or the worry over mistakes yet to come.

Chapter 13

Estelle's home was nestled in the opulent neighborhood of Highland Park, close to the campus of Southern Methodist University. With green, manicured lawns, bright gardens bursting with colorful flowers, and palatial mansions, the premium real estate in this section of Dallas was considered by many to be a necessity when entering the ranks of the city's social scene.

Trent eased his car up to a stunning French Provincial home tucked behind an overgrown lawn cluttered with unkempt gardens of tall juniper trees, red azalea bushes, and gardenias.

"There's a side entrance." Rayne pointed to a small cement road that meandered through the overgrowth in front of the property.

"Estelle, you have quite a place," Trent commented as the car drew closer to the impressive structure.

Four huge, white colonial windows with stylized cornices on top, and ten-foot high double front doors that were carved with long swirls and stained in a very dark birch, accentuated the façade of the home.

"My father bought it when I was in high school," Estelle recounted from the back seat. "When my parents died, they left everything to me. I used to have lovely gardens in front, but they got to be too much. It costs a small fortune to keep this place going."

"A small fortune you don't have," Rayne piped in as the front of the house passed before her passenger window. "I've told you a million times to sell it."

Estelle clucked disapprovingly. "And live where, Raynie, with you?"

"You could get something smaller that you could afford with the money you would make unloading this place," Rayne suggested with an equally contentious tone.

"Move to Carrolton or Richardson? You must be joking? I'll never leave Highland Park. Only the best people live here. I need to be among my kind."

"They're not your kind anymore, Mother."

"Bite your tongue, Raynie. They'll always be my kind, and yours, too."

Trent gave Rayne a lighthearted grin as he steered the car around the side of the wide home.

"Just drop me at the door," Estelle directed.

"Mother, I should stay with you."

Estelle waved a thin hand at her daughter. "Nonsense. I'm fine, and you two need time alone."

Rayne sighed with frustration, only making Trent's humorous grin even bigger.

Pulling under a high portico with a stucco and stone archway, Trent glimpsed the smaller replica of the wide front doors at the side entrance.

"How big is this house, Estelle?"

"The lot is two and a half acres, and the house is almost seven thousand square feet," Rayne volunteered.

"That's a lot of house for one person," he remarked.

"Well, you never know when you might have guests," Estelle added.

"Your days of having guests are long gone, Mother." Rayne opened the rear car door for Estelle.

"One always needs extra rooms," Estelle argued.

Trent came around from the driver's side of the car. "I've got only about four thousand square feet and I've got a maid that comes twice a week. How do you manage?"

Estelle retrieved her keys from her leather purse. "Oh, I manage." She marched up a small flight of cement steps to the darkly stained doors. "Let Raynie give you a quick tour before you head out."

"You shouldn't be alone, Mother."

"I don't want you to stay. I'm fine." Estelle then pushed the double doors open and walked proudly into her home, like a queen entering her castle.

The accentuated sway of the hem of her aquamarine dress made Rayne swear the woman was putting a little more swing in her hips, probably for Trent's benefit.

"I'm sorry," Rayne softly said as she climbed the back steps with Trent. "Mother is sort of like a sixty-year-old version of Scarlett O'Hara. She hasn't quite come to terms with the fact that she isn't the belle of the ball anymore."

"How has she held on to this place? The taxes alone must be a small fortune," he whispered as they stepped into an elegant marble entranceway with oak hardwood floors and high ceilings.

Rayne waited as her mother disappeared around the corner of the entranceway, and then turned and shut the heavy double doors behind Trent.

"The taxes haven't been paid for two years, and the city of Dallas has been threatening to auction the house off unless she comes up with the taxes in the next six months."

She walked with Trent to the end of the entryway. A long hallway with parquet wood floors had several high doors running along either side, and was painted in alternating panels of taupe and white.

"Mother has struggled for years to hold on to this house." Rayne motioned to a bright room at the end of the hallway to her right. "There used to be a gardener, and a maid to help keep it clean, but she let Mattie go a few years back."

As they walked down the hallway, Trent inspected the impressions in the walls where long pictures had once hung. The nails were still left in some places, and dotted along the detailed wood floor, small dents could be seen where furniture once sat.

They entered a rectangular living room with a vaulted wood ceiling and a wall of glass doors that opened on to a slate-covered patio. There was not a stick of furniture anywhere, and more dents marred the hardwood floor. Along the walls were additional impressions where paintings had once hung.

Trent gestured about the room. "It seems rather…empty."

"It's how she has held on to her home. My grandfather was an avid antiques collector. This house was crammed with them when we moved here from New Orleans. Now, there's barely any furniture left. She sold off his collection of paintings shortly after he and my grandmother died in a car accident."

He went to one of the windows that looked out to a matted garden of weeds and shrubbery. "How long ago was that?"

"A little over eight years. It happened after I was married to Foster."

Trent turned to her in astonishment. "And she has been keeping this place going since then?"

Rayne walked over to his side and stared out to a tall oak just beyond the gardens. "Foster helped some when we were first married. He sent over his gardener to keep up the grounds and paid the bills, but after a few years of putting up with her drinking escapades, he stopped helping." Rayne nodded to the living room entrance. "I'll just check on her, and then we can go."

"I'll be right here," he told her.

Rayne took in the curve of his square jaw, the rise of his Adam's apple, the way his blue T-shirt hugged his wide shoulders, and the fit of his jeans around his round butt. Like a mirage to a thirsty traveler across a wind-torn desert, he seemed too good to be true. But as she relished the memory of their morning together in her bed, the fantasy of Trent Newbury began to blur into a newly unwanted reality; this was a man she could really fall for.

Hastily leaving Trent, she proceeded down the hallway to one of the tall doors at the far end. When Rayne stretched for the dull brass handle, she squared her shoulders, preparing to take on the cantankerous beast inside.

The door opened with a slight creak, and the only light from inside was from a lamp set on a simple wooden desk to the side. In the center of the crimson-painted room, elevated on a platform, was an unmade king-sized walnut bed. The only other furniture in the large circular room was a thick oak dresser with dulled brass handles, set against the far wall. The creamy carpet was worn and frayed in sections, and the white baseboards contained a thick layer of dust.

"I told you to go," Estelle fussed as she sat on the corner of the bed, undoing the buttons on one sleeve of her dress.

"I think I should stay, at least for a little while." Rayne closed the bedroom door.

"And pass up the opportunity to spend time with that fine man? You're not that dumb, Raynie." She kicked off her black heels.

"This isn't about Trent. It's about you."

"Of course it's about Trent. It's always about men. Everything we do as women is to impress them." Estelle stood from the bed. "I can't believe you brought him to the hospital in the first place. That's a terrible impression to give a man. You need to be charming and attractive, not bringing him to see your injured mother and ex-husband."

"Trent insisted on going to the hospital. He said he wanted to be there for me." Rayne stepped closer and when her eyes lit on the assortment of liquor bottles on the floor by the head of the bed, she shook with rage.

"Be there for you?" Estelle's raspy laughter bristled against Rayne's skin. "Honestly, Raynie, do you think that man cares about your problems? You need to use your head to nab this one. Don't smother him like you did Foster. Let him have his freedom and don't monopolize his time. And if he has an indiscretion like Foster did, then look the other way for Christ's sake."

"Mother, let's not discuss that again. Foster cheated on me, and I could not stay with him after that."

"So what? All men cheat. It's part of their nature." She went to a pair of white pocket doors across from the foot of her bed.

"Dad never cheated on you. You didn't know how it felt."

Estelle pried apart the pocket doors to reveal a huge walk-in closet bursting with clothes. "I knew. Your grandfather ran around with every woman he could get his hands on." She flipped on a switch on the wall and the closet's interior glowed with a soft light. "But Momma always had to put up with it to keep a roof over her head. You could have learned to live with it just like she did." Estelle tugged at the sleeves of her dress, inching it off her shoulders. "Then you would still be married to a wealthy man." She advanced into the closet.

"I'm not going to stay with a man who runs around on me. I'd rather make my way without a man than live a lie."

Estelle emerged from the closet wearing only a full beige slip. "Sometimes I can't believe you're my daughter. Who in their right mind would want to give up security and comfort to work like a dog?" She yanked the bandage off her forehead.

"Working is not all bad, Mother. I like my job, and I feel productive earning a paycheck."

Estelle tossed the bandage to the floor and strolled toward the head of the bed. "You sound just like your father. You remind me of him more and more every day." She then picked up a half-empty bottle of scotch from the floor.

The acrid taste of disgust burned in Rayne's mouth. "I'll go then. I have a lesson to teach at the stables." Rayne headed to the bedroom door, refusing to watch as Estelle put the bottle to her lips.

"You would do better to spend your time catering to that man out there. Pamper him and make him feel like he's in charge. Remember that. It makes them feel like a man when they can dominate you. I hope you at least satisfy him in bed."

Rayne's humiliation rose to her cheeks as she placed her hand on the doorknob. "Good-bye, Mother."

"I'll call you later to see how it's going with Trent. Don't blow this, Raynie. He's just what you need."

Rayne pivoted around. "How would you know what I need?"

Estelle gripped the bottle in her hand. "I'm your mother, darling. Of course I know what you need. Now go on, and make sure you keep that man happy."

Refraining from slamming the door to her mother's bedroom, Rayne stepped into the hall and stormed off toward the living room.

"I take it you're not staying," Trent quipped when she burst through the living room entrance.

"No." Rayne took a second to compose herself. "Sometimes she can be so…." She threw her hands in the air, grimacing.

"I know the feeling."

Rayne's hazel eyes soaked in his bemused smirk. "You do?"

"Yeah. I'm beginning to get that same feeling all the time with you." He took her hand. "Come on, we'll have to haul ass back to the stables to make your lesson."

Allowing him to lead her to the side entrance, Rayne felt the angst created by the conversation with her mother slowly evaporate. It was as if Trent's presence replaced her strife with a strange sense of contentment. Foster had never elicited such a response, and the last time she could remember feeling that way with anyone was with her father. She spied their intertwined hands and wondered what George Masterson would have made of Trent. Rayne could picture her father's long face and warm hazel eyes glowing with happiness for his daughter. She did not know why, but somehow she just knew her father would have approved. And that certainty made Rayne smile.

***

After her morning lessons and a quick cup of coffee with Rebecca to discuss changes to the lesson schedule, Rayne was in her tack room, pulling on her boots for an afternoon ride on Bob, when Trent came barreling in the door. Slightly disheveled with windblown hair, dust-streaked jeans, and a damp brow, Rayne's lust for the man quickly shoved away all reason.

"I think you've been avoiding me." He shut the tack room door with a thud.

She stood from a bale of hay. "I have not. I've been busy." She pointed to the door. "Leave that open."

He eyed the door. "Why?"

"Because last time you closed it, Rebecca and a few others heard us and...well, we don't need to give people more to gossip about around here."

"To hell with what other people think. Let them gossip." He came toward her and scooped her into his arms. "Why have you been avoiding me?"

Rayne lightly stroked her hands along the front of his sweaty blue T-shirt. "I haven't been avoiding you. I thought you might want to...."

"What?"

"I don't know...." Her finger played with the collar on his T-shirt. "Spend some time apart? Maybe you've had enough of me for one day."

He lifted her off the ground and kissed her neck. "Fat chance, baby."

She gripped his shoulders as her insides exploded with heat. It took everything Rayne had to push him away. "If you start that, neither one of us might get out of here," she warned, trying to sound practical and not desperate for him.

He put her back down on the floor. "I would like nothing more than to throw you on that bale of hay right now, but I'm afraid duty calls." He let her go. "I have to observe Selene's dressage class."

"Does Selene know you're observing her class?" She arched a wary eyebrow at him.

"No. If I told her I was coming, she would just make more excuses."

"Have fun with that…she hates having an audience. Doesn't even let the families of her students watch; claims it distracts them."

"So I've heard." He rested his hand on the saddle rack next to him. "Any word from your mother?"

"If she needs me, she'll call. But I'm sure she's fine. Mother is like a cat with nine lives; she always lands on her feet."

His long fingers drew a few circles on a saddle in front of him as his eyes pondered Rayne. "I can't believe you've been dealing with her on your own all these years. A lot of daughters would have written her off."

"I've tried, believe me, but every time I swore I was done with her, I would hear my father's voice in my head. He's the reason I haven't deserted her completely."

"That's your conscience, Rayne, not your father. You're just not one of those people who can disregard someone because they don't fit into your life. You have a good heart."

"I'm not good, Trent. I've done a lot of things I regret."

"So have I, but that doesn't make you bad, it just makes you human. Besides, you have all those wonderful assets I was telling you about this morning before we were interrupted." His eyes wandered over her figure. "I guess I'll have to spend tonight reminding you of every single one of them; but until then…." He sighed and checked his stainless watch. "I have to head back to the schooling ring." Trent kissed her forehead. "When I'm done with Selene's class, I can meet you in the jumping ring to school Bob. We need to get started if we are going to get you ready for October."

"About that...." Rayne rubbed her hands together, avoiding his eyes.

"What is it? Are you afraid of showing him?"

"Afraid? Hell no. He's a great horse. It's just been a long time since I've competed. I'm not so sure I'm up to it."

"I know that's not true." He stared into her eyes, analyzing her. "Why don't you tell me what's really going on with you?"

Rayne itched to bolt from the tack room. "Forget it. I'll show in October," she affirmed, pulling away from him.

He held her arm. "Oh, no you don't. What is it?"

"Nothing." She jerked away. "I told you I will ride in the show, so there's—"

He threw his arms about her. "Talk to me," he urged against her cheek. "What will it take for you to trust me, Rayne?"

What would it take? She wished she knew the answer.

He kissed her ear. "Come on, what is it?"

Rayne wavered, unsure of what to tell him. Ever since they had left her mother's home, she had been stewing over Estelle's warning about smothering Trent. How long could it last if they spent their days together training Bob, and their nights sharing a bed?

Trent suggestively rubbed his hips against her. "I'll get it out of you one way or another."

"Damn you." She hated her body for wanting him. "All right. I think maybe we shouldn't spend so much time together. With our personal relationship, and our professional one, it might make things difficult."

Trent's bellowing laughter stung her ears. "Nice try, baby, but you're not getting rid of me so easily. I'm going to pester you every day until you let me in that stone cold heart of yours. Being around all the time is one way of getting you to lower your defenses."

She wiggled in his arms. "I don't have any defenses to lower."

He held her tighter. "Rayne, please. You're about as boarded up as an abandoned house." He ran his hands over the curve of her butt. "Now, you get Bob warmed up and meet me in the back ring in one hour. We have a lot of work to do." He slapped her hard on the ass.

"Hey!" Rayne shouted.

Trent kissed her mouth. "Tonight I promise I will do a hell of a lot more to you than that." He let her go. "Now get Bob ready."

As he opened the tack room door, Rayne added, "Have fun with Selene."

He smiled back at her. "Oh, I plan on it. I think she is about to get a very rude wake-up call."

After he had departed, a twinge of worry ate at her. Despite his vast experience with women, Rayne doubted Trent had ever run across the likes of Selene.

"I think you're the one in for a rude wake-up call, Trent. I just hope you survive it."

Chapter 14

The sun was sinking below the horizon when Trent's BMW drove into his wide glass and stone three-car garage. The aroma of the loaded meat and extra cheese pizza they had stopped to get on the way back from Rayne's house wafted through the car.

"I still don't understand why Frank couldn't come with us," Trent debated, turning off the engine.

"I will not be held responsible for the disaster he would have made of your lovely home."

Trent scooped up the pizza from the back seat. "Or is he your excuse to leave early and not stay the night with me?"

As if on cue, Rayne's stomach noisily rumbled. "I'm starving," she admitted, purposefully avoiding his question as she turned to the car door.

"There you go again. Running from me."

She opened the door, laughing off his comment. "I'm hardly running. I'm hungry, there's a difference."

"Your mother warned me about you. She said you liked to push men away." He climbed from the car.

Rayne gawked at him. "Estelle is the last person on earth you should take advice from." She stood from the car. "And I am not pushing you away."

Trent came around the front of the car, carrying the pizza box in his hand. "You could have fooled me. But meeting your ex today gave me a little more insight into why you are the way you are." Trent walked to the garage door that led to the house. "He's a real cold bastard, your ex."

The slight took Rayne off guard. "That's a cruel thing to say, Trent."

"It's true." Trent fumbled with his keys in the lock of the back door of his home. "Foster immediately struck me as a man without loyalty."

"But he was there last night for my mother when he could have ignored her. That was pretty damn loyal."

"Yeah, and I saw the way he was looking at you when you walked into the exam room. He wasn't helping your mother out of kindness, Rayne. He still has feelings for you."

Rayne chuckled as he pushed the back door open with his foot. "You're exaggerating."

"Am I?" Trent entered the darkened house.

After stepping past a small utility closet with a second refrigerator, a selection of rain gear on the wall, and a row of dirty riding boots on the floor, they negotiated down a narrow corridor that eventually led to his open kitchen, overlooking the wide living room and adjoining dining room.

"You do know I have no feelings for Foster, don't you?"

He slid the pizza box onto the stone and cedar breakfast bar. "I know." He turned to the natural wood cabinet behind him and took out two white plates. "But I think Foster may be regretting letting you go."

"How did you know that?" Rayne dropped her purse on the kitchen counter. "He hinted at something like that when we were talking outside of the exam room."

Trent put the plates down and went to the built-in refrigerator. "Your mother told me. When she called Foster, she was certain he would blow her off. Even she was surprised when he came to her rescue." He withdrew a bottle of white wine from the refrigerator. "He asked her a lot of questions about you. Your mother suspected he was growing tired of his new girlfriend." Trent brought the wine, along with two wineglasses from the rack under the cabinet, to the breakfast bar.

"I can't believe she told you that."

"She likes me." Rummaging through a drawer, he found the wine opener. "She wanted to give me some tips on how to handle you."

"Yeah, that sounds like something she would say." She eyed the bottle of zinfandel. "Do you have anything other than wine? I think I had plenty last night."

"There's some bottled water in the fridge."

While leaning into the refrigerator and searching for her water, an unsettling curiosity nagged at Rayne. "What kind of tips did my mother give you?"

"Oh no." He worked the opener into the bottle of wine. "I'm not telling you. I plan on using that information to win you over."

Rayne found a bottle of water and stood up. "Win me over? You've already slept with me, what more could you want?"

He expertly extracted the cork from the bottle. "Is that all you think I'm in this for? To sleep with you?" Slapping the opener on the counter, he grabbed a wineglass. Trent filled the glass halfway with the golden liquid, and then handed it to her. "You need this more than I thought."

She pushed the glass away. "I told you I don't want to drink."

"Those pesky little defenses of yours are already starting to show." He banged the wineglass down on the countertop.

"Like the way you ignored my question about wanting to use Frank as an excuse not to stay with me tonight."

Rayne put the bottle of water on the bar and snatched up the wine. "You're good." She took a sip from the wine. "And I didn't ignore your question. I think it would be best if I slept in my bed tonight and not yours."

"Best for whom? You or me?" Lifting the bottle of wine, he poured another glass. "Admit it; you're still nervous about being with me."

"Trent, I'm not nervous, and I'm not putting up any of my 'so-called' defenses." Rayne took a bigger gulp of wine.

"Then why are you suddenly drinking the wine?" He raised his glass to his lips, all the while keeping his eyes on her.

"I'm thirsty, not nervous."

He grinned. "Prove it."

"What?"

"Prove I don't make you nervous, Rayne."

She took another swallow of wine. "How do I prove that?"

He held his glass in front of his mouth as he considered the question. "Take off your clothes," he finally stated.

Her hazel eyes grew wide and her mouth fell open. "You're not serious?"

"I am serious." He put his wine on the stone countertop. "Take off your clothes."

She whacked her wineglass down. "Let's eat first."

He held her wrist when she reached for the pizza box. "There will be no pizza for you until you take off your clothes for me."

The sudden emptiness in his eyes frightened her. "Why do I need to take off my clothes?"

He kept his hand on her wrist while he closed the pizza box. "Because I want you to learn that you can trust me."

Pushing down her fear, she calmly said, "I trust you, Trent. I wouldn't be here if I didn't trust you."

"That's not the kind of trust I'm talking about, Rayne."

Still holding her wrist, he dragged her into the living room. She wanted to vehemently protest, but bit her tongue. There was something exciting about the way he took control.

Arriving in front of his brown leather sofa, Trent let her go. "Take off your clothes," he commanded in a husky tone. He sat down on the sofa and folded his arms over his chest. "While I watch."

Rayne remembered that voice from their night of phone sex. It had the same sexy quality that had driven her to do something unexpected and totally out of character. She rubbed the heel of her hand over her forehead, fighting to reign in her libido. "Trent, I'm really not in—"

"Do as I say, Rayne." His voice was rough and dangerous. "Strip for me. I want to see you, every inch of you."

She stared at him, weighing the possibility of running for her car still parked outside. Then, her mother's words from earlier that day came back to her. She considered what would happen if she did let him take control. What if for once, she handed herself over to a man completely? Stopped thinking, stopped worrying, and just let events unfold.

Mesmerized by the unyielding resolve reflecting in his eyes, Rayne started undoing the laces of her tennis shoes. After she had kicked off her shoes, she pulled her white T-shirt over her head. She threw the shirt to the sofa, where it landed next to Trent, but his attention never left her. Keeping her focus on him, she wiggled her jeans down her hips. Stepping out of her jeans, she unclasped her bra. Her excitement began to build as she undressed for him. She was not trying to be seductive…if anything, she felt clumsy and awkward, but the way his eyes stayed riveted on her made Rayne want him even more.

By the time she dropped her panties to the floor, her heart was beating wildly. He examined every inch of her, from her lean legs to her small waist and full breasts, and then up to her slender shoulders. The scrutiny was agonizing, and made Rayne cover her nakedness with her hands.

"Lower your hands," he ordered. "Stand perfectly still and keep your hands at your sides."

After several more minutes, he finally stood from the sofa. When he came up to her, she could not detect any hint of desire in his eyes or flush on his tanned cheeks. He appeared unmoved by her nudity, adding to Rayne's discomfort. He stepped behind her, but never laid a finger on her.

Leaning over her shoulder, he whispered, "Get on the sofa."

She turned her head slightly to the side, to look for a glimmer of what he had planned, but saw nothing in his expression. His gray orbs were cold, ruthless, and intimidating as hell.

Repeating her mother's advice in her head, she went to the sofa and sat down. She shivered when her naked bottom touched the chilly leather.

"Now lie down, on your back," he directed.

She stretched out on the sofa and the goose pimples rose on her skin.

He came forward and gazed down at her. "Close your eyes."

She opened her mouth to question whether this was a good idea or not.

"Just do it," he growled.

Rayne's anxiety rose with her eyes closed. Not being able to see what he was going to do, or gauge the sincerity in his face, was even more nerve-wracking for her. When his hand rested on her thigh, she jumped.

"Easy, baby," he cooed into her ear.

Slowly he caressed her left leg, moving his fingers up and down in a rhythmic motion. The cool air swirled around her, but Rayne did not mind anymore. She was no longer cold as his hand eased along her inner thigh. His fingers lighted over the small mattering of hair between her legs, and then gently tracked over her lower belly. Moving up, he traced the outline of her right breast and crept closer to her nipple. Rayne's body was beginning to hum, and her anxiety receded as her yearning rose.

She let out a surprised gasp when his mouth grazed her right breast. His tongue circled her nipple, and when his teeth teased her flesh, her breath caught in her throat. His bite began to get a little more intense, and the gentle nipping turned into tugging. The funny thing was, Rayne liked it. The harder he clamped down, the more her flesh rippled with delight.

"Do you like that?" he panted against her cheek. His fingers pinched her left nipple. "Do you like it when I'm hard or gentle?"

"Hard." Rayne found her lips forming the words before her mind even considered the question.

"I knew it," he moaned against her.

Both his hands began running up and down her hips, inner thighs, and kneading her breasts as Rayne imagined Trent pulling her from the sofa, throwing her body to the floor, and taking her from behind.

"What are you thinking about?" His fingers dipped between her legs.

"All I can think about is you."

His fingers roughly forced their way inside her. "That's not true, Rayne. Tell me what you are thinking."

Her body arched when he pushed further into her. "I'm thinking about how you would feel."

"That's not explicit enough. I want details."

"I…I'm thinking about you throwing me to the floor…and taking me."

His fingers darted in and out of her as his thumb rubbed her sensitive nub. "How do I take you? Describe it to me." His voice was menacing, and yet intensely alluring.

"Oh God…from behind. You throw me to the floor and take me from behind." She quaked as spindles of electricity flew through her gut.

"Why do you want it that way?"

"I…I don't know." Her hand squeezed the leather arm of the sofa.

"Yes, you do."

"Because…." The heat from her coming orgasm hit her.

Trent's fingers slowed. "You need to tell me the truth."

Her body collapsed against the sofa. "Please, don't stop."

He traced the top of her thighs with his fingernail. "Tell me why that excites you."

Her pulse was resonating in her ears while her body was screaming for release. It took everything she had to make her brain focus. "Because no one…has ever been…that way with me," she stammered. "I want to know how it feels to just…just…."

"Let go and hand yourself over to someone?"

"Yes," she sighed, opening her eyes.

The fire in his eyes shocked her. She knew he was passionate, but what Rayne saw at that moment was disconcerting. He appeared as if he were possessed with some unholy spirit. His attractive face held not a single hint of the attentive, caring man she had come to know.

He stood from the side of the sofa and wrestled his T-shirt over his head. Rayne sat up on her elbows as he undressed. When he finally slipped his briefs down to his ankles, she could see he was fully aroused.

Without warning, he flipped her over. Pinning her to the back of sofa, he bit down on her shoulder as his fingers spread her folds apart. He drove all the way into her with one forceful thrust. The sensation made Rayne tremble. It was raw, powerful, and utterly intense.

She held on to the sofa back as he pounded into her. Her insides exploded, and she grunted against the waves of pleasure. As he moved faster, her climax came tumbling forth. She tried to shift her hips, allowing him to go deeper, but he responded by crushing into her. She was helpless against him, and that feeling amplified her rush of adrenaline.

"Yes," she cried out, as he stabbed into her with such force her body rocked forward.

When she shuddered, Trent did not ease up and rammed into her even harder than before. Rayne had not even felt the first orgasm receding when the next one came over her. She tried to grip the back of the sofa, but her arms were like wet spaghetti. When the second release rocketed forward, she screamed and wilted into the sofa, but Trent relentlessly kept up his assault.

By the time she heard his ragged breath and felt him tense, Rayne was already covered with a light sweat and her insides were throbbing with satisfaction. Groaning into her back, he lurched against her and then went limp.

Pulling her down on the sofa with him, Rayne could not fathom where this side of Trent had been hiding. She had believed him to be kind, gentle, and strong, but had never pictured such a primal side to him.

His arms embraced her as he settled behind her on the sofa. "Did I hurt you?"

Rayne giggled. "No, God no. That was…."

"Just what you needed," he inserted.

"How could you tell?"

He kissed the back of her shoulder. "You need a man to take control, especially in bed. I got that from you this morning."

She rolled over on the sofa. "I don't understand. How did you get that?"

He flipped on to his back. "When you didn't get turned on and I had to change positions. I sensed it wasn't the position that needed to change but my approach."

She settled her head on his chest. "Is that something you acquired from your other lovers?"

"No, I think it came from riding. You can tell the horses that need to be led, and those that want to lead." He rested one arm behind his head. "Somewhere down the road I started noticing the same thing in women. Not to compare women to horses," he quickly clarified. "But just to say, I started to see some women needed a man to take control, and others wanted to be in control, especially in bed."

"Which do you prefer?"

He stroked her blonde hair draped across his chest. "Doesn't really matter to me."

Rayne sat up. "But you must have a preference. Some way you like being in bed."

"The way we just did it is my favorite. I like taking a woman. I like being in control." He ran his fingers along the round curve of her cheek. "But I should have been responsible with you. I got carried away and forgot to use a condom. Is that going to be a problem?"

"We're safe. But we shouldn't make a habit of it. I'm not on anything."

"Next time I promise to be more vigilant."

Rayne noted the subtle hint of warmth had returned to his eyes. "You were different before. Not like now. Why is that?" She rested her head against him.

"How was I different?"

"You were…colder."

He ran his fingers down her back. "I was turned on, baby. Very turned on."

"Turned on because you were in control?"

He sat up slightly. "Turned on because I finally got you to tell me what you were thinking."

"Why would that turn you on?"

"Because sex begins in the mind, and moves to the body, Rayne. To please you, I had to figure out what you wanted, but now that I know…." He kissed her lips, gently at first, but as his kiss continued, his mouth became more demanding.

He careened his mouth past her cheek to her ear. "I think it's time to try something a little different." He nibbled her earlobe, and Rayne's body instantly wanted him all over again.

"What did you have in mind?"

He spanked her butt and jumped from the sofa. "Pizza."

"Why you…." Rayne stood up and was about to collect her clothes when he stopped her.

"Uh, no." His arm went about her waist. "You're going to eat naked with me." Then he practically carried her to the kitchen.

"Naked? Why?" she challenged when he deposited her next to the breakfast bar.

"Because I'm not finished with you yet." Trent opened the pizza box on the countertop.

"You do realize I have a dog to get home to?"

He placed a slice of the loaded pizza on one of the white plates he had left sitting next to the box. "Frank will keep. Now, eat. You need to keep up your strength for what I have in mind."

"And what is that?" Rayne took the plate from him.

Reaching into the box for another slice of pizza, Trent grinned, but remained silent.

Rayne munched on her pizza while her imagination overflowed with all kinds of wonderful notions. Never before had sex been so intriguing with a man. Rayne looked ahead to the rest of their evening together, and was eager to find out what Trent had planned for dessert.

Chapter 15

Rayne's eyes fluttered open as shards of morning light streamed through the skylights above Trent's king-sized platform bed. When she sat up, she was wrapped in light blue sheets and lying below a dark wood ledge that served as a headboard. On the ledge were an alarm clock, a few books on riding, and one man's stainless watch. Next to her, tufts of black, wavy hair were protruding from beneath the sheets and resting on a light blue pillow.

Images of their passionate night together galloped across her mind. Glimpses of moments in the kitchen, dining room, in the pool, and finally in his bedroom made Rayne turn several different shades of red. Each time had been just as intense and exciting as the first on the couch. Every time he had taken command, manipulating her into different positions that had brought her to dizzying heights of climax.

Whenever she had searched for her clothes, he had taken her again to a different part of his house and threw her onto the dining room table, or pinned her against the kitchen counter. When she swore she needed to go home to Frank, he had lugged her to the pool, tossed her in, and made love to her in the shallows.

After he had carried her to bed, she remembered feeling so safe and complete with him that her urge to leave had been completely stifled. They had drifted off to sleep in each other's arms, and at one point in the night when she had attempted to climb from the bed and sneak out on him, he pulled her back into his arms and took her with such ferocity that when she came, she swore her screams could be heard by the neighbors.

But now, in the light of day, she considered whether all that passion had been worth it. Not only was she sore as hell, she had slept very little and had a full day at work ahead of her. Reclining back in the bed for a few more minutes of rest, she felt him stir next to her.

When arms wrapped around her, Rayne smiled.

"You can't leave," he insisted, biting her shoulder.

"I have to." She stretched out her arms. "I have to get home to Frank, who has probably done God knows what to my house. Then, I have to get ready for work."

"I know." He kissed her neck. "By the way, last night...." He sighed into her skin. "It's never been like that with anyone."

"Is that what you usually say the morning after?"

He shook his head as he sat up next to her. "What makes you think I could possibly go five times in one night with any other woman?"

"Six," she corrected. "We did it twice in the pool."

He dramatically slapped his hand over his forehead. "I feel so cheap."

Rayne tossed the covers aside. "I think that's my line."

Trent sat up as she walked to his open bathroom door. "I'm glad you stayed."

"Like I had a choice?"

He climbed from the bed and went to her side. "You had a choice, Rayne." He kissed the tip of her nose. "Tonight, I'll make it easy on you and Frank, and sleep at your place."

Rayne leaned back against the bathroom doorframe. "Are you sure about that? Perhaps you might want to have a break from me."

"Stop it." He glared at her, enraged by the suggestion. "I know what I want, and time away from you isn't it."

"What if I need time?"

Trent's anger disappeared and he anxiously searched her features. "Do you?"

Her eyes outlined the square cut of his darkly stubbled jaw, and the concise line on his thin lips. She knew she should play hard to get, perhaps leave him wondering where her feelings stood, but in her heart Rayne could never be so calculating. Despite her fears of him growing bored and walking away, she decided that she would not hold back anymore. It was time to take a chance.

"After last night, I'm not sure how I'm going to get through the day without…wanting you again."

The smiled that curved along Trent's lips was so heartwarmingly genuine that Rayne was uplifted.

"Finally, an honest answer about your feelings. Didn't that make you feel good?"

She shook her head. "No, it made me feel…vulnerable."

"Vulnerable? You're standing naked in my bathroom doorway, baby. You'd better be feeling something other than vulnerable."

Rayne inclined her head to the side. "What should I be feeling?"

"Relieved that you're opening up to me. I can't make you happy unless I know what you want, Rayne."

"And last night you were trying to make me happy?" she asserted in a suspicious tone of voice.

"I was trying to show you what it feels like to open up to someone."

She noted the grin on his lips as a question that had been eating at her since their first date came to mind. "Can I ask you something?"

His eyes hungrily glided over her naked body. "You can ask me anything."

"Why me?"

He appeared taken aback. "What?"

"Why me, Trent? In the brief time we have been together, you have fought very hard to make me feel…." She paused, searching for the right words. "It's like you have been on some kind of quest to woo me."

"You should know the kind of man I am. Competitive, driven, and I get what I want. Right now what I want is you." He cocked a single dark eyebrow at her. "Is that a bad thing?"

"No, but to someone as distrusting as me, it makes me feel like you have some ulterior motive for wanting me; that this isn't just about sex, or getting to know me." She folded her arms over her chest and perused his face. "It's like you want something more."

Trent rested his back on the doorframe opposite her and his eyes lost their friendly glint. "I do want something more, Rayne, but as long as you think I have an ulterior motive for taking you to bed and spending time with you then you will never believe me." He leaned forward and put his hands on the wall behind her, bringing his face to within inches of hers. "From the moment I met you, you have been pushing me away. For once, stop pushing and let me in."

Her hazel eyes challenged him as her doubt surged forward. "What if you turn out to be like all the rest?"

"I've told you before, I'm not Foster." His arms slid down the wall to her waist. "I'm not looking for a woman to make me look good. I'm looking for someone I can build a life with."

"What makes me any different from all the other women you've been with?"

A fleck of frustration surfaced in his eyes and then vanished. "Well, for starters, you don't have an agenda," he began. "You're the first woman I've met that didn't try to impress me with your looks or influence. You're stubborn, nervous, distant, make no excuses for who you are, and most important of all, you don't wear lipstick to the stables."

"Lipstick?" Rayne giggled, startled by the admission. "You're kidding."

"No." He shook his head, sporting a comical frown. "Big turn off for me."

"I don't get it. Why is that a turn off?"

"It means you're not serious about being there." He let her go. "Next time you go to the stables, look around to see how many women are wearing lipstick."

Rayne silently ran through a list of women she knew from the stables, but only one name stood out. "Does Selene wear lipstick?" she questioned, leaning on the doorframe.

"Deep red," he said, walking to his wide shower stall. "She keeps it in the front pocket of her riding pants and reapplies it frequently."

As he turned on the shower, Rayne admired the curve of his firm ass. "You've seen her do that?"

He tested the water temperature with his hand. "Yesterday, when I observed her class."

"Some men might find that a turn on."

Trent chuckled and held the shower door open, motioning inside. "Perhaps, but not me."

Rayne confidently sashayed up to the wide shower stall door, accentuating the sway of her hips just like Selene. "Are you sure about that?"

Trent rested his hand against the outside of the stall door, mesmerized by her movements. "I'm not interested in her. I've told you that before."

Rayne directed her eyes to the cascading water flowing from four different showerheads into the middle of the wide stall. She was still not completely convinced of his sincerity, but her reasons for staying with the man were beginning to outnumber her excuses for walking away. "I guess I'm still a little mystified that you want to be with me," she divulged, turning her attention to the ripped muscles in his abdomen.

"Stop questioning my motives, and just relax. I'm a one-woman man, Rayne. I gave up juggling women when I was a teenager. It's too hard and you create a lot of enemies."

Her fingers traced the muscles in his abdomen. "Then why are you so different from other men?"

He nodded to the shower. "Get in there, and I'll show you just how different I am."

"Yes, sir." She gave him a flirty smile and then stepped into the shower. "Just remember I have to get home to Frank."

"Eventually," he murmured, following her under the spray of water. "Once I'm done with you."

***

Rayne spent the morning at the clinic, chugging down coffee and catching up on a backlog of paperwork. It was well past lunch when she finally pushed away from her desk in the cramped, broom closet of an office she had next to the lab. Desperate for food, she made her way to the break room to warm up the leftover pizza Trent had sent home with her.

Thankful to have the break room to herself, she popped her leftover pizza in the microwave. While waiting for her food, Rayne went to the coffeepot on the trolley, but found it empty. She began to make another pot, hoping maybe her next cup of coffee would be the one to finally jump-start her floundering body.

"Are you making more coffee?" Lindsey admonished as she stood in the break room door. "Haven't you already had like four cups?"

Rayne went back to the microwave. "They didn't help."

"What was it; another late night of phone sex with the hot riding guy?"

Rayne blushed at the mention of Trent.

"Ohhh." Lindsey dashed to her side, the nursing paraphernalia weighing down her pockets jingling as she ran. "That doesn't look like phone sex to me. You're as red as a can of Coke. Could this mean you and the horse guy were up all night doing the nasty?"

Rayne turned to the counter. "Not all night."

"You had sex with the guy and never told me about it. What kind of friend are you?" Lindsey rested her hip against the counter, edging her face in front of Rayne. "I need to hear everything," she insisted.

The timer went off and Rayne opened the microwave door. "It's not like that, Lindsey. We had pizza and talked."

"Uh, huh. Is that the pizza you ate last night?" She pointed to Rayne's slice of pizza.

"Yeah." Rayne put her plate down on the counter next to her.

"Then you didn't eat pizza and talk. On those dates, there are no leftovers, because all you do is eat. On the dates where you have sex, there are always leftovers."

Rayne picked up her slice of pizza. "I've never heard that."

"That's because you weren't a slut in high school like me." Rayne took a bite of pizza while Lindsey waited. "So, come on. Let's hear it. What happened?" she besieged with a roll of her hand.

Rayne hurriedly swallowed her pizza and put it back down on the plate. "You know." She yanked a paper towel from the dispenser hanging on the wall by the sink. "We had a good time."

"Good time? Honey, by the bags under your eyes and the amount of coffee you have consumed, I suspect you had more than a 'good time.' So how was he?"

Rayne wiped her hands on the paper towel. "He was not a…how do I put this…a gentle kind of lover. This guy was—"

"Knock you into the headboard until you saw God kind of lover?"

"Not the headboard, but more like the dining room table, kitchen counter, edge of the pool," Rayne smiled slyly, "and then the headboard of his bed."

Lindsey let out a boisterous howl. "Thank you, God. You've only been with an old man who probably had to take Viagra to get it up. What you needed was a guy who took you to bed and showed you how it's done."

Rayne flashed back to how assertive and demanding Trent had been the night before. "Is it always like that with guys? You know, a kind of take what they want attitude."

Lindsey stared at her for a moment, grinning. "Was he strong, dominated you, and treated you like his woman? You know, caveman-like?"

Rayne nodded her head, grinning happily. "Yeah, he was a total caveman."

Lindsey clapped her hands in jubilation. "Finally, you got a man who knows how to handle you."

"Handle me? What are you talking about?"

"Rayne, I know you're a good girl and all. You never cheated on your husband and you probably have a perfect driving record and never had a cavity, either. But women like you keep so much locked up inside. I see it every day when you come to work. You're reserved, quiet, don't have any friends, other than me, and you spend every other moment when you're not at work with your horse. You need a man who is going to take control, and it sounds to me as if this guy is perfect for you."

Rayne had never considered Trent to be the perfect guy. Sure there were parts of him that she thought perfect, and the fact that he loved horses was an added bonus, but was that enough? "What if he is just taking me for a ride, Lindsey? He's never been married, and there have been a lot of women in his past; a whole lot. Don't you think I should be cautious?"

The beeping of the coffeemaker distracted Lindsey, and she stepped over to the trolley to hit the off button on the machine. "Stop looking for problems where none exist, girl. You have a man that wants to make you happy. That should be all that matters. Besides, if he wasn't in it for the long run, he wouldn't have given a damn last night about whether you were satisfied or not."

The break room door flew open and a short, bald man with a thick gray moustache peered inside.

"Lindsey, I need you to recheck the blood pressure on Mr. Dominguez in room two, and call Dr. Lender again with that consult for Mrs. Bennet."

"Yes, Dr. Moffet," she chirped.

"Is that fresh?" The doctor pointed to the coffee pot.

"Sure is. You want your usual two sugars?"

"Thanks, Lindsey." Dr. Moffet left the break room door open and turned away.

Lindsey removed a white mug from a tray next to the coffeemaker. "At least I won't have to smell his breath if he drinks this."

While Lindsey poured Dr. Moffet's coffee, the black iPhone in the front pocket of Rayne's scrub top played its jazzy ringtone. When she saw the number on the caller ID, Rayne frowned.

"Bad news?" Lindsey inquired, easing the coffeepot back on the warming plate.

"No, just my mother." Rayne put the phone back in her pocket.

"How is the mother of the year?" Lindsey joked with a snort.

"Oh, ha ha." Rayne walked across the break room to Lindsey's side and selected a mug from the trolley. "She fell over the weekend, hit her head, and called Foster to take her to the hospital when she couldn't find me."

Lindsey's jaw dropped. "All that happened in addition to your night of caveman sex with the horse guy?"

Rayne poured the fresh coffee in her mug. "Trent and I were having dinner at his place Saturday night. I drank too much and fell asleep. Sunday morning I got home and Foster left a message on my machine."

"Is Estelle okay?" Lindsey took two packs of sugar from a dish next to the coffeemaker.

"She's fine, but the ER doctor said her blood work was pretty bad. He wants her to see her internist for follow-up."

"How did she react to that news?" Lindsey dumped the sugar in Dr. Moffet's coffee mug.

"She wasn't happy about it. But honestly she wanted to know more about Trent than what tests they were going to do to her."

"Wait?" Lindsey took a breath. "She met him?"

Rayne drank from her mug. "Trent went with me to the hospital Sunday morning."

"And you're wondering if he's serious? Honey, you're really in the dark when it comes to men. If he went with you to the hospital, met Foster and the notorious Estelle, and still wants to be with you, you'd better hang on to him."

"He seemed really worried about how it all affected me," Rayne admitted.

"I want to meet this one." Clutching Dr. Moffet's mug of coffee, Lindsey headed to the open break room door. "He sounds like those guys I read about in my books. The kind you live happily ever after with."

After Lindsey had disappeared out the door, Rayne carried her coffee mug to the counter and collected her plate of pizza. Getting comfortable at the faux wood table, Lindsey's comments about Trent circled like a hawk in Rayne's head. Munching on her pizza, she debated if he was her "happily ever after" or just a man who would make her "happy for now."

Rayne was certain that the most she should count on was some great sex and a few happy memories before Trent Newbury inevitably walked away. But as the idea of having more with the addictive man tantalized her, the slightest glimmer of hope awakened in Rayne's soul. Maybe she had to start with "happy for now," before she could arrive at "happily ever after." After all, true happiness, like trust, took time to build.

Chapter 16

After work, an exhausted Rayne opted to let Bob out in the paddock for exercise instead of tacking up for an afternoon of jumping fences. The cool nip in the air combined with the warmth of the sun had a sedative effect on her. Deciding to stretch out on the grass next to the paddock, Rayne closed her eyes and took a few moments to rest her weary body.

"What do you think you're doing?" a smoky voice griped.

When she opened her eyes, Trent was standing over her, scowling. Wearing gray dress slacks, a long-sleeved pale blue shirt, and black leather loafers, he appeared as if he had just come from the office.

"You've got a show in less than a month. You can't afford to lounge around."

Rayne sat up. "Well, if someone had not kept me up all night, doing unspeakable things to me, I might have the energy to get on my horse and jump a few fences."

Trent took a seat on the grass next to her. "Try a mid-afternoon nap. Worked wonders for me." He kissed her lips and Rayne was instantly rejuvenated.

"I can't nap in the lab," she complained, pulling away. "I don't own a business like some people." She motioned to his clothes. "Did you come from work?"

He reached into the front pocket of his trousers. "Yeah, I have a meeting with Rebecca in a few minutes." He handed her a folded slip of paper.

"What's this?" She unfolded the paper, scrunching her brow.

"A copy of your entrance form for the Golden Farms Horse Show next month. I entered you and Bob." He ripped out some of the blades of grass poking up around him. "Southland Stables is picking up your fee. You'll be showing under our stable name as an instructor."

"Did Rebecca agree to that?"

"Not yet."

Rayne held up the paper in her hands. "She's not going to like footing the show fees for her instructors."

"If she doesn't pay it, I will. I want you in that show. You need to start showing again, Rayne. It's time."

Despite his confidence in her abilities, Rayne still had reservations. As her mind rumbled with refusals, she gleaned over the paper in her hand. "Wait a minute. The name of the horse on this entry form is 'One of a Kind.' Who is that?"

Trent wiped the grass from his hands. "I told you I would come up with a great name for Bob. What do you think? It reminded me of the two of you; simple, classy, but says it all."

Rayne kept staring at the paper, soaking it in. "I can't believe you actually came up with a name."

"Do you like it?"

She was touched that he had not only done as he promised, but he had actually found a name she loved. "It's wonderful."

His gray eyes twinkled and he proudly bobbed his head. "See? I told you I would come up with something perfect."

"Thank you, Trent. I really don't know what to say."

"Just win the damn blue ribbon. That will be thanks enough." He kissed her cheek. "I better not leave Rebecca waiting. She sounded pretty upset on the phone when we talked earlier."

"What could she be upset about?"

"Selene. Seems she contacted her ex-husband after I chewed her ass out the other day. Apparently the judge wasn't too happy about it."

"What did you say to her?"

"What didn't I say to her?" Trent snickered. "She was belligerent with her students, and didn't know how to properly execute many of the required maneuvers in the dressage show ring. So I told her to straighten up or I'd fire her ass."

"You shouldn't have done that." Rayne crumbled the paper in her hands, her joy short-lived. "See, I told you. She's already starting problems."

"Nothing that I can't handle." He patted her thigh. "You look wiped. Go on home, take a nap, and I'll see to Bob."

"I can't ask you to take care of my horse, Trent."

"Rayne, part of letting someone in your life means allowing them to help you out every now and then." He stood from the grass. "When I'm finished here, I'll grab some take-out and come over to your place. So get some rest. I don't want you falling asleep on me. I'm hoping for a repeat performance of last night."

Rayne sarcastically raised her eyebrows, doubting either of them was up for another night without sleep. "We'll see. But I think that will all depend on what kind of take-out you get."

"Any preference?"

She shook her head. "Surprise me."

"Dangerous words to a man with a very adventurous palate."

"I'll take my chances."

He leaned over and kissed the top of her head. "See you later, baby. Get some rest. I have a feeling you're going to need it."

As Trent strode away from the paddock, Rayne took in the curve of his round backside in his fitted slacks. She flopped back on the grass and let out an exuberant sigh, feeling like a sixteen-year-old with a big crush. Lifting her hand still clutching the crumpled entrance form, she took the paper and began smoothing it out.

Interested to see what she was doing, Bob poked his head through the railing of the paddock and sniffed at Rayne's ponytail. Rubbing her hand along the soft flesh on his nose, she gazed up at the white star on his head.

"One of a Kind," she softly said to the horse. "What do you think of that?"

The jazzy ringtone from her phone in the front pocket of her jeans interrupted her moment with Bob. While shoving the copy of the entry form into her back pocket, she spotted her mother's number on the cell phone.

"Hello, Mother."

"I tried calling you earlier," Estelle began in her craggy voice.

"I was busy at work, I couldn't talk." Rayne stroked Bob's nose.

"Are you at the stables? Riding that horse of yours?"

"Not riding. I'm sitting with Bob at the paddock. I'm too tired to ride today."

"Why? You're never been too tired to ride. What wrong?" Estelle almost sounded worried.

"Nothing. I just didn't...get a lot of sleep last night."

"I hope that was because of Trent and not because of your usual worries."

"My 'usual worries'?" Rayne suppressed the cutting remark she wanted to make about Estelle's drinking, deciding it was better not to go down that road again.

"Lord have mercy, child," Estelle drawled. "Ever since you were five years old you have worried about everything from global warming to not having fire extinguishers in the house."

"You make it sound like I was psychotic, Mother."

"Sometimes I think you were. Your father thought it was cute. I found it annoying as shit."

"I'm surprised you didn't tie me in a burlap sack and drown me like an unwanted puppy."

"Really, Raynie. You can be so dramatic. So, tell me, is he the reason for your fatigue?"

Rayne's edginess returned. "That's not your concern, Mother."

"When you get testy, it's because I've hit a nerve." She paused for a moment, making Rayne cringe with anticipation. "Is he any good in the sack?"

"God, you're impossible." Rayne angrily swiped at a few blades of grass. "I'm hanging up now."

"Dr. Emerit's office called to confirm my appointment for next Monday," Estelle edged in. "I had no idea what they were talking about. Did you call them?"

"Yes, I did," Rayne confessed. "And don't tell me you canceled the appointment. You need to have those tests done to find out about your liver."

"My liver is fine."

"Your liver is probably pickled, Mother."

"Oh, humor." Estelle's voice rose with amusement. "You must have gone to bed with that fine man; otherwise you wouldn't be so funny."

"Did you cancel the appointment?" Rayne demanded, ignoring her jab.

"No. I'll go just to show you that I'm fine."

"Go ahead, Mother. Prove me wrong. It's what you live for."

"One day I hope you and I can have a civil conversation. When you have children, you might understand why I am the way I am with you."

Rayne gawked at her cell phone in surprise. "Children? You told me you never wanted to be a grandmother."

"Perhaps, but you've always wanted to be a mother, Raynie. At least I know that much about you. I hope you get the chance."

Disturbed by her mother's insight, Rayne shifted uncomfortably on the grass. "I have to go."

"You always do." Estelle hung up before Rayne could add anything else.

Determined not to let the conversation with her mother dampen her mood, she focused on a pleasant evening ahead with Trent. Standing from the grass, she withdrew her car keys from her back pocket and gave Bob another pat on the neck. Crossing the grassy pasture that led to the shell-covered parking lot, Rayne remembered the name Trent had chosen for Bob.

"One of a Kind. How did he know?"

As the late afternoon sun cast long stretches of red, orange, and yellow across the expanse of the western sky, Rayne smiled. For the first time since her father's passing, she believed she had found a kindred spirit who seemed to know exactly how to touch her heart.

***

It was after seven when the cascade of bells from Rayne's front door echoed across her living room. Unable to rest after she had returned from the stables, Rayne spent the afternoon and early evening cleaning. She changed the sheets on her bed, mopped the floors, vacuumed, and even lit some candles about the living room to add a romantic ambience.

But as she darted across the living room to the front door, she concluded the candles were a bit much. She knew he was coming over intending to have sex, but maybe the candles appeared a little too…desperate. Wanting to give the right impression, Rayne quickly scurried about the living room, blowing out the candles she had spent twenty minutes arranging to give off just the right mood.

"What took you so long to answer the door?" Trent stood on her front porch, balancing two brown paper bags in his arms.

"I didn't hear the doorbell in the bathroom. I was putting on my makeup." She hoped that at least sounded reasonable.

"You don't need makeup for me." He walked in the front door and handed her the larger of the bags. "Chinese." He hugged the smaller one to his chest. "Dessert."

The aroma of the Chinese food made Rayne's mouth water. "What are we having?"

He deposited his keys on the round table close to the door. "Boneless fried chicken with veggies, shrimp fried rice, egg rolls, beef stir fry, and a few fortune cookies thrown in. I hope that's enough."

"Smells wonderful." Rayne gestured to the other bag. "What's for dessert?"

"It's a surprise."

"A surprise dessert?" She turned away, carrying the bag of Chinese food. "Does it have to be set on fire or something?" she joked over her shoulder.

Trent followed behind her. "Just might."

Leaving the entryway, she was about to cross the living room to the kitchen when Trent stopped.

"Why does it smell like smoke in here?"

Rayne placed the bag of food on the kitchen counter and tried to act casual. "Oh, I was just burning some candles to get rid of the eau de Frank."

"You sure you don't want to relight them?" Trent put his bag on the counter next to her. "Might help get me in the mood." He embraced her from behind.

Rayne spun around in his arms. "Somehow I don't think you need any help with that."

He kissed her hard on the lips, and when he finally came up for air, he asked, "Where is the mangy mongrel?"

"Still outside." Rayne opened the cabinet behind her. "He discovered a squirrel in one of the small trees I have out back. He's been staring at it for over an hour."

Trent put the paper bag containing his "surprise" dessert in the freezer. "I'll go and get him."

He opened the back door that led to a small patio and the yard beyond. Trent clapped his hands and Frank came galloping up to greet him. The easygoing familiarity between man and beast made Rayne smile. It was as if they had been living together for years. All the comfortable domestic habits you learn to share with another seemed so easy with Trent. She could not recall ever having such a feeling with Foster.

"He's excited to see me," Trent declared as he and Frank came bounding in from the patio.

Rayne unpacked the cartons of Chinese food from the paper bag as Trent and Frank played in her kitchen. When

Frank jumped up and placed his dirty paws on Trent's nice pale blue shirt, she grimaced.

"Frank, get down." She went to Trent's side and began wiping away the mud stain Frank had left behind.

Trent stayed her hands. "Don't worry about it."

"But it will ruin your shirt." She patted her hand on his chest. "Take it off and I'll wash it for you before the stain sets in."

"Are you undressing me already?"

"Maybe," she returned with a winsome grin.

As Trent unbuttoned his shirt, Rayne's eyes lingered over his smooth chest and ripped abdominal muscles. He eased the shirt from his shoulders and handed it to her. Preoccupied with his spectacular chest, she took the shirt from him, and was about to toss it to the side when something caught her eye. On the collar of the shirt was a lipstick stain…deep red.

"What's this?" She pointed to the stain.

"What's what?" He furrowed his brow at the shirt.

"Lipstick. How did you get this on your shirt, Trent?"

"I guess I got it when I was meeting with Rebecca and Selene."

"Selene? I thought you were only meeting with Rebecca."

Trent went to the counter. "So did I." He deftly flipped open a white lid on a carton of Chinese food and peeked inside. "But when I walked into Rebecca's office, Selene was there. Rebecca was trying to get us to set aside our differences."

"And did you?" Rayne placed his shirt on the countertop, suddenly more interested in the outcome of his meeting than running her hands over his chest.

"I was forced to." He rested his hip against the counter. "I need someone to teach the dressage class, at least until I can find a replacement. Plus, Selene vowed she would work hard to get up to speed with all the dressage requirements for the show ring. She promised things would be different, and Rebecca assured me that if they weren't, she would fire Selene."

Rayne tossed her hands up, furious. "So she got her way after all."

Trent pushed away from the counter and came toward her. "So what if she did? At least now she will do as I ask."

"No, Trent. She'll only let you think that for a while, but then she will return to the same old Selene she has always been. A leopard does not change its spots."

His arms slinked about her waist. "As far as I'm concerned, she is on probation. And I insisted she had to compete at Golden Farms next month."

Rayne felt all of her excitement for the coming show wane. "Selene will be impossible until then. She'll demand time with you to help her train, and try to come...." She let the words die on her lips, not wanting to sound like a meddling wife.

"You mean she will try and come between us, is that what you were going to say?" He fervently searched her eyes. "So there is an 'us' now?"

She stroked his chest, her aggravation relenting to his charm. "Yes, there's an 'us.'" Rayne glanced back at his shirt on the counter, thinking.

"I'm glad to hear that." His lips gently nuzzled her neck.

"I still have one question."

"What is it?"

"How did you get that lipstick stain?"

He laughed, seeming pleased with the lilt of jealousy in her voice. "Selene must have left it when she kissed my neck after our meeting in Rebecca's office. It never occurred to me that there was a lipstick stain on my shirt until you pointed it out. It was nothing, Rayne."

"I know I sound like a—"

His arms tightened around her. "Forget it, baby. I don't run around and I told you before, I could never be interested in a woman like Selene." He lowered his head to her. "See what I mean about women who wear lipstick at the stables? It gets you in trouble."

She relaxed against him as her concerns faded. When his lips began to tempt the flesh on her neck, Rayne handed herself over to the rising furor of her desire. Her hands skimmed the firm muscles in his chest and back.

Trent closed his arms about her hips and in one smooth motion, lifted her onto the kitchen counter. "I don't think I'm ready to eat yet."

Rayne giggled against his chest. "But the food will get cold."

"That's what microwaves are for."

He pulled the loose-fitting T-shirt over her shoulders, and expertly unclasped her bra. When her breasts fell free, his hands were all over them. He lowered his lips to her right nipple and bit down hard, making Rayne moan.

"That's what I like to hear." He picked her up from the counter and carried her to the living room floor.

After setting her down on her burgundy carpet, he unzipped the fly of her jeans and worked the thick denim fabric down her legs along with her panties.

Naked on the floor beneath him, Rayne waited as he kneeled over her. Before Trent she would have been anxious about being with a man, but now she wanted nothing more than to feel him inside her.

"What are you going to do with me, Mr. Newbury?"

Leaning over her right thigh, he kissed her knee. Slowly, deliberately, his mouth followed the course of the taut muscles along her thigh. As he inched forward, his hands spread her knees wide apart.

Rayne's heart slammed in her chest as his lips snuck closer to the mound of flesh between her legs. Placing her hands over her face, she anxiously anticipated what was to come. But when his kisses ceased, Rayne uncovered her eyes and saw his face hovering over her hips.

"You look nervous." His fingers gently tracked along her folds.

"I...I've never done this. Heard about it, but I've never actually had anyone...."

He kissed her belly. "Foster never tasted you."

"Not like I think you're about to. It was something...he never wanted to try."

"Relax, baby. I promise you will love it."

The instant his lips clamped down on her flesh, Rayne almost screamed out loud with surprise. The sensation shooting up her spine was unlike anything she had ever known.

"Oh, God," Rayne cried out as her back arched against the thrill of electricity.

Soon Trent's tongue was tracing circles over her tender nub, and Rayne forgot herself completely as she moaned and gyrated against him. When his teeth gently nipped her, a slam of white heat blasted up her back and her orgasm exploded. She screamed with every ounce of energy she felt bursting out of her, and as her body fell back against the carpet, she broke out in a fit of giggling.

"Oh my God." She slapped her hand over her mouth, embarrassed by her reaction.

Trent chuckled and stood beside her. "I guess you liked it."

"I never expected it to be so...good."

He slipped out of his trousers and briefs. Before tossing his pants to her nearby white leather sofa, he took out a condom packet from his pocket. He saw her staring at him and held out the condom to her.

"Come and put this on me."

Rayne rose to her knees and crawled over to him. She took the condom in her hand and looked up at him.

"Just roll it down over the tip," he instructed, guiding her hands.

When she cupped her hands about his erection, Trent closed his eyes and groaned. After she gently slid the condom over him, he hurriedly pushed her to the floor.

"I can't believe you've never done any of this before."

"I'm beginning to see there are a lot of things I have missed out on when it comes to sex." She wrapped her lean legs about his hips.

"I'm going to have a lot of fun expanding your sexual horizons." Trent kissed her chin as he rubbed his hips against her.

She rolled her head back, laughing with happiness. "You mean there's more?"

He grabbed her firm butt, raising her hips higher in the air. "Lot's more." Slowly, he pushed all the way into her. "Now, let's see if I can make you scream even louder." He pulled out and thrust into her wet flesh.

Rayne bit down on his shoulder. Her folds were so sensitive that even the slightest touch from him made her body tremble.

"Yes, again," she cried into his chest as he dove into her, even harder than before. "Don't stop."

"I won't, baby." He kissed her neck. "I promise."

Chapter 17

They were sitting naked on the burgundy living room carpet, with Frank spread out between them, snoring, while cartons of half-eaten Chinese food were littered about.

"I think we killed Frank." Trent gestured to the large dog.

Rayne wiped the crumbs from the egg roll she had just eaten from her hands. "After the amount of boneless chicken you fed him, he'll probably sleep for a week."

"Well, I felt guilty. I forgot he was in the kitchen while we were out here rolling around on the carpet like two teenagers."

Rayne blushed. "Yeah, I think all my screaming might have scared him just a tad."

Trent leaned over and kissed her cheek. "You didn't scare me. I love it when you scream."

Her blush quickly turned into a warm burning on her cheeks and chest.

"I love it when I can make you blush, too." Trent's beaming smile lit up his face. "I still can't believe that…well, that Foster was such a neglectful lover."

Rayne rested her back against the edge of a white ottoman behind her. "He was just set in his ways. I realize that now. Maybe if I had been more experienced in bed, I might never have settled for him."

Trent reached for a glass of water next to him on the floor. "I've been meaning to ask you about something, but every time I want to bring it up I get…distracted."

Rayne pensively furrowed her brow. "What is it?"

He rolled the glass in his hands. "Perhaps you should consider going on birth control, because we have slipped up once, and probably will again. We should discuss it. Just in case."

"In case I get pregnant?"

He took a sip of water. "It has crossed my mind."

"Don't worry, Trent. If that did happen I wouldn't expect you to be responsible. It would be my problem, not yours."

He put his glass down and nestled in beside her. "Our problem, Rayne. I would never shirk my responsibilities, and I would always be there if we did have a child…that is, if you wanted to keep it."

Keep it? How could she tell him what a baby would mean to her? After all the years she had spent alone, to have someone who would forever be a part of her life was beyond imagining.

"Foster was not capable of being a father. He had undergone a vasectomy during his first marriage to ensure his wife would never get pregnant again." She let her eyes wander back to Trent. "I could never entertain the idea of having a child until…."

Trent nudged her shoulder. "Until what?"

"Until…you." Dreading his response, Rayne shrank from his side. "I shouldn't have said that. That was probably more than you wanted to hear."

His arms went about her, pulling her close. "That is exactly what I wanted to hear."

She avoided his penetrating gaze. "Is it?"

"Here I am practically throwing myself at you, and you can ask such a question?" He shook his head, chuckling. "You're one tough cookie to crack, but I think I'm finally starting to get through."

She settled into his strong arms. "Perhaps a little."

"Just a little?" His hand stroked suggestively up and down her naked back.

"Okay, a lot."

"That's better." He kissed her forehead and let his lips meander their way to her mouth. As his kiss intensified, he pushed her body down on the floor.

"Again?" Rayne giggled.

"I can't get enough of you."

"Yeah, I'm beginning to feel exactly the same way." She then raked her nails across his round ass.

He sucked in a gasp of air. "You're gonna pay for that."

She pushed her hips into him. "I'm counting on it."

***

Rayne awoke with a start and rolled over in her queen-sized brass bed to the digital alarm clock on the nightstand next to her. It was a little after one in the morning and she questioned what had roused her from such a sound sleep. Then, Frank's snoring started up from the floor next to the bed. When she sat up and saw Trent asleep beside her, a warm, fuzzy feeling of contentment tugged at her heart.

He had been so tender the second time he had taken her that night. His kisses and even the way he moved inside her felt different. It was almost as if she could feel his emotions. If that was making love, it was something she had never experienced with Foster. How could she have wasted all those years with such a man?

As she watched the rise and fall of Trent's chest, Rayne caressed the wavy black hair about his temples. Fleeting images of waking up beside him every morning for the rest of her life were soon replaced by her voice of reason, squelching her daydreams.

A loud snort from the floor next to the bed made her jump. A gray eye popped open, and Trent bolted upright.

"What was that?"

She smiled apologetically. "Frank. I told you he snored."

Trent peered over the edge of the bed to the sleeping ball of fur on the floor. "That's not snoring, that sounded like vacuuming."

"He is rather loud. I have to poke him a few times during the night to get him to stop."

Trent ran his hand through his hair. "Ever consider a dog house?"

"Of course not."

"I'll put one at my place. He can sleep there when you stay with me." He pulled her back down in the bed.

Rayne snuggled against his bare chest and smelled the last hints of his cologne on his skin. "Maybe I'll just leave him here. He might get upset being stuck outside in a dog house."

Trent closed his eyes. "I'll put it in the kitchen then, if that will make you happy."

"Or you can just stay at my place when you want to see me," she sheepishly offered.

"No way. Your bed is too small. We can work out some kind of arrangement between both our places."

"You sure that isn't moving too fast for you?"

"Rayne, stop putting up road blocks."

She raised her head slightly, resting her chin on his chest. "I'm not putting up road blocks; I've just never done this before. You know, juggling the sleeping arrangements."

"Sometimes you remind me of a little girl, and then at other times you are so determined and self-reliant."

"You've met Estelle, so you know why I've had to be self-reliant."

"What about your father? What was he like?"

"Dad?" She sighed, remembering the lanky, easy-going man. "He was nothing like my mother. In fact, he was the total opposite...kind, willing to help anyone, and funny. Dad was always cracking jokes for Jaime and me at the dinner table. Every night when he would get home from the office, he would have a new joke for us. I still miss his jokes."

His fingers combed through her unruly hair. "I think you're more like him than your mother. I just don't see you when I look at her."

"Jaime was the one who favored my mother. She was the pretty one all the boys followed around."

"Do you have a picture of her?"

Rayne shook her head. "After she and Dad died, Estelle burned every picture in the house, every memento my sister had collected, her stuffed toys, and all the papers from my father's desk, everything." A single teardrop cascaded down her cheek. "I have nothing from either one of them. What she didn't burn, she sold. The clothes, jewelry, and even Dad's collection of antique law books he had once prized. Everything is gone."

"But why?"

"Because they were dead, and Mother said we had to forget about them. After that, the drinking sort of took over her life."

Trent sat up next to her and wiped the tear from her cheek. "I can't imagine what it must have been like to lose your family. I know mine helps keep me sane."

"I hoped when I married Foster I was getting a family. But he was never close with any of his relatives. He claimed they were all after his money. So holidays were spent with friends. Foster always had a lot of those. Funny thing was, every holiday there was a whole new set of friends. I guess he never kept anybody in his life for long."

"You know what would make you feel better?" He kissed her neck.

"I think I'm getting an inkling."

"Dessert," he announced.

"Dessert?" She was not sure if he was talking about the actual food or the alluding to another round beneath the sheets.

He scooted across the bed and threw off the covers. "I'll be right back."

A little mystified, Rayne watched as he jogged out of the darkened room and into the hallway. She sat up and flipped on a small lamp on the carved night table next to her bed. After a few minutes he reappeared in her bedroom doorway, flaunting a red and white ice cream carton and two spoons.

"We forgot my surprise dessert." He came toward the bed and Rayne ogled over the rippled muscles in his abdomen, and the size of his…. "I went to the best ice cream place in Lewisville," he went on, distracting her.

"The one you told me about on the phone?"

He climbed back in the bed and handed her a spoon. "Braum's Ice Cream and Dairy." He tore the top off the red and white carton. "Mocha chocolate chip. You need to be adventurous."

Dipping her spoon into the ice cream, she smiled. "Thank you."

As she tasted the ice cream, a dull thumping arose from the floor next to the bed, followed by a large, furry brown head staring up at them.

"What? Does he only move when there is food close by?"

Rayne nodded her head. "Basically. If he's not eating, he's sleeping."

"What about the squirrel he was obsessed with earlier?"

"Isolated incident." Rayne licked her spoon. "He's never that energetic for very long."

Trent scooped a large chunk of ice cream from the container as Frank's big brown eyes concentrated on him. "What do you do with him when you have to go out of town?" He placed the carton on the night table next to Rayne, noting how the dog's eyes fixated on the ice cream.

"I've never gone out of town since I got him."

Trent lapped the coffee-colored ice cream from his spoon. "What if I wanted to take you out of town next weekend?"

"To where?"

"My friend, Tyler Moore—the one I did that consulting job for—has invited us to a party at his house in North Dallas next weekend. We could get a hotel room close by and stay the night after the party, so we wouldn't have to drive all the way back here."

"Invited *us*?"

"His wife Monique wants to meet you. So yes, he invited us."

"Why does she want to meet me?" Rayne's concern permeated her voice.

He polished off the last of the ice cream on his spoon. "Monique is curious about you. She claims you bewitched me."

Rayne laughed and put her spoon on top of the carton of ice cream. He leaned across the bed and rested his spoon next to hers.

"I don't know. You're pretty bewitching, especially with an ice cream stain on your chin." He licked the spot of ice cream away from her chin.

"Perhaps I should find some other places to spill ice cream."

"Don't give me any ideas."

"Wouldn't dream of it."

He lowered her to the bed. "Say you'll go with me next weekend."

"What about Frank?"

Trent careened his head to the side as Frank was inching closer to the open carton of ice cream sitting on the night table. "I think I know the perfect babysitter for the monster."

"Who is that?"

Trent gazed down at her naked body. "I'll tell you later." His hands slipped behind her back and ran down to her round butt. "It's time to try something different for dessert."

"No more ice cream?" she playfully teased, reaching for his erection.

Trent kissed her belly button, and then slowly spread her legs apart. "This is going to taste much better than ice cream."

Chapter 18

"I don't babysit dogs!" Rebecca howled, standing before Rayne's tack room door a few days later. "But when your boyfriend basically threatened to quit unless I took your oversized fur coat, I had no choice."

Rayne walked out her tack room door, carrying her English riding saddle and blanket in her arms. "I can't believe he talked you into babysitting Frank this weekend."

"He insisted you two needed to get away for the weekend and that you wouldn't go unless you knew that thing you call a dog was cared for. Why can't you just board him like a normal mongrel owner?"

Rayne hefted the saddle and blanket onto Bob's back and turned to Rebecca. "Frank is not a mongrel, and I could never leave him in a kennel with strangers. He knows you."

"He hates me," Rebecca countered. "Every time you bring him to the stables he looks at me as if I'm a slab of ham."

Rayne tightened the saddle girth beneath Bob's belly. "He looks at everyone that way. It's a sign of affection."

"It's a sign of inbreeding." Rebecca stepped over to Bob and patted the horse's long neck. "Where is that handsome riding master of mine, anyway? He hasn't been here the past two afternoons."

"He's got another consulting job in Louisiana. He'll be back Saturday morning."

Rebecca ran her hand over Bob's thick shoulder and down his front right leg. "He's looking real good, Rayne." She stood up. "Did your boyfriend tell you I sent in the entry fee for you and Bob for the Golden Farms Horse Show next month?"

"No, he didn't tell me." Rayne secured the buckles of the girth without looking up at Rebecca. "And that's the second time you have called him my boyfriend."

"I was wondering if you were going to say anything." Rebecca wormed closer to her side. "So how is it going with the two of you? That he wants to take you away for the weekend is a good sign."

"It's not what you think. We're going to a formal party in the city and he wants to stay overnight in a hotel so we don't have to drive all the way back to Lewisville in the middle of the night."

"Same room or adjoining rooms?" Rebecca's playful brown eyes glistened with curiosity.

"You're joking, right?" Rayne went back to her tack room door.

"So what are you going to wear to this party?"

"I still have some gowns in the back of my closet from my days with Foster. I'm sure I can find something," Rayne reasoned from inside the tack room.

"Just make sure you look amazing, Rayne. I have a feeling he's taking you to this gig to show you off."

Rayne came out of the tack room clutching a dark leather bridle. "I think I might have just the right dress. I only wore it once years ago, but it should do."

"If it clings to your ass and shows off your boobs, it will be the right dress." Rebecca gave Bob's neck a celebratory slap. "That will get his engine revving."

Rayne shook her head and veered back to Bob. Unclasping his blue halter, she placed the flat of her hand under the bit and gently pushed it into Bob's mouth. After he had taken the bit, she slipped the bridle up his long head and secured it behind his black-tipped ears.

"Well, I may not be the only one around here trying to rev his engine." Rayne rubbed the white star on Bob's head as Rebecca gave her a questioning glance. "He told me about his meeting with you and Selene. I thought you wanted to get rid of her."

"I did, until Judge Kendrick begged me to intervene on his ex-wife's behalf and smooth things over with Trent. And that is one man I want to owe me a favor, if you know what I mean."

"I understand. It's business." Rayne shrugged her shoulders. "Trent made it sound like Selene was happy about keeping her job. I even found a lipstick stain on the collar of his shirt after your meeting. She must have been real grateful."

"Grateful?" Rebecca snorted with contempt. "The slut basically used Trent's body as a stripper pole after she kissed his ass to keep her job." She paused and eyed Rayne for a moment. "When you saw his shirt was it coming off or going on?"

"Rebecca," Rayne chastised with a scolding gaze.

"All right, none of my business." Rebecca apologetically held up her hands. "And don't worry about Selene, sweetie. If you ask me that lipstick stain was probably planted on his shirt, hoping you would see it. She wants your guy, there's no question about that, but he only has eyes for you."

221

Rayne wished she could wholeheartedly believe in Trent, but still doubts still plagued her. "Sometimes I think he's still too good to be true."

"Why? You're a hell of a catch, Rayne. I've always told you that, and Trent sees it. He's lucky to have you."

Rayne grasped the reins in her hand. "If I'm such a catch, then why didn't Foster want me?"

"Foster was a back-stabbing, conniving, selfish pig, who was stupid to let you go. Forget about him." Rebecca patted her arm. "Now you'd better get out to the ring before it gets dark. You have a show to get ready for, and you had better bring home the blue ribbon."

"Thanks for the extra pressure, Rebecca. Not only do I have to please Trent, now I have to please you, too."

"Yeah, but I only need to be pleased vertically, kiddo," she chuckled with a wink. "Your man requires a different kind of horizontal pleasure."

"Christ, Rebecca. Are you always thinking about sex, or do you just pretend to be?"

Squinting her brown eyes, Rebecca pondered the question. "No, I'm not pretending. I'm always thinking about sex."

Clucking to Bob, Rayne urged him to follow her to the stable entrance. "You should have been born a man."

"Maybe in my next life. In the meantime, bring your flea motel to my place before you two head into the city Saturday. I'll have my grandkids come over and wear his furry hide out."

"Frank will like that. He loves kids." Rayne started down the shed row with Bob.

"And Rayne?"

Rayne halted and turned to Rebecca.

"He won't hurt you. It's real obvious he's crazy about you."

Rayne drew in a shaky breath. "Yeah, I'm crazy about him too, Rebecca. That's what scares me."

***

The following Saturday night, Rayne was caressing the soft fabric of her dark green gown as Trent opened the passenger door of his car. The empire-waisted, halter design hugged the curves of her hips and accentuated her full breasts, making Rayne feel more self-conscious than attractive.

"Did I tell you how beautiful you look tonight?" Trent articulated as she stepped from his car.

"No. When you picked me up, your first words were 'Let's not go,' and, 'Take off that dress.'"

Trent shut the car door and fidgeted with the black tie of his tuxedo. "I was excited. Any man seeing you in that dress would be excited."

"Thank you...I think." She brushed a speck of lint from the lapel of his black tuxedo jacket. "And you look pretty damned handsome in that."

His hand ran around her back and rested on her butt. "I'll let you strip it off me later."

"I'm counting on it," she taunted, tracing the curve of his clean-shaven jaw with her finger.

Letting out a ragged breath, Trent took her hand. "You're going to be the best-looking woman in the place."

Rayne cast her eyes to a contemporary one-story, natural stone home nestled on two lush acres. With a myriad of pricey imported cars parked before it, the house seemed out of place and better suited for a Texas ranch rather than a luxury mansion.

"It's not what I expected from an oil tycoon," she admitted, eyeing the array of trimmed white crape myrtle, white birch, and dogwood trees in front of the structure.

"Just wait." Trent nodded to the house. "It's a lot like Tyler Moore; simple on the outside, but very impressive on the inside. He bought it after he married Monique a few months back. But don't be fooled; he and Monique are really down-to-earth people. Especially Monique. She's from New Orleans, like you." He took her elbow and guided her to a walkway that meandered through the trees, leading to the home.

"You didn't tell me she was from New Orleans." Her high black heels clicked on the cement as they strolled along.

"Her professional name is Monique Delome. She writes romance novels."

"*The* Monique Delome?" She glanced over at Trent. "I can't believe it. I've never read her books, but Lindsey, my friend at work, has."

The idea of a party sprinkled with celebrities and the socially well-to-do brought to mind her life with Foster and all the misery she had endured.

Trent stopped in mid-stride. "You're shivering. Do you want my jacket?"

"No, it's just that…well, this reminds me of my marriage. I feel like I've gone back in time; the fancy clothes, fancy cars, expensive homes, and famous guests."

"Do you want to leave?"

"Of course not." She clasped his hand. "This is your friend, not some business associate or charity event where I have to smile, say nothing, and look like attractive arm candy."

"Well, you definitely look like candy to me." His eyes glided over her outfit. "I'd eat you."

"Are you sure you and Rebecca aren't related in some way?"

His brow crinkled. "I don't get it."

"Forget it." She waved off his confusion. "I just hope Frank survives the night with her."

"I hope she can sleep through his snoring." Trent's troubled eyes inspected her face. "Are you sure you want to do this?"

She started down the walkway, ignoring his concern. "I want to meet your friends. It might give me a little more insight into you."

He came alongside her and hooked her arm through his. "You already know everything about me."

His comment ricocheted about in her heart, reawakening her uncertainty. "I don't know everything, Trent."

"Well, you know a lot, Rayne. And just tell me if tonight gets to be too much. We can sneak out and head over to the hotel."

"I will." Rayne took in a fortifying breath when she spotted the flowing gowns and tuxedos of the other guests heading toward the entrance of the home.

"Promise? I don't want you putting up with something that makes you uncomfortable for my sake, Rayne."

A little stunned, Rayne gave him a perplexed side-glance. "That's a first."

"What is?"

"Being with a man who cares more about my feelings than his."

He patted her hand as they came to the edge of the gardens on the side of the portico. "That's the way it should be."

They made their way under a wide porch to a pair of open dark red double doors with circular, bright brass knockers. As they waited for guests ahead of them to trickle inside, Rayne rolled Trent's words over in her mind. Maybe this was how it was supposed to be with a man. Never before had she known such contentment and such happiness. As long as Rayne lived, she would treasure this moment; that nanosecond where long-wished-for dreams merged with the reality of one's life, making everything seem absolutely…perfect.

Chapter 19

After wading through the crowds at the entrance and passing a bottleneck of colorful gowns, shimmering jewels, and varying cuts of black tuxedos, Rayne and Trent managed to squeeze their way into the home. They meandered along a narrow corridor with gray marble floors and thick glass windows on one side. Glancing out the windows, Rayne slowed, awestruck by the view.

A center patio, edged with thick green shrubbery and gray slate, surrounded an I-shaped pool and spa that was lit with ethereal blue and green lights. On either side of the pool, twenty-foot high walls of glass and thick wood beams allowed a clear view of symmetrical living rooms and fireplaces.

"It's stunning," Rayne remarked.

"The home backs to Turtle Creek and was designed by an old friend of mine, architect Hayden Parr of Parr and Associates. Behind the house are wandering paths of gardens, stone walls, and ponds that lead to the creek." Trent urged her further into the home. "Let's find our hosts."

Guiding her past a drawing room of high peaked ceilings, hardwood floors, and another wall of windows, Rayne took in the airy use of space and light around her. But when they stepped into one of the living rooms, her eyes grew round with astonishment.

Rectangular in shape with a fire pit fireplace at one end topped by a colossal tarnished metal hood, the living room had an iridescent pearl-covered bar with an elongated fish tank built into the wall behind it. Soft taupe leather sofas and chairs complemented the pale paneling on the walls, while metal and glass tables sat atop a muted beige Berber carpet. Guests were seated at high backed leather stools about the bar, where a black-tied bartender was serving drinks. Others were taking in the serene views of the gardens and grounds through the windows that made up two of the twenty-foot high walls in the room.

"I don't see them." Trent swept the room with his eyes. "Let's try the kitchen."

Taking her arm, he escorted her back into the narrow hallway and passed doors of opaque glass with veins of metal that looked like sticks of wood embedded in them. Rayne browsed a few black and white framed photographs of New Orleans landmarks on the walls, and wanted to stop and study the pictures in detail, but Trent encouraged her onward. Soon, Rayne was standing at the entrance to one of the most spacious rooms she had ever seen.

One long, rectangular room was comprised of a family room, kitchen, and dining area. There were no walls or partitions between sections, only two oval islands of oak cabinets topped with black granite were set in the center, designating the kitchen area. Three of the walls were inlaid with windows, overlooking gardens bathed in amber and yellow light. The remaining wall was covered from floor to ceiling with oak cabinets and inlaid niches for knickknacks and family photos. In the kitchen, the cabinets were broken up by black granite countertops, and then a Viking cooktop, double oven, and built-in glass refrigerator created a shiny centerpiece.

The crowds were thickest in this room, hovering over silver chaffing dishes set out on the two kitchen islands, and clustered in groups as black tie wait staff served hors d'oeuvres on silver platters.

"There they are," Trent pronounced to be heard over the noise of the other guests, and then began pulling Rayne toward one of the kitchen islands.

Rayne's eyes settled on an attractive older gentleman standing next to the counter with his arm around the waist of a very petite woman with an upswept coif of dirty-blonde hair.

The woman had pale, almost translucent skin, an oval face, rosy cheeks, and sleek cheekbones that complemented her small pink mouth and daintily curved jaw. Her pleated light red gown reminded Rayne of a Greek statue. It attached at one shoulder, clung to her trim waist, and fanned out into a cascade of sweeping material that gathered behind her in a small train. The thick gold bead and diamond choker about her slender neck made Rayne raise her hand to her woefully inadequate emerald and diamond necklace. It was one of the few expensive pieces Foster had given her for their fifth wedding anniversary.

The handsome man beside the elegant blonde laughed at something one of his guests had said, and then discretely rubbed his hand over his chin, attempting to hide his cocky grin. When his eyes pivoted about the room, he spotted Trent, and his grin spread into a sincere smile.

"Trent," he shouted in a friendly tone.

"Tyler Moore," Trent whispered to Rayne.

Attired in a black Armani tuxedo that shimmered beneath the recessed lights above, Tyler Moore's fit body screamed of grace, sophistication, and long hours at the gym. Black, wavy hair tinged at the sides with gray outlined his chiseled cheekbones, determined, square jaw, and high forehead. As his deep-set, dark eyes lingered over Rayne's dress, her stomach tied into a thousand knots.

"Finally, you made it." Tyler Moore held out a tapering hand to Trent.

Trent gripped his hand. "Yeah, we had to drop Frank off at his babysitters."

"Frank's the dog that snores, right?" Tyler turned to Rayne. "Trent has told me quite a few entertaining stories about your dog, Ms. Greer."

Rayne extended her hand, a little awestruck that such an important man would be bothered remembering stories about Frank. "Please, call me Rayne, and thank you for having me tonight. You have a beautiful home."

"Thank you, Rayne." Tyler tapped the shoulder of the woman beside him. "Moe, Trent and Rayne are here."

Shady gray eyes turned to Rayne, surprising her with their intensity. Up close the woman's beauty was even more breathtaking, and at the same time unexpectedly fragile. In that instant, Rayne was reminded of her sister Jaime. She had shared the woman's coloring and captivating beauty.

"Rayne, I'm Monique Delome." She offered a delicate hand to Rayne. "Trent has told us so much about you."

Rayne shook Monique's hand and immediately knew she liked this woman. Her warm, welcoming manner had completely erased the knots created by her husband's disturbing eyes.

"It's a pleasure, Ms. Delome. I must say I have a friend that simply adores your books."

"You must call me Monique." Her attention shifted to Trent. "You have a very good eye, my friend." She kissed his cheek.

"You don't have a drink." Tyler pointed to their empty hands. "Come with me." He patted Trent on the shoulder. "I'll take you to the bar."

Trent's fingers caressed Rayne's hand. "What would you like?"

"Wine is good."

"Champagne," Monique proposed. "You must have champagne. We have two cases of Bollinger RD for tonight."

Rayne bowed her head graciously. "That is my favorite champagne."

"See?" Monique waved at Rayne. "She is already fitting in."

Trent displayed a proud smile. "I'll get you champagne then."

As Trent and Tyler walked away, Rayne could not help but watch their lean bodies sway beneath their tuxedos. Almost the exact same height, both men cut an impressive figure from behind, but Trent's body boasted a thicker set of shoulders and much better butt.

"Good-looking men, aren't they?" Monique spoke out behind her.

Rayne blushed slightly as she turned around, embarrassed that she had been caught staring. "I'm sorry, I was just admiring the—"

"Don't worry about it. You wouldn't be female if you didn't look." Monique's grey eyes skimmed over Rayne's features. "Trent told me you're from New Orleans. What part of the city are you from?"

"Uptown," Rayne replied. "My parents had a house on Second Street just off Prytania."

"I've got a house on Prytania. Ty keeps bugging me to put it up for sale, but I just can't make myself."

"Do you get back often?"

"Not so much anymore," Monique conceded. "Since our daughter, Eva, was born, I've been staying close to home."

"Your daughter? How old is she?"

"Six months." Monique gazed about the crowded room. "I was going to sneak away to check on her, if you would care to join me."

Rayne heartily nodded, excited at the prospect. "I would love to meet your little girl."

"Come on, but don't tell Ty. He'll just scold me for taking you away from Trent." Monique crooked her finger at Rayne and then slinked away from the kitchen island, carrying the train of her light red dress in her hand.

She led Rayne down a hallway away from the kitchen, and as they went along, the noise of the party dimmed behind them. On the walls, Rayne noticed more old photographs of New Orleans.

"I love these pictures," Rayne told her.

Monique lovingly smiled. "I collect old photographs of New Orleans. Keeps home in my heart."

They came to an ash-stained door at the end of the corridor, and Monique pushed down on the long silver handle. As the door opened, pink light seeped into the hallway. The room beyond was awash in the soothing light, coming from a single lamp set beside a pink crib with a turning mobile of pink and white angels above it. On the walls were painted white, wooly lambs, small pink piglets, doves, and creamy ponies, and amid the animals, chubby cherubs were tying slender red ribbons on the tails of each and every creature. White shelves on a far wall were packed with stuffed toys and assorted bottles of lotions, creams, and powders.

"Is she still sleeping, Trisha?" Monique inquired, turning to an older woman in a white scrub suit.

"She's been sleeping soundly, Mrs. Moore." Trisha stood from the chair she had set up in a corner of the room. "She hasn't made a peep."

Monique motioned for Trisha to return to her seat. "I just wanted to check on her." She glanced about the room. "Where is he?"

Trisha pointed to a pink pillow on the floor to the side of the crib. Rayne lowered her eyes to the pillow to see a small dog with patchy white fur sleeping on his back as his pink tongue hung from the side of his mouth.

"Bart, my dog," Monique explained. "He never leaves Eva's room."

Gentle snores could be heard coming from Bart, making Rayne smile. "I've got a snorer, too. Mine is named Frank."

Trisha returned to her chair as Rayne and Monique crept up to the crib. The aroma of baby powder blended with sweet honeysuckle floated by Rayne's nose as she peeked over the railing of the crib. Inside, a very small head with faint, wispy yellow hair was jutting out from beneath a pink blanket. The infant had her thumb in her mouth, but her eyes were closed and she appeared as peaceful as anything Rayne had ever seen.

"She's been so good." Monique stroked the child's head. "Tyler keeps claiming that she can't possibly be ours."

"She is adorable." Rayne regarded the baby with awe. "She's so tiny."

"She was early. Took us both by surprise. We had just gotten married a few days before I went into labor."

The infant yawned and squirmed in the crib, then went right back to sleep.

"We'd better not wake her." Monique directed her eyes to the nursery door.

After they had stepped back into the hall, Monique regarded Rayne. "Trent told me you two met at the stables where he works."

"Yes, he's the riding master there and I teach the children's classes."

"He's quite something, isn't he?"

Bewildered by the question, Rayne asked, "Who? Trent?"

"Yes, Trent." Monique grinned, entertained by her response. "I met him when I married Tyler, but he has become a good friend to both of us." She gestured down the hall, indicating for them to return to the party. "I may not have known Trent very long, but I have never seen him so confounded by anyone." She gathered up her train.

Rayne fell in step beside her. "Confounded?"

"Yes. From the moment he first mentioned you, it has been obvious how he feels."

"Has it?" Rayne shook her head, convinced otherwise. If anything, she was more confused than ever by the man.

"It's a bitch, isn't it?"

Rayne hesitated, staring at Monique's profile. "What is?"

"Trusting someone." Monique slowly turned to her. "I was once where you are now. Tyler came back into my life after twenty-one years apart. We dated briefly when I was in college at SMU, but we never forgot about each other. It was hard when we reunited. I doubted his intentions and he had reservations, too. We almost didn't make it, but there comes a point when you just have to throw caution to the wind and say 'To hell with it. I'll trust him.'"

"That's good in theory, Monique, but sometimes hard to apply to real life. Scars have a way of tempering us, or at least me."

"Trent mentioned that you were married to Foster Greer."

Rayne gritted her teeth with annoyance at the mention of her ex. "For eight years."

"I was married for ten years to a surgeon in New Orleans. Mat, my ex, ran off with an assistant in his office, so I understand how hard it is to trust again. We think if one man didn't want us, why would another? But they're not all the same, Rayne. Some are truly unique."

"And Trent is one of those unique ones, is that what you're telling me?"

Monique started down the hall. "He said you were stubborn."

Rayne followed behind her, suddenly intrigued. "What else did he say?"

"That you reminded him of me. We were two tough women who had made our way in the world despite the ruthlessness of others."

Rayne smiled, relaxing a little. "That sounds like a pretty fair assessment."

"Yes, it does." Monique noted her smile and shifted a little closer. "Let him in, Rayne. He's a good man."

A tweak of suspicion cut through Rayne. "Did he ask you to tell me this?"

Monique shook her head. "No. I wanted you to come tonight so I could find out what kind of woman you are. Now, having met you, I can see he was right; we are the same. You just need a bit of reassurance that you're not repeating your past mistakes. I guess it's just the romance writer in me. I want to see every couple have their happy ending." Monique halted at the end of the hallway, just as the noise from the party rose around them. "And if he asks, we never had this conversation. We Sacred Heart girls have to stick together."

Rayne's mouth dropped. "You went to Sacred Heart School?"

Monique laughed. "Your maiden name was Masterson. I was teaching freshman English when you were there, and I remember hearing about you. You were the girl who rode horses and won every horse show she entered."

"I can't believe you taught at Sacred Heart."

"New Orleans is a real small town, Rayne. Always has been, always will be." She turned toward the hallway ahead. "We better head back before they come searching for us."

As they entered the kitchen, Rayne spied Tyler and Trent standing by one of the oval islands, flourishing champagne flutes in their hands and laughing.

"You two look like you've been up to no good," Monique offered as she took the champagne glass from her husband's hand.

"Where were you?" Tyler questioned, skeptically eyeing his wife.

"Eva," she answered, and then took a sip from her glass.

Trent picked up a glass of champagne on the black granite countertop and handed it to Rayne. "You met their daughter?"

Rayne took the flute of golden liquid from him. "She's precious."

"You need one of those, Trent," Monique assured him. "It keeps you humble."

"It keeps you awake at night," Tyler joked.

Monique nudged her husband with her elbow. "But you love it, don't you, darling?"

Tyler happily grinned. "Absolutely."

***

After they had dipped their fingers in the pool, explored a few of the trails behind the house, and sampled the chicken pasta primavera along with more champagne, Rayne felt her enthusiasm for the party waning. Her shoes pinched, her dress was growing uncomfortable, and her yearning for her favorite sweats and smelly dog were getting hard to ignore.

As if sensing her restlessness, Trent began slowly herding her through the crowd of partygoers toward the entrance of the home. "I think we should head to the hotel."

"We need to say good-bye to Tyler and Monique."

"Already taken care of." He gripped her hand. "I told them we would be sneaking out later and that if we didn't see them, we had a wonderful time."

"Trent, that's not polite."

"They understand, Rayne. They're not into formality. Kind of like us."

Just as they were leisurely making their way through the entrance hall to the double doors, a strong hand come down on Rayne's shoulder.

"Rayne?"

When she heard that thundering voice, she let go of Trent's hand and wheeled around.

He had slicked back his gray hair, and the black Brioni tuxedo he wore emphasized his wide shoulders and narrow waist. He smelled of his sweet and very expensive Clive Christian cologne, and his "only for special occasions" diamond and gold Rolex shone on his right wrist.

"Foster," Rayne all but yelped.

Trent's reassuring arm curved about her waist, but Rayne could not turn to him. She was almost petrified to her spot on the gray marble floor.

"You look stunning." Foster's eyes swept over her gown. "I remember the last time you wore that dress. We were celebrating our seventh wedding anniversary."

Trent stepped out from behind Rayne. "Foster. Good to see you again."

"Trent?" Foster sounded surprised. "What are you doing here?"

"I do consulting work with Propel Oil and Gas. Tyler Moore is a friend."

"Really?" Foster's gray eyebrows went up. "Tyler and I play tennis together every now and then. He never mentioned he knew you."

"Since when do you play tennis with Tyler Moore?" Rayne demanded.

"Connie made a point of getting to know him at the Dallas Country Club. She was always the social climber and introduced us. Much to my surprise, we hit it off."

Rayne struggled to curb her growing anxiety. "Where is Connie? Is she here?"

"No." Foster took a step closer to her, putting his back to Trent. "Connie left me. It seems I was too old for her after all. Just as you had warned."

"I said she was too immature for you, Foster, not that you were too old." Rayne shifted her attention to Trent. "We should be going."

"Have you been here long?" Foster persisted with that lilt of insistence that Rayne recognized when he was getting impatient.

"Yes," Rayne told him. "That is why it's time for us to go."

"Foster, there you are!" a woman's captivating voice called from just down the hallway.

When Rayne's eyes swerved past her ex-husband, a pair of almond-shaped, bright green eyes glared back at her.

Sashaying seductively between the guests, and barely covered in black velvet, the woman smugly came up to the trio, flashing a perfect, white-capped smile and waving a flute of champagne. Her strapless gown had slits running up both sides, and she appeared dangerously close to having a wardrobe malfunction. Dark brown hair was teased and tossed about her white shoulders, while a stunning platinum and diamond necklace sparkled on her long neck.

"Trent!" she screeched, drawing the interest of a few other guests. "What are you doing here?"

Trent's body tensed. "Lisa, this is unexpected."

Foster appeared genuinely shocked. "You two know each other?"

Trent curtly nodded and motioned to Rayne. "Lisa Shelby, this is Rayne Greer."

Rayne instantly recognized the name of Trent's former lover, and gave the woman another thorough going over. Catlike in her movements, with long legs, a very slender waist, and full breasts, Lisa Shelby's body was the kind usually found in the centerfold of a male magazine. However, her sallow, oblong face, flat cheekbones, round lips, and wide chin dramatically contrasted with her svelte figure, making Rayne wonder how much of her body was actually hers and not reconstructed from silicone.

"So you're Foster's ex." Lisa had the kind of deep, breathless voice that men swooned over. "How do you know Trent?"

"We ride together at Southland," Trent quickly added.

Lisa's inquisitive eyes drifted down to where Trent's hand hugged Rayne's waist. "Just ride?"

Rayne raised her head to her ex-husband, ignoring Lisa. "I didn't realize you two were acquainted."

Lisa looped her arm about Foster's waist and he nervously cleared his throat. "Oh, we never met before tonight," he revealed.

"Yes." Lisa snuggled up against Foster. "But we've discovered that we have quite a lot in common."

"I'll bet," Trent muttered under his breath.

"We're just friends," Foster insisted.

But Lisa's wicked grin spoke volumes to Rayne.

"Well, I must admit," Trent professed with more than a hint of disbelief in his voice. "I never suspected you two would get together."

Lisa's eyes hungrily devoured Trent's body. "My, you look quite dashing in that tux, Trent. It's been a while since I've seen you in it."

"So how do you two know each other exactly?" Foster pursued, eyeing Lisa.

Lisa wavered as the champagne glass in her hand tipped dangerously close to spilling. "Oh, we're old friends. Trent used to work for me at Shelby Stables. He's an excellent riding master; don't you agree, Rayne?"

"Yes, very good." Rayne took Trent's hand. "We really need to go."

Trent nodded to Foster. "Foster." He veered his eyes to Lisa. "Lisa, good to see you again."

She tilted her voluminous cleavage toward Trent. "Always a pleasure, Trent."

Foster eagerly searched Rayne's face. "How's Estelle?"

Rayne cast her eyes to the floor. "She's fine."

"I'll call you, so we can talk."

"Sure, you do that, Foster." Rayne spun away, pulling Trent behind her.

"I'll see you soon, Trent," Lisa exclaimed as they proceeded to the front doors.

Once they were out on the path that led to the street, Trent started laughing. "I can't believe those two have hooked up."

Rayne perused the sea of cars for his BMW. "If you ask me, they deserve each other."

"I'm sure they do," he agreed. "But Foster better be careful with that one. Lisa Shelby only sees dollar signs when she looks at men."

"Is that why you called it off between you two?"

He dug out his keys from his jacket pocket. "Let's just say we wanted different things."

Rayne noted the twitching muscles in his jaw. "Do you still care for her?"

"No, of course not. I was the one who ended it." He paused, observing her wary reaction. "You're not letting her get to you, are you? She was drunk, Rayne, and I think making a play for your ex was more for your benefit than his."

"She was making a play for you, Trent, not for Foster."

"Let it go, Rayne. I don't want her to ruin the rest of our evening." Trent escorted her away from the glowing lights of Tyler Moore's refined home. "Let's get the hell out of here."

Chapter 20

The chic Joule Hotel in downtown Dallas was not where Rayne was expecting to stay when they walked into the ultra-modern lobby with its contemporary design and collection of modern art. After checking in at the elegant Italian wood front desk, with the enormous bronze artwork of a chambered nautilus mounted behind it, Trent and Rayne headed to their room on the fifth floor.

"Any particular reason you chose the best hotel in the city for tonight?" Rayne interrogated as the dimly lit glass elevator car rose upward.

He rearranged their overnight bags on his shoulder. "I wanted to make tonight special. How am I doing so far?"

She grinned at him. "What are you up to?"

"Patience, baby." He patted her butt. "You'll just have to wait and see what I have planned for us."

The elevator doors opened on their floor, and Trent ushered her into the hallway.

Colorful modern paintings of different geometric shapes lined the dark blue and gold-painted walls. At a white door with gold piping and the number 567 on it, Trent ran the room key through the electronic lock. But when Rayne stepped inside, it was not an ordinary hotel room she found, but a two-story loft suite. "You got a suite?"

Trent followed her in the door. "I told you I wanted to make tonight special."

Done in the ultramodern theme of the hotel, the living room had sleek chrome and leather furniture, spherical light fixtures that hung from the intricately tiled ceiling, and walls decorated with black and white photographs of Dallas landmarks.

"But Trent, this is so expensive."

He dropped the bags on the red, gold, and beige carpet. "I can afford it."

"I'm impressed." Rayne viewed the glass and steel balcony railing on the second-story. "But why did you go to all of this trouble?"

He came up behind her and ran his fingers along her bare arms. "First of all, it wasn't any trouble to pick up the phone and make a reservation. Second, I wanted to bring you some place memorable for our special night."

Turning to him, she wrinkled her forehead with curiosity. "That's the second time you referred to this as a 'special night.' Why?"

"You don't miss a thing do you?"

She angled away from him. "So you are up to something."

He twisted one corner of his mouth into a leering smile and then abruptly stood back from her. "I have something for you."

He went to his black overnight bag on the floor and zipped it open. Returning to her side, he had something gripped tightly in his right hand. "I want you to think about this before you say we're moving too fast, or that you want me to reconsider." He held up his hand and opened it. Sitting in his palm was a gold key with a single red ribbon tied around it.

Rayne stared at the key, not sure what it meant.

"It's to my house," Trent clarified. "I want you to know you can come and go at any time. Bring Frank as well. I want you to be a part of my life."

She took the key and fingered the red ribbon. "I'm touched, Trent."

He lowered his head, contemplating her eyes. "But…?"

Rayne clutched the key to her chest. "No buts. I think this is…pretty great."

"And here I was worried you would think I was pressuring you."

She shook her head. "You don't pressure me. If anything you…never mind."

He shimmed up to her. "Talk to me."

"I was going to say that…." She halted, fearful of his reaction. "You make me feel confident. We can go as fast or as slow as you want. As long as I can be with you, it doesn't matter."

Trent picked her up in his arms. "Now, that's what I want to hear."

She giggled against him with relief. "It is?"

He carried her to the recessed stairs toward the back of the living room and bounded up the steps two at a time. Hurrying along the second floor landing, Rayne looked ahead to the open loft bedroom. A wide king-sized bed covered with white and burgundy bed linens beckoned. When Trent gently lowered her on to the bed, his hands were instantly reaching for the zipper at the back of her dress.

"Ever since I saw you in this, I've wanted to take it off you." His lips hungrily kissed her neck and sped downward.

Rayne pushed his black tuxedo jacket over his shoulders and let it fall to the floor. As she became undone by his kisses, the key in her hand tumbled to the floor beside his jacket. She was tugging at the buttons on his white shirt as Trent eased the gown from her body. Once he had put her dress to the side, his hands crept down her legs to her black pumps. One by one, he dropped the shoes on the floor with a dramatic flourish, making Rayne laugh. But when Trent quickly discarded his shirt and climbed onto the bed, her laughter subsided. He held her close and his mouth came down hard on hers.

His kisses were like fire, scorching her lips. She opened her mouth for him, and wantonly ran her tongue along his. Incensed by her, Trent became even more insistent. His hands avidly roamed every inch of her. Pulling at her strapless bra, he threw it to the floor, and when his fingers hooked her lacy black underwear, Rayne was sure he was going to rip them away, too. Instead, he gently lowered the panties down her legs and haphazardly tossed then aside. His hand immediately went to the mound between her legs, and felt her folds.

"You're so wet," he mumbled into her hair. "I can't wait."

His strong hands gripped her hips and without warning flipped her over. Rayne's excitement for him took over as his body pinned her against the bed.

"Do it," she groaned, shoving her butt into his crotch.

She heard the distinct sound of a zipper being lowered, and then felt his hands on her folds, spreading them apart. When he thrust into her, it was brutal, hard, and exhilarating.

Her head shoved into the mattress as he forced his body weight into her. Rayne's insides were screaming for him. When he pushed further in, she moaned with satisfaction. His lovemaking was rough and had none of the calculated restraint she had felt from him in the past. He held nothing back as he relentlessly pounded into her, rutting behind her and grunting with exertion. She gave herself completely, wanting him to take her in any way he needed. When her orgasm started, it hurtled up from her belly, faster than she had expected, and as it took over, it became so intense that she lost all sense of reality.

She stretched out like a cat in the sun, and a deep, guttural scream echoed in her ears as her insides clamped down with release. Rayne could feel the perspiration on her face, hear Trent crying out on top of her, smell the air thick with a mix of her floral perfume and his musky aroma, but she was helpless against the sweet torment taking over her body.

After her waves of climax had retreated, she sank into the bed. Her hands ached and she realized she was gripping the comforter with such force that when she let go, her fingers were stiff.

"That was…unbelievable," Trent sighed behind her.

Rayne let out a long breath. "Yeah."

He rubbed his hand over her back and then turned her to him. "Was I too rough?"

She wiped the dampness from her face. "No."

He traced his fingers along the top of her left thigh. "Are you sure?"

"Positive," she affirmed.

He climbed on top of her and held her hands out to her sides. "I don't believe you."

She wrapped her supple legs about his waist. "What will it take to convince you?"

His hand dipped between her legs, fondling her folds. "Let's say I need more proof."

Her skin pulsated with his touch. "Oh, Trent," she cried out as she gripped his shoulders.

"We've got all night, baby," he whispered into her cheek. "All night for you to prove it to me over and over again."

***

Monday morning Rayne walked into the employee break room to find Lindsey with her nose in another romance book. Sitting at the faux-wood table with her white coffee mug in front of her, she never looked up when Rayne went to the coffeemaker.

"What's this one about?"

Lindsey gaped at her, appearing disoriented for a second. "Oh, hey Rayne. I didn't hear you come in."

"How could you with…." She paused and read the cover of the book. "*The Lady's Gentleman.*"

Lindsey put the book down on the table and snatched up her coffee. "This one is pretty steamy." She took a sip from her mug. "How was your weekend? You and the horse guy do anything fun?"

Carrying a mug of fresh coffee, Rayne had a seat at the table across from Lindsey. "Actually, we went to a party Saturday night in the city. A formal affair at the home of one of Trent's business associates. Beautiful place in Highland Park."

"And you didn't invite me?"

Rayne raised her mug to her lips, smirking. "Wish I had. There was someone there you would have loved to have met."

Lindsey put her coffee down. "Really? Who?"

Rayne let a dramatic pause settle between them before she announced, "Monique Delome."

The scream that filled the break room was earsplitting.

"You met Monique Delome!"

"What is it? Is everything okay in here?" Dr. Moffet shouted at the break room door.

Lindsey pointed to Rayne. "She met Monique Delome at a party."

Dr. Moffett rolled his tired brown eyes. "Jesus, is that all, Lindsey? You scared the crap out of me and Mrs. DeBois."

Dr. Moffett disappeared from the doorway and Lindsey turned back to Rayne.

"I need to hear everything! How did you meet her? What was she like? Was she nice, mean, a real bitch to you? I've met her once at one of those book signing things and she seemed real nice, but you never know if they are like that in real life or is it just something she puts on for her fans. I had a friend of mine go to one of her conferences in South Carolina and she says she never showed up, and after that—"

"Lindsey, you need to take a breath." Rayne broke in, putting her mug on the table. "Yes, she was very nice. She's married to one of Trent's friends, Tyler Moore, and that is how I met her. We talked for a while about Trent, she introduced me to her baby girl, and then...that was it."

"I don't believe it! You got to pal around with Monique Delome, meet her little girl, and your boyfriend is friends with her husband. You know what that means, don't you? You'll be able to get copies of her books before they hit bookstores." Her blue eyes burned into Rayne. "I hate you."

"If I see her again, I'll ask her to sign one of your books. Will that make you unhate me?"

Lindsey, obviously disgusted, grabbed for her coffee mug. "Only if you take me with you and I get to grovel at her feet."

"I'll think about it," Rayne teased, grasping her mug.

"So what did she tell you about your horse guy?"

Rayne nonchalantly shrugged. "She confided that Trent really cares for me and I should give him a chance."

"I could have told you that," Lindsey scoffed, then sipped her coffee.

"You already did."

Banging her mug on the table, Lindsey eyed Rayne. "So what happened after that? Did you run into his arms and profess your undying love?"

"You really don't have to tell anyone you like romance novels," Rayne lightly tittered, nursing her warm mug in her hands. "And no, it didn't quite turn out like that."

"So how did it turn out, Rayne? Did you at least tell him how you feel?"

Rayne refrained from sharing the wisecrack poised on her lips. "Yeah, I think he knows how I feel." She ran a finger along the rim of the white mug in her hand. "He gave me a key to his house. Told me he wants me to come and go as I please."

"Oh, I see." Lindsey's blonde eyebrows went higher. "And did you give him your key?"

Rayne plopped her mug on the table. "Was I supposed to?"

"Ah, yeah. He lets you have access to his life, and you are to allow him access to yours. First, you exchange keys, and before you know it you're having that 'we need to consider living together in one place' discussion."

Feeling like an idiot, Rayne sagged into her chair. "I didn't know that was what was expected."

"Lord, woman," Lindsey admonished with a roll of her blue eyes. "You really are a babe in the woods when it comes to men. Didn't you learn anything after all those years with Foster?"

"Foster." Rayne grimaced as she pictured her ex. "He was at the party, too. He found me just as Trent and I were leaving. He told me Connie left him."

"Hallelujah." Lindsey loudly applauded. "The bitch finally wised up to him."

"And he was there with someone else. Trent's former flame, a woman named Lisa Shelby. Trent used to ride for her at Shelby Stables."

"And how did that go? An uncomfortable time had by all, I suppose."

"Yeah, you could say that," Rayne admitted. "Lisa Shelby was in this black strapless dress that let everything hang out, and was drooling all over Trent. Foster said they were just friends, but Lisa made it pretty clear that there was more to it than that."

"You mean Foster might actually be sleeping with someone over the age of twenty-one?" Lindsey clapped her hands over her cheeks, feigning utter shock.

Rayne chuckled at her friend's performance. "I know, it sounds incredible."

Lindsey lifted her coffee mug. "Yeah, well, the Catholic Church might want to investigate that little undocumented miracle."

"Anyway, it was really nerve-wracking meeting Trent's former lover. We left right after that."

Lindsey took another pull of coffee. "What did your guy think about Foster and this Lisa woman?"

"He broke out in a fit of laughter as we were leaving the party. I don't think I've ever seen him laugh so hard."

"That's good. That means he doesn't care about her anymore. If he had been mad, then I would be worried." Lindsey stood from her chair and made her way to the sink. "So when are you going to give him your key?"

"I can give it to him this weekend when we see each other at—"

"Honey, he gave you that key to use. You go over there tonight and give him your key."

Rayne pivoted around in her chair to her. "You don't think that would be…rude?"

Lindsey placed her coffee mug in the sink and scowled at Rayne. "Girl, he gave you that key hoping you would just show up at any time during the day, and especially the night. Now you go over there after work and give him your key. That will let him know you're just as interested in moving ahead with this relationship as he is."

"But I've got to go to the stables and ride Bob after work. I've got a show in two weeks and a lot to do to get him ready."

"Rayne, the sooner you give the key to Trent, the better."

"I know, you're right," Rayne sighed, turning back to her coffee on the table. "I'll stop by his place after work and see if he's home. If he isn't, I'll just leave it on his kitchen counter."

"Tie your underwear to it," Lindsey chimed in.

"What?" She whirled back around.

"I read it in a book once. The heroine tied her hotel room key to a pair of sexy underwear so the guy knew exactly what that key was for."

"Jesus, Lindsey. What kind of book was this?"

"Hey, you can't have a good romance without a whole lot of sex, at least that's the way I like my romances."

"I should introduce you to my friend Rebecca," Rayne quipped. "You two would have a lot in common."

Lindsey ran some water over her mug in the sink. "Hey, Casey loves that I read romance books, especially when I finish them."

"Why is that?"

Lindsey set out for the open break room door. "Because after I finish a book, I usually like to practice the love scenes on him."

After Lindsey was gone, Rayne picked up her coffee and slinked down in her chair. When her eyes spotted the book Lindsey had left on the table, she stared at it. The scantily clad woman on the cover was in the arms of a man who reminded her of Trent. His black, wavy hair and intense gray eyes were identical. With her curiosity ignited, Rayne put her coffee down and flipped the book over. Reading the page where Lindsey had left off, she soon became engrossed in a heated love scene. Getting comfortable in her chair, Rayne inched the book closer to her face, eager to take a few more minutes to discover what other things a woman could do to a man.

Chapter 21

After work, Rayne drove to Trent's, anxious to see his reaction when she handed him the key with lacy, red thong underwear she had purchased at a lingerie store on the way to his home. Her mind was exploding with vivid images of things to try with him after reading excerpts from Lindsey's racy book. A whole world of possibilities had opened up to her between the pages of that novel; possibilities she was eager to explore with Trent.

Her jazzy ringtone suddenly interrupted her steamy daydreams. Spying her mother's number, Rayne's excitement quickly disintegrated.

"Hello, Estelle."

"Where are you?" Estelle's raspy voice sounded unusually flat.

"Heading to the stables," Rayne lied, not wanting to tell her mother anything about Trent. "I have a show I have to get ready for."

"A show?" Estelle sounded surprised. "You're going to start that nonsense again?"

"Yes, Mother. I want to start showing again. Trent has been working with me and encouraging me to…never mind. Why are you calling me?"

"Well…Raynie, I was wondering if you could go to the doctor with me later this week."

"Wait, you had an appointment today." Rayne gaped at the iPhone in her hand. "Did you change it?"

"No, I went, and they drew a lot of blood and he did some other tests and told me to come back Friday to go over the results. But I need you to help explain things to me. You know that business and what those tests mean. All that stuff is lost on me."

"It's not lost on you, Mother. You just choose not to pay attention to it, like everything else in your life."

"Fine. Think what you like," Estelle huffed. "I'm sorry I bothered you."

Rayne wanted to scream out loud, but then she heard her father's voice in her head. "Wait, Mother. When on Friday?"

There was a long break, and then Estelle sweetly answered, "Ten at Dr. Emerit's office."

"I'll take off work and pick you up."

"I can take a cab, like I always do," Estelle smugly asserted

"You can't afford to keep taking cabs everywhere, Mother."

"Well, how do you expect me to get around? I don't have a car."

"You don't have a car because…never mind. I'll pick you up Friday," Rayne insisted, raising her voice.

"I'll see you then, Raynie."

Tossing her iPhone to the passenger seat, Rayne shook her head, fascinated at how the woman was still able to push her buttons. She sometimes contemplated what things would have been like if Jaime and her father had not died that winter's day so long ago. But as visions of the life that could have been materialized in her mind's eye, Rayne brushed them away. Better not to think of what might have been, and deal with what was.

"Christ, I sound like my mother," she muttered.

Pressing her foot down on the gas pedal, she was more anxious than ever to get to Trent's. She needed to forget about her mother and her past, and invest her energy in her possible future with the man who was beginning to take up a permanent place of residence inside the confines of her heart.

***

After parking in front of Trent's wood and stone contemporary home, she peeked around the side of his front gardens to discover that one of his garage doors was open and his dark blue BMW was parked inside. Hoping to surprise him, she took the key he had given her along with the one she had tied with the fancy red underwear from her backpack and exited her car.

At the double doors to his home, she put her gold key in the lock.

"Trent?" she called out as she opened the doors.

The short entrance hall was dark, but the lights were on in the grand living room and she could hear the strains of soft music coming from within. Entering the living room, she found a CD player in a recessed wall to the far right of the stone hearth filling the home with a mellow jazz tune. Rayne searched the connecting kitchen and dining areas, but when her eyes went to the open patio doors, she froze. Draped over one of the cedar chaise lounge chairs, beside the rectangular pond, was a pair of black riding breeches, a black T-shirt, and black, lacy underwear. Rayne's fist closed over the key tied to the panties in her hand. A wave of nausea came over her as she began to jump to a number of conclusions.

"Rayne?"

When she reeled around, Trent was behind her, clutching a white envelope in his hand. The smile on his face held not the slightest hint of deception.

"You used your key." He came up to her and kissed her cheek. "I'm so glad. I didn't know if you—"

The sound of splashing and hurried footsteps outside made him turn toward the patio doors.

Rayne followed his eyes and recoiled when she spotted the reason for his sudden loss of words. Standing outside on the deck, and naked as the day she was born, was Lisa Shelby. Her long brown hair was wet and clung to her shoulders, and although she pretended to be embarrassed and hide her nudity, Rayne could tell by the evil grin on her red lips that she was more delighted than upset at being seen that way.

"What in the hell are you doing?" Trent shouted.

"I was waiting for you to join me in the pool." Lisa came into the house, leaving tiny wet footsteps on the bamboo floor.

Trent jogged out the patio doors. "Are you mad?" He hastily collected her clothes from the chaise lounge. "I never said anything about you swimming in my pool. Honestly, Lisa, what is wrong with you?" He went up to her and shoved the clothes at her. "Get dressed."

But Lisa made no attempt to dress as she kept her almond-shaped eyes on Rayne. "Remember how much fun we used to have in your pool, Trent?"

Trent's eyes swiveled around to Rayne, and his anger turned to bitter concern when he saw her face.

Common sense told Rayne that the whole incident was nothing more than cruel manipulation by a spiteful ex-lover. But as the naked woman's green eyes bore into her, Rayne began to consider all the other women who had come before her; all the women he had made love to in the shallows of his swimming pool. She had always been aware of Trent's history with the opposite sex, but it was not until she saw Lisa naked in his living room that Rayne began to carefully question why he had such a history.

"Rayne, don't you for one minute believe that I knew—"

"I'm sure she knows better than to trust you, Trent," Lisa interrupted as a scheming smile spread across her red lips. "I could never trust you, so why should she?" She frowned at Rayne. "You see, he asked me to come here. He wanted me, even though he already had you." She laughed, sounding cold and empty inside. "They're all the same, Rayne. They'll say anything to get you into bed, but they don't mean it. They never mean it."

"Shut up!" Trent yelled. "You backstabbing bitch." He rushed across the living room to Rayne's side. "You can't believe a word she says. She came here begging me to return to Shelby Stables. She even wrote out a check for a year's salary." He threw the white envelope still in his hand to the floor.

Lisa just stood in her spot inside the patio doors, dripping all over the finely polished wood floors and with her clothes strategically positioned over her naked body.

"Get out," Rayne growled to Lisa.

Lisa opened her mouth to object.

"You heard her, get out of my house," Trent hollered.

Lisa indignantly raised her head. "At least allow me to put my clothes on and—"

But before she could finish, Trent seized her wrist. He dragged her wet, naked body toward the living room entrance.

Interested in what would happen next, Rayne slowly followed them and stopped just short of the hallway.

"We're over, Lisa. Don't ever come back here," Trent went on as he practically carried her down the hallway.

"Let me go," Lisa squawked.

"If you ever say anything negative about me or Rayne, I will be sure to let everyone know about all those disgusting affairs you bragged to me about."

"You better think twice about that, or else—"

"Or else what?" Trent opened the front doors. "By the time I'm done with you, no one will ever want to go near Shelby Stables. You'll be ruined." He shoved her, still naked, outside to the porch. "Don't threaten me, Lisa. Don't ever threaten me." Trent smashed the doors closed.

An uncomfortable quiet settled in the hallway as Trent leaned against the closed front doors with his back to Rayne.

She did not know if his reluctance to face her was a sign of his guilt or innocence, but the cold stab of anguish in her gut made Rayne think that no matter his explanation, it would not help his cause.

"You know nothing happened." His voice was strained as he continued to lean against the doors.

Rayne stood riveted to her spot on the hardwood floor. "I know nothing happened today...but what about tomorrow?"

When he turned around, the fury in his eyes jarred her. That ever-present confidence he always seemed to possess had disappeared. "What is that supposed to mean?" He pointed his finger determinedly at the doors. "Do you think I still want to be with Lisa? The reason I ended it was because she confessed to me that she had been sleeping with the husbands of half her tenants at the stables. After hearing something like that, I couldn't stay. It sickened me. She sickened me."

"I can understand that. But perhaps if you had told me that before—"

"Before?" Infuriated, he slapped his hand against his chest. "Now you don't trust me because I didn't want to tell you the truth about why I left her?"

Rayne studied his rigid posture, the icy anger in his eyes, and the way his ropelike muscles were bulging in his arms. She found it odd how in a split second everything she had come to know about him, all the idiosyncrasies she had grown used to, could simply vanish without a trace. The man before her was nothing like the one she had let into her life. This Trent Newbury was almost a stranger.

"Trust?" The word tumbled from her lips as its meaning tore at her heart. "I don't know if I ever trusted you."

"Where is this coming from? You can't be jealous of her. She is nothing to me."

Rayne felt his house key in her hand. "Not jealous, perhaps…just seeing the real you for the first time."

"What in the hell are you talking about?"

His ugly tone made her flinch. "I guess I'm just beginning to wonder where I stand in that long line of women you've been with." Rayne moved to the Shaker table by his front door. "I don't want to end up being just another meaningless fling."

He came up to her, holding up his hands as if she were a nervous horse about to bolt. "You're upset and not thinking clearly."

She placed his key on the table while hiding her key tied with the panties in her other hand. "I am thinking very clearly, Trent. For the first time since we met, I'm beginning to understand." Focusing her eyes on the bright gold key she had put on the table, she refused to look at him.

"Understand what?" He stood next to her, resting his hand on her arm. "What is there to understand? I care for you, Rayne. I don't want anyone else."

Her eyes shifted to the floor. "You know, I have always wondered why me? Why would someone like you be interested in me?"

"You know why. You're not like her. You don't see me as a meal ticket." He gestured to the front doors. "You're different from all the rest."

"All the rest of what, Trent? The women you have been with?" She pointed to the key on the table. "I was coming here to give you your key back and ask for a little time apart, but now I think we're done."

He reached for her, but Rayne shied away from him.

She stepped around him to the doors. "I have to go."

"No, Rayne." He pulled her to him. "I know this is not what you want. You can't doubt me, not after all we've shared."

All we've shared? Infuriated by his words, she broke free of his embrace. "What did we share, Trent? A few rolls in the sack to what…break that skittish horse you so desperately wanted to ride? Well, you got what you wanted." She yanked the doors open and ran outside.

Rayne did not remember running down the wide steps to the street, or even climbing into her car. When her mind began to register what had just happened, she was already driving away from his house, pressing her foot down on the accelerator and desperate to put as much distance as possible between her and the man who had just broken her heart.

***

Instead of going home, Rayne drove to the stables. She needed to get out in the brisk fall air and occupy her mind with something, anything other than Trent. After pulling into the shell-covered parking lot next to the red and white barn, she wiped away the tears that had stained her cheeks.

Not since she had walked in on Foster and Connie had she felt such heartache. In a way, Lisa Shelby had been right; all men were the same. And even though he may not have treated her quite like Foster, in the end she was convinced Trent would have tossed her aside just as her ex had done.

Walking up to Bob's stall, she was sure that she had made the right choice. But still the ache in her heart endured, creating that speck of doubt that maybe she had been wrong about the man and his intentions.

"No. I'm right, aren't I, Bob?"

Bob's long face held no answers, no hints of wisdom, making Rayne almost laugh at her question.

"Come on, buddy. Let's go jump some fences and I can tell you all about it."

The time with Bob worked wonders for her. As they jumped fences she had set up around the ring, her mind went over the confrontation with Trent. As she rode, she talked to Bob, told him the entire story and voiced her concerns about Trent. It was what she had done in high school with boys that confounded her, and after fights with her mother. She had spent hours on her horse, talking out her problems. During her divorce, she decided her horse was cheaper than a psychologist, and a lot less judgmental. Through the years, all the time she had spent in the saddle had kept her grounded and sane. And now, when she needed him most, Bob was there like a close friend, willing to listen to her every word.

After an hour in the jumping ring, her body and her mind were weary. She had run through all possible scenarios with Trent, but every conclusion had reinforced her decision. Sometimes you had to fight to protect your heart, no matter how painful the outcome. For Rayne, love always ended badly, and all those she had loved had left her. Better never to love, and avoid all the misery.

***

It was late in the evening when Rayne returned home from the stables. Determined to put the past with Trent behind her, she greeted Frank with a hearty pat on the head and went to her refrigerator, eager for orange juice.

As she was chugging from the carton, she heard the answering machine in her bedroom click on.

"I've left you ten voice mails on your cell phone, and now I'm resorting to this goddamned machine. I know I have been with a lot of women, and that you're scared, but you can't just walk away. I want a chance to show you that I'm not the man I was. You have changed me. Please pick this up. I know you're home, probably drinking your orange juice and telling Frank what a shit I am."

Rayne looked down at the carton of orange juice in her hand and then to Frank's fuzzy face on the kitchen floor next to her.

"Just talk to me, Rayne. Let's work this through. I can come over or you can come back here. I'll do whatever it takes. Please, think about this." The machine clicked off, and once again the house was still. She stood in the kitchen, considering his plea. After several minutes of deliberation, she replaced the juice on the refrigerator shelf, walked into her bedroom, and deleted Trent's message.

"It's for the best."

Without looking back at the machine, she hurried to her bathroom, eager to wash the dust, sweat, and tears from her body. She was not healed, but Rayne knew she would grow stronger. Soon, she would be able to resist him completely, or at least she hoped she would. Parts of her body still longed for him, but years of dealing with Estelle had taught Rayne that the head must rule the heart; otherwise you would just end up a lonely old drunk with an empty house, a broken spirit, and a lifetime full of regrets.

Chapter 22

The rest of the week, Rayne spent her days hiding in her lab. She stayed away from the break room to avoid running into Lindsey. She did not want to have to explain what had happened with Trent, nor did she want to lie to her friend and tell her everything was fine. Rayne retreated to her broom closet of an office for breaks and skipped taking her lunch hour. Her desire for food had waned considerably since leaving Trent's house, and she wanted nothing more than to be buried in work and to forget about her life. At the end of her workday, she would dash out the back office door to the parking lot, hoping to get away unseen.

Afternoons were spent with Bob. She came to cherish the few hours she spent with him working over fences in the back ring. His steady demeanor and gentle nature comforted her during those first few days. Thankfully, Trent never made an appearance at the stables when she was there, and he gave up calling her cell phone and house. Rayne hoped that it was over, and she could get back to her life.

Bob was making rapid progress over the fences, and Rayne itched to tell Trent about it. He had encouraged her, schooled her, and offered a lot of advice. There were times when losing the friend who had supported her hurt more than the giving up the man who had made love to her.

But the nights were the worst for Rayne. After the activities of the day had faded, and her mind was left to wander in the darkness of her bedroom, her thoughts would always stray back to Trent. The way he had held her, kissed her, and made her feel so content. It was when she was inundated by those emotions that the tears would creep over the edges of her eyelids and trickle down her cheeks. And after the tears came the inevitable self-loathing. She was ashamed to admit that despite her best efforts, she had not been able to completely close off the walls of her heart.

***

By Friday morning, Rayne was feeling better. The crying bouts had ended, and her appetite had returned, at least a little. When her gray Highlander drove up to the side entrance of her mother's mansion, she felt certain she could tell Estelle everything without falling apart.

"You look like shit," Estelle commented as soon as she climbed into Rayne's car. "What happened?"

Rayne glimpsed her mother's bright yellow shirt dress, black, low-heeled pumps, and matching black handbag. She found it amazing that no matter where the woman went, drunk or sober, she always looked her best.

"Nothing happened, Mother. I'm just…tired." She squared her shoulders, ready for another altercation, and put the car into gear.

"Something happened. Was it with Trent? I bet it was. You always used to get that same sour face when something was wrong."

Rayne kept her eyes on the road. "If you must know, Trent and I are done. We were not well-suited."

Estelle's pale, powdered face fell. "You're kidding? You expect me to buy that bullshit? He was crazy about you." She tossed a hand in the air. "You see, Raynie, there you go. You chased off another one, didn't you? What was it? Did he get too close? Want more than you were willing to give? Which I'm sure wasn't much, knowing you."

"Christ, Mother! Why are you always attacking me? And what makes you think it was me? Maybe the guy was a pervert, maybe he was seeing other women on the side, and maybe I just didn't like him. Did you ever figure on that?"

Estelle's cold snicker made Rayne's blood turn to ice. "You never were a very good liar, Raynie. I can see it in your face. So what happened?"

Perturbed that the woman who was as motherly as boiled cabbage knew her so well, Rayne shifted in her seat as her hands clenched the steering wheel. "I went to Trent's house last week and found his former lover naked in his living room."

Estelle sat back as her big blue eyes scoured her daughter's profile. "And where was Trent?"

Rayne kept her attention on the street ahead. "Coming out of his office, fully clothed. He claims nothing happened and that she just showed up wanting him back, but I'm not completely convinced."

"I'm sure he was telling you the truth."

Rayne gawked at her mother. "How can you say that? You weren't there. You didn't see them together."

"I saw how he looked at you. He would never jeopardize what he had with you to jump into bed with another woman. Trent wants someone strong, capable, sophisticated, and who can make him proud…he wants a woman like you."

"Me?" Rayne balked. "What makes you think he ever wanted me?"

"Because he's a lot like your father. Men like your father and Trent are never interested in playing games. They speak their minds, tell you what is in their hearts, and once committed, never sleep around." She patted the black handbag in her lap. "I knew the day I met your father what kind of man he was. That's why I married him, because I wanted an honest husband, not a rich one."

"Then why were you so unhappy with Dad? If he was what you wanted, why did you make his life hell?"

"I never made his life hell. I was happy with him, in the beginning." Estelle's pink-painted mouth slanted downward. "After being courted by so many men, I never thought I would miss the attention when I married. But I did. My father made me believe I was only good for marriage. He wanted to use me to tie his business to some prestigious family, and when I married a nobody from El Paso, he never forgave me."

"Grandpa John was a spiteful, selfish man who resented everyone," Rayne vented.

"Yes, he was," Estelle agreed with a nod of her head. "But he was still my father."

"But you lived your life on your terms, Mother. You married for love."

Estelle smiled. It was a warm, emotional gesture, the likes of which Rayne had never seen on her mother's face. All her life, she remembered scowls, frowns, and looks of complete disgust, but she could never remember such a smile.

"Do you know the real reason why I married your father?" Estelle asked with a hint of melancholy in her voice. "When he looked at me he saw me…not the pretty socialite, the wealthy meatpacker's daughter, or the party girl. He saw Estelle, the real one on the inside. I knew I'd better marry a man who loved me, because no matter what happened he would always be able to put up with my crap. And your father did. Until the day he died, he put up with my drinking, my tantrums, my shopping binges, and my outbursts."

Despite all of her mother's embarrassing moments, and the pain they had brought her family, Rayne recalled how her father would always smile, kiss her mother's cheek, and take everything in stride. Up until that moment, she had believed it was just his nature and never his love for his wife shining through.

"When I look at Trent, I see the same thing I saw in your father," Estelle went on. "He sees you, Raynie. Foster saw the pretty woman who could bolster his ego and his business, but he never knew you. That inquisitive, driven girl who always had to show the world that she was worth the effort." Estelle let go a long sigh as she turned to her window. "But that's probably my fault. Maybe if I had praised you more, and gone to those horse shows of yours, you would never have fought so hard to be noticed."

Rayne gulped back the lump forming in her throat. "Well, you made me tough. You taught me I needed to fight to get ahead in life. That helped me to win state championships. It made me competitive."

"But it has also made you stubborn, and that has kept you from Trent."

"Trent and I are over. It's for the best, Mother."

"You keep telling yourself that, Raynie. I know better."

Rayne did not bother to argue. There was no point. She never could win an argument with Estelle and was not about to try. Some rocks were never meant to be budged.

***

The despair in Rayne's heart skyrocketed when she read the blood work results Dr. Emerit handed to her. Sitting in the chair across from his walnut desk with framed pictures of his wife and two sons scattered about, Rayne shook her head. The findings were worse than she had feared.

"Mother, you have to stop drinking right this minute."

"I'm afraid Rayne is right, Estelle," the chubby figure of Dr. Charles Emerit concurred from his chair behind the desk. He pushed the thick black glasses back on his pasty, round face. "If you don't stop, you'll be deathly ill in less than a year."

Estelle's glowered at Dr. Emerit. "Charlie, you've been telling me that for years now, and I'm still here."

Dr. Emerit leaned his arms on his desk and pensively studied Estelle. "This is different. Your liver is dying. If you stop drinking now, you'll buy some time." He held up his pudgy, short hand. "Only buy some time. The damage is done, and eventually your liver will fail."

Estelle twisted the strap of the black handbag resting in her lap. "Then I'll get another one. They do liver transplants all the time, right?"

"Estelle, you might not be a candidate for that." Dr. Emerit frowned and sat back in his chair. "Your body may be too weak at that point to take on a new liver, and I know you're too damn set in your ways to stick to the regime necessary to maintain a new liver. There are pills, frequent medical checks, blood work, and a whole host of issues to consider." His bloodshot hazel eyes returned to Rayne. "You know what I'm talking about."

"Mother, you just don't stick a new liver in someone and think that's it. There are a lot of things that have to be done to keep your body from rejecting the foreign tissue."

Estelle did not bat an eye. She sat demurely in her chair, smirking at her daughter. "I'm not a complete idiot. I have a computer you know, and have researched this on the Internet."

"Did you actually read any of it?" Rayne demanded, raising her voice.

"Perhaps it's best if you two take this information home and talk about it," Dr. Emerit suggested. "Estelle, you already know what you need to do. I've told you a hundred times before, but if you choose to continue drinking, you need to be prepared for the consequences. Liver failure is a slow, painful death."

Estelle's mouth dropped open. "Charlie Emerit, that is too much."

He shook his head and stood from his chair. "Nothing is too much with you, Estelle. I've known you since you were in high school with my older sister, and you were just as stubborn then as you are now." He buttoned up his white coat. "I'll care for you no matter what you decide, but you have to know the truth."

Estelle stood up. "Fine. Raynie, let's go."

Rayne placed the lab results on Dr. Emerit's desk. "Thanks, Uncle Charlie." She smiled for him. "We'll talk soon."

"Don't be nice to him," Estelle scolded. "He's an old coot."

"Takes one to know one, Estelle." Dr. Emerit came around to Estelle's side and kissed her cheek. "You should have taken me up on my marriage proposal. Imagine all the health care bills you would have saved on."

She swatted his arm. "You were fourteen and had a crush on me, Charlie Emerit."

Dr. Emerit winked at Rayne. "Still do." He kissed Rayne's cheek. "Call me if you need me."

Rayne nodded. "I will."

Dr. Emerit's worried eyes veered back to Estelle. "Please think about this. You can't just ignore this problem like you do everything else in your life, Estelle. This will kill you if you don't do something now."

Estelle offered no reply, made no argument against his concerns. She simply patted down the skirt of her yellow shirt dress, attempting to wipe away the imaginary wrinkles. After slinging the strap of her purse over her thin arm, she marched toward the office door. A dull thud rocked the office as the door bashed against the wall after she flung it open.

Rayne sighed and lowered her head.

"Talk to her, Rayne, sooner than later," Dr. Emerit pleaded after Estelle had exited the room. "You know what those lab results mean. We don't have a lot of time."

Rayne gave him a curt nod and trudged toward the door. She did know what those lab results meant, and somehow she suspected her mother did, too. She questioned if Estelle was ready to face death the same way she had faced life, on her terms.

***

In the car on the way back to Highland Park, mother and daughter spoke little to each other. But when Rayne's SUV parked beneath the portico by the rear entrance, Estelle dropped a bombshell.

"I'm selling the house."

Rayne was too stunned to respond.

"Don't look so surprised, Raynie. You've been bugging me to sell it for years."

"When…when did you decide this?" Rayne managed to get out.

Estelle placed her hand on the car door. "After we left Charlie Emerit's. I figure if I'm dying, it's time to sell."

Exasperated, Rayne crashed her head back into her headrest. "You're not dying. I mean you won't die, if you give up drinking. If you stop, you could arrest the damage, and your liver might improve. I've seen it before in alcoholics."

"I am not an alcoholic," Estelle loudly proclaimed.

Rayne shook her head, snickering. "Yes, you are, Mother. You drink too much, you've got the bad liver to prove it, and you've been in and out of how many rehabs? You're a drunk. You've always been a drunk. When are you going to start admitting it?"

Estelle said nothing, and Rayne was almost as shocked by her lack of words as she had always been by her scathing rebukes. As she slumped in her seat, Rayne swore she could see a crack forming in her mother's stubborn determination.

"I guess when you hear your daughter say it, it must be true."

Rayne pretended to view unkempt gardens along the side of the house, quashing the swell of pain in her heart. "You needed to know the truth...isn't that what you always say to me?"

"Yes, it is." Trembling, Estelle reached for the door handle. "I'll let you know when I put the house up."

"You do that." Rayne balled her hands into fists, choking off her hankering to soothe her mother's distress.

"Thank you for coming to the doctor with me, Raynie." Estelle stood from the car. "I appreciate it."

Rayne put the car into gear. "Just stop drinking, Mother, for both our sakes."

Once Estelle had made it in the double doors of her side entrance, Rayne turned the car back down the driveway.

"I bet she goes right inside and pops open a bottle of scotch to celebrate."

With visions of Estelle's long, debilitating decline from alcoholism infusing her ire, Rayne made the trek home to

Copper Canyon. She had enough to worry about without adding her mother's bitterness to her sordid pile of troubles.

Chapter 23

Saturday morning, Rayne was at the stables with the rising sun. Eager to get in a brief workout before her morning classes, she was tacking up Bob when a throaty voice interrupted to her.

"Man, do we need to talk."

Standing by her tack room door and wearing her usual beige jodhpurs, black boots, and a dark red T-shirt, Rebecca looked as if she had just come from an early morning ride. Her bleached blonde hair was tossed about her head, her boots were dusty, and her pink lipstick was faded.

"In one week, I've seen you go from floating on air to looking like the world is ending. My riding master has been distracted as hell, and keeps asking if I've seen you. You want to tell me what is going on with the two of you?"

Rayne secured the girth on her saddle. "It's over between us."

"Over? Oh, no!" Rebecca's pudgy hand clamped down on Rayne's wrist. "We're going to talk about this."

As Rebecca dragged her away, Rayne waved back at Bob, still tied to the post by her tack room door. "Wait, I have to get in an early work out before my lessons."

"Forget it." Rebecca pulled Rayne to her open office door. After letting her go, she pointed inside. "Get in there."

Glancing back at Bob, Rayne figured he could keep for a few minutes. Walking into the air-conditioned office, she went to a chair beside the small wooden desk, folded her arms, and flopped down.

Slamming the office door, Rebecca sprinted across the room to her desk, but did not take her seat. "So what is this crap about calling it off? Last time we talked, you were walking on cloud nine after your night in the city."

Rayne took in a deep breath and sat up in her chair. "Last week, when I went over to Trent's, Lisa Shelby was there."

Rebecca's dyed blonde eyebrows went up ever so slightly on her forehead. "Lisa Shelby?"

"Yes. She was naked and dripping wet from skinny-dipping in his pool."

Rebecca stared down at Rayne, seemingly unimpressed. "And was Trent with her?"

"He came out from his office and acted surprised to see her. She was there trying to get him to come back to Shelby Stables. When he wasn't looking, she took off her clothes and jumped in his pool. That was about the time I used the key he gave me and walked in the door."

"Wait, he gave you his key?"

"Last weekend, when we spent the night at The Joule."

"But you never told me he gave you his house key." Rebecca edged forward, intrigued.

"Doesn't matter now. When I saw Lisa Shelby there I—"

"Rayne, you can't honestly believe anything happened between the two of them." Rebecca sat down in the chair behind her desk.

"Perhaps, but seeing Lisa Shelby in his house, naked…something just snapped. I suddenly pictured all the other women he had been with, and there have been quite a few." Rayne shook her head and set her eyes on the top of the desk. "All I could see was this long line of naked women parading about his living room, and I thought...what in the hell am I doing with this guy?"

"Having great sex," Rebecca laughed.

Racked by doubt, Rayne leaned forward with her hands clasped tightly together. "But how do I know I'm not just another woman he will eventually grow tired of?"

"You don't. Nobody knows that. You just go into every relationship hoping for the best, but expecting the worst." Rebecca's lips curved into an understanding smile. "Searching for someone is masochistic in a way; we know we may get hurt, desperately want to believe we won't, and when we do get dumped, we aren't surprised. But that's what everyone does when the goal is happiness. You do whatever it takes to get there, and pray this will be the one who makes the world feel like the wonderful place you know it can be." She stood from her chair. "That's what Trent did for you and still does for you, doesn't he?"

Rayne bit her lower lip, attempting to look tough. "No. That's all over and done with."

"You can't fool me, kiddo. You're still crazy about him, and if you ask me, he hasn't given up on you, either."

Rayne stood up, shaking off Rebecca's observation. "You're wrong. I think he has given up."

"No, he hasn't," Rebecca argued, her brown eyes swimming with concern. "Trent is a very competitive man. He doesn't walk away from what he wants, and he wants you. I would hazard a guess that he's hanging back and giving you some space for a while. You always were the kind that needed to be approached cautiously."

The comment astonished Rayne. "He called me a skittish horse once."

"How right he was." Rebecca shook her head as she walked to the office door. "You may not like what I'm going to say, but I think you need to hear it. Trent Newbury is good for you, Rayne. I watched you during the years you were married to Foster and then after the divorce. You always seemed so withdrawn, like you were afraid to be a part of the world. But with Trent, you became confident, and I got a taste of the young woman you were, that championship rider who was an aggressive competitor and took chances. Now if a man can do that for you…he might just be worth hanging on to."

Rayne knew part of what Rebecca said was true, Trent had given her back the confidence Foster had taken away, but she could never trust him with her heart again. "Nice try, Rebecca, but we're finished."

"And what happens when you see him again? You two are going to run into each other sooner or later. What will you do?"

Rayne went to the door, contemplating the question. "I know it might be uncomfortable at first, but maybe after a while it will get easier for us to be together."

"What about the Golden Farms Horse Show next week?" Rebecca went on. "Are you're still going?"

Rayne stretched for the handle on the office door. "I'm an instructor at your stables and expected to show. I'll go."

Rebecca clucked like a mother hen and waved her out the door. "You're a stubborn fool, Rayne Greer. I hope you know that."

"So I've been told." Rayne pushed the door open and stepped outside.

Her determination against Trent was now more ardent than ever. She had to keep her resolve steadfast and stick to the course she had set. Rayne knew it would not be easy, but she could not imagine handling it any other way.

***

It was after five that evening when Rayne pulled into her single car garage and turned off the engine. Taking a minute to close her eyes and set her head back against the seat, Rayne dreaded the long, lonely Saturday night ahead without Trent.

A gentle rapping on her passenger window made her jump.

Standing outside of her car was her ex-husband. With his gray hair neatly slicked back, and wearing a white dress shirt, Foster looked as if he were going out for a casual night on the town. His everyday stainless Rolex on his wrist shimmered in the dull garage overhead lights.

"What are you doing here?" Rayne demanded, climbing out of her Highlander.

He motioned to the street. "I saw you pull in and I wanted to talk to you."

His red Porsche Cayenne Turbo was parked along the curb in front of her house, and Rayne brooded over how she had could have missed it. But her mind had been somewhere else for days, and guessed a masked gunman could have walked up to her and she would never have noticed.

After taking her blue backpack from the front seat, she stepped back from the car. "What do you want, Foster?"

"To talk," he declared. "Estelle phoned me. She told me about the tests."

Aggravated that her mother had called her ex, yet again, Rayne smacked her car door closed, causing a loud "whump" to echo about the garage. "Why did she call you?"

"She said she needed a real estate agent because she was selling the house." He kicked at something on the garage floor with the toe of his black leather loafer. "We ended up talking a good bit about you," he softly confided.

"Me?" Rayne went around her car toward the short walkway that led to her back door. "That woman never wants to talk about me." She fumbled with the keys in her hand.

Foster followed her along the walkway. "She also told me you broke up with Trent."

Damn that woman! Gritting her teeth, she placed her key in the lock of her back door. "She shouldn't have said anything to you."

"Well, she did." He paused behind her. "I wanted to make sure you were all right."

The lock gave way and Rayne pushed her back door open. Once inside, she hit the code on her alarm panel. "You didn't need to drive all the way up here to check on me."

He stepped in the back door. "No, but I wanted to."

When Rayne walked through the hallway toward her kitchen, she could hear Frank's heavy feet scampering from the living room. Stepping into the kitchen, she threw her backpack onto the countertop.

"I'm fine, Foster," she gnarled.

After Frank galloped into the kitchen, he halted and studied Foster with his soft brown eyes. Then, without hesitation, he bounded up and put his front paws all over Foster's black trousers.

"Frank!" Rayne grabbed for the dog's black collar.

"I didn't know you got a dog." Foster hurriedly wiped his pants and then began meticulously picking at stray Frank hairs.

Rayne observed the man's fastidious movements, and for a moment missed Trent's relaxed attitude.

"Let me put him outside." With a great deal of effort, she finally got a bouncing and excited Frank out the kitchen door that led to the yard.

After Foster was appeased that his clothes were once again pristine, he pulled up a wooden stool and had a seat at her breakfast bar.

"I have to admit, the place appears rather…homey." His disapproving blue eyes surveyed the living room furniture and smattering of framed travel posters on her eggshell-painted walls.

"You hate this place. You told me that the day I moved in."

He turned back to her. "I hate that you chose to live here. I would have given you money for a bigger house."

"You know I did not want you buying me a house after the divorce." She went to her refrigerator. "Besides, I couldn't keep up with the taxes on anything bigger than this."

"I told you I would take care of you, even if we weren't married. I promised you that I would always be there for you."

Rayne took out the orange juice from the refrigerator. "You also promised to 'honor and keep' me 'until death us do part,' yet here we are, divorced."

He sighed and had a seat on the stool. "You know I didn't want the divorce."

She pounded the orange juice carton on the granite countertop, wishing it was his head. "I found you with Connie in our bed. What in the hell was I supposed to do? Look the other way?"

He rested his arms on the breakfast bar, shrugging. "Why not? You knew I would grow tired of the girl. She wasn't you."

"Jesus, Foster. We were married for eight years, but I have to wonder if you ever really knew me. I would never have looked the other way when it came to cheating."

"All right." He held up his hands, assuaging her fury. "I was wrong. Connie was a stupid mistake, and I have paid my dues for getting involved with her." He put his hands down on the beige granite countertop and wistfully smiled. "I knew the moment you found us in bed together that I had screwed up, but I never meant to hurt you, Rayne."

"The minute you took that woman into our bed you hurt me, Foster. You knew that."

"You're right." He bowed his head penitently. "I'm sorry; I didn't come here to rehash the past."

Trepidation nibbled at Rayne as she looked over her ex-husband. "Why did you come here?"

He splayed his hands on the countertop, never raising his head. "To say I was wrong to let you go. I don't think I comprehended how wrong until Connie started living with me. She had none of your class or easygoing manner, and she was hard as hell to live with."

Shaking her head, she picked up the orange juice. "Then why let her move in?"

"You left, and I...." His eyes meet hers. "I was lonely without you."

She smirked and then took a swig of the orange juice.

Foster rose from his stool and went to the oak cabinets behind her. He opened a few cabinet doors until he found the one containing the glasses. Taking a tall iced tea glass, he walked over to Rayne's side.

"I'm glad to see some things haven't changed," he stated, placing the glass on the countertop next to her.

She ignored the glass and continued drinking from the carton.

"You know how that used to drive me crazy, Rayne."

She lowered the carton from her lips. "Perhaps you should just get to the point, Foster."

"Fine." He let out a long breath, plucking up his courage. "I'm here because I want us to work this out and start over. I want you back home."

She put the carton down on the countertop, considering his statement. "What about Lisa Shelby? At the party, you two looked real cozy. Maybe she wants to move in with you."

He chuckled, a sinister sound that used to make Rayne cringe when they were first married. Now, she just found it annoying as hell. "I have no interest in that woman," Foster protested. "Lisa Shelby is well-known by several of my business associates. She has quite a reputation as a gold digger. I only met her at that party because of Selene."

A slow, unsettling feeling rose from her toes. "Selene? What has she got to do with you and Lisa Shelby?"

"I was at Tyler Moore's because Selene had phoned me and said that you were going to be there, but I never expected to see you with Trent. After you left, Lisa let it slip that the real reason she was hitting on me was because Selene had suggested it in order to make Trent jealous. It seems Selene told her Trent was going to the party with you. I heard all about their affair and how he ended it when he found out about her reputation. Lisa wanted him back, and was only at that party because she thought she could win him away from you."

"But how did Selene know I was going with Trent to that party?"

He leaned back against the bar. "I don't know. Maybe she talked to Monique Delome. You know what a pathological little social climber she is."

"Yeah, I know." Rayne's mind filled with questions as she stared at her ex-husband's surly countenance. "So Selene planned the whole thing?"

"Looks that way." He bobbed his head in agreement. "But after seeing the way you were with Trent at the party, it was obvious you two were pretty serious."

"Why did you think that?"

"You looked happy, Rayne. Real happy."

Images from the night of the party came back to her, and that warm feeling of contentment Trent had always evoked blanketed her weary body.

"So when Estelle told me you two had split up, I was kind of surprised, but also relieved." He crept closer to Rayne's side. "I'm not asking for you to move back in right away. I was hoping we could start seeing each other again; dinner, a few parties; maybe even go on a trip together…wherever you want. I'll do whatever makes you comfortable."

"Comfortable?" She retrieved her carton of orange juice from the counter. "But not happy."

"Happiness will come, Rayne. We have plenty of time to find happiness."

Rayne walked back to her refrigerator and replaced the orange juice on the shelf. "I'm sorry, Foster, but I can't go backwards. I'm not the same woman you married." She slowly faced him. "I'm different, a lot different, and I want so much more."

He cast his eyes to the floor. "Perhaps you need some time to—"

"All the time in the world won't change my mind," she broke in.

When his blue eyes rose to her, the same cool, contentious look she had always associated with his dismissive nature stared back at her. Even on their wedding day, he had appeared as aloof, as disconnected from his emotions as he did at that moment.

"All right." With an air of indifference, he shoved his hands into his trousers pockets. "But I want you to know I'm always here for you, and for Estelle. She is going to need help down the road, and I want to be there for both of you."

"I appreciate that, Foster."

She showed him to the door, and after he had left, Rayne settled back against the wall in her hallway. Ever since the divorce, she had dreamed of Foster coming back to her and making amends. Now that dream had come true, but she felt not an ounce of satisfaction. He was not the man she wanted...Trent was.

That certainty almost knocked her to the ground. "No, that can't be. He's going to turn into another Foster. He doesn't care about me...he can't...." But as a montage of her time with Trent skipped across her heart, her resistance faded.

Her mother, Rebecca, even Lindsey had been right. Trent was not Foster, and the emotion she had shared with him had never compared to the emptiness she experienced with her ex. Maybe all she had needed was to put her life with Foster behind her before she was ready to embrace a relationship with Trent.

"What have I done?" She slowly sank to the floor. "What in the hell am I going to do?"

Chapter 24

The morning of the Golden Farms Horse Show, Rayne was adding the finishing touches to the tight braids arranged in Bob's mane. Her fingers smarted from working the coarse horsehair into the decorative circles tied up with white yarn, but she was pleased with the results. Gliding her hand over his shimmering bay coat, she listened to the sound of other riders preparing their horses in the stalls surrounding her.

Rebecca had transported Bob, along with the other horses competing, from Southland to the guest stables at Golden Farms the evening before. Located to the side of the main green and white barn, the large guest stables housed over a hundred horses for the show, with entrants coming from all over Texas.

Rayne had done a good job avoiding Trent during the chaos of transporting horses the previous evening, and all the show prep that morning. He had been busy dealing with Selene and her dressage riders. Rebecca told her he had opted to oversee Selene's activities, complaining that he was not comfortable with her abilities, while Rayne was left to supervise her beginner students who were entered in a few of the flat classes.

Having stuck to the shadows whenever he appeared, Rayne had managed to avoid him. But when he was not looking, she would sneak peeks at him stamping in front of her stall as he went up and down the shed row checking on his riders. Every now and then, she would hear his voice and her stomach would shrink to the size of a pea. Sooner or later, Rayne knew they would have to confront each other; she just hoped that eventuality could be postponed for as long as humanly possible.

While leading Bob from his stall to the post where her polished saddle and bridle were waiting, she saw Rebecca off to the side in a corner of the stables, waving angrily. When a figure across from Rebecca retreated from the shadows, she sighted Trent's wide shoulders slouching forward, along with the nasty scowl on his face.

Tugging on Bob's lead rope, hoping to make him move faster down the aisle, Rayne wanted to run for cover when Trent spotted her. Instead of confronting his gaze, she lowered her head and pulled with all of her might on Bob's lead rope, making the stubborn animal come to a grinding halt.

"Shit, Bob, don't do this to me."

"Rayne, get over here," Rebecca's masculine voice ordered. "We need to settle some things."

She smiled sheepishly and kept on pulling at Bob's lead. "I have to get him ready."

"I'll do it." Rebecca marched down the barn aisle toward Rayne and wrenched the lead rope from her hands. "Talk to him. Do something, for Christ's sake. I can't have the two of you not speaking to each other in the middle of a show." Rebecca pointed at Trent. "Go and fix this."

The color drained from Rayne's face. "Please don't ask me to—"

"Go!" Rebecca yelled. "Or I'll fire your ass."

Quickly pulling Bob away, Rebecca left Rayne in the middle of the aisle with nowhere to hide. When she finally looked up, Rayne saw Trent's arresting eyes taking in every inch of her.

"Son of a bitch," she cursed under her breath as her dread dissolved into a spark of desire.

Squeezing her hands together, she very slowly walked toward him. With every step, she could feel his eyes burning into her. When she stood before him, Rayne proudly raised her head. She could not let him know that this was killing her.

"Trent." She was thankful her voice did not crack under the pressure.

He tipped his head to her, keeping the cruel scowl on his lips. "Rayne."

"I guess we should discuss how we plan on breaking up the schooling schedules with our students." She unclasped her hands. "I have three kids in the flat classes in the afternoon, while at—"

"That's not what we need to talk about and you know it," he grumbled, cutting her off.

A thick silence formed between them, making Rayne wish she could be swallowed whole by the ground below her feet.

"I know we didn't end on the best of terms," she began. "But I—"

"End?" He angled closer. "What in the hell makes you thinks we have ended?"

She took a step back from him. "I told you that I needed time to think."

He hurriedly closed the distance between them. "And I gave you time to think. But you need to know that I'm not going to let you go."

"It's not your choice, is it, Trent? It's mine."

"You're mine," he hissed under his breath.

Rayne took two steps further back from him, her mouth slightly open. "You arrogant asshole. Where the hell do you get off, telling me—"

"Drop it, Rayne." He grasped her arms, his fingers squeezing into her flesh. "Why did you run away? You thought I slept with Lisa, didn't you?"

She shirked off his grip. "I know you didn't sleep with her."

"Then why run out on me like that?"

"Because…." She faltered, too afraid to tell him the truth about her misgivings.

"Because why? And don't lie to me. Tell me what it is and let's work this out."

Work this out? His words hit like a battering ram against her heart. How could they work this out? For Rayne, they had seemed doomed from the start. "There's nothing to work out," she calmly insisted. "You're a man who…needs a lot of women to feel satisfied, and I will never be enough for you. Don't you see that?"

He folded his arms over his chest and the thick muscles in his exposed forearms twitched. "No, I don't."

"When I saw that woman in your living room, I wondered how many other women had been in your home before me. I knew then that I would never be enough for you."

"That is the most ridiculous thing I've ever heard." The silliest grin etched its way across his lips. "Admit it, you're afraid. Afraid of being with me because you think I'm going to turn into Foster."

"Well, aren't you?"

"No." He uncrossed his arms. "Not every man is going to become your ex. We're not all the same, despite what a lot of women believe."

She shook her head. "Well, I can't take that chance."

"You'd better take that chance with me; otherwise you will be making a big mistake."

"I made a mistake once with a man, and my heart can't afford to repeat it." She turned away, showing him her profile. "In the future, please keep all conversations strictly limited to the lessons and the students." Without another word, she walked away.

Rebecca was tightening the girth around Bob's belly when Rayne walked up to her.

"So when's the wedding?"

"Why did you do that to me, Rebecca? You knew how I felt."

Rebecca patted Bob's back. "That's why I did it. Because you're just too stubborn to admit that you want him—God forbid, even need him—in your life."

"I don't need anybody," Rayne fiercely defended, checking her fancy show bridle next to the post.

"That's where you're wrong, Rayne. For someone who has taken so many chances in the show ring, don't you think that perhaps it is time to take a chance outside of it?"

Rayne wrestled the bridle from the post and walked over to Bob. "Last time I took a chance on a man...." She slipped the blue halter from around Bob's ears. "You know what happened." Easing the snaffle bit into Bob's mouth she edged the bridle over his head, securing it behind his black-tipped ears.

"He's not Foster, Rayne."

"Yet." She flipped the reins over Bob's neck. "He's not Foster, yet."

"So that's it. You're just going to let him walk away."

She clucked for Bob to move forward. "I have to go and warm him up before our class."

"I hope you and Bob are very happy together. Because that's the only man I know you won't chase away."

Reminded of her mother's words, Rayne spun around to Rebecca. "I'm not chasing him away."

Rebecca took a few steps closer to her. "That is exactly what you're doing." She patted Bob's sleek neck. "You need to stop comparing every man to Foster, and start living your life again. You deserve to be happy; even though you may not be convinced of that fact, you do deserve it."

"My father always said that to me, 'you deserve to be happy,' and then after he and Jaime died, I didn't think I would ever be happy again. I hoped Foster could make me happy…you know, make me feel…whole again, but he never did. How do I know I won't end up living the same kind of emptiness I had with Foster?"

Rebecca lovingly placed one hand against Rayne's cheek. "Because you love Trent, and you never really loved Foster, did you?"

Rebecca's words ripped into Rayne's gut, spilling out the truth that she had for so long been too afraid to admit. "How…how did you know?"

"I suspected from the beginning." Rebecca offered a reassuring smile. "The way you spoke of him, especially when you first started riding at my stables, you never had love in your heart. You withdrew from him long before the divorce, and it wasn't until Trent that I saw a part of you I had never seen before, the side of you in love. You never glowed with Foster, never blushed during your time together…you were always reserved, always calm. And I think with Trent, you're absolutely terrified that another human being can have that kind of control over you."

Rayne nonchalantly shrugged. "I think you're reading way too much into my relationship with the man."

"You know I'm right."

Rayne urged Bob along. "I have to get ready for the competition."

"I hope you're ready for a showdown, Rayne."

"Bob's ready."

"I wasn't talking about that kind of showdown," Rebecca objected with a grunt.

After clearing the shade of the barn, Rayne led Bob out into the early morning sunshine. "Never mind her," she mumbled to the horse. "We've got a blue ribbon to win."

But as she rode toward the warm up area, Rayne kept looking over her shoulder for Trent. Suddenly, she was terrified that what Rebecca had told her might actually be true.

***

Atop Bob and decked out in her tight white jodhpurs, shiny black boots, black velvet riding hat, black jacket, and white, high collar shirt, Rayne memorized the course posted for her jumping class outside the show ring gate. Nervous butterflies danced in her belly as a competitor on a dapple-gray gelding took a turn over the fences.

"You better keep off his neck when you're clearing the water fence, otherwise he'll tip the edge," a smoky voice directed next to Bob.

Over Bob's right shoulder she saw Trent with a condescending sneer plastered on his face. "Remember to give him at least three full strides before that touch and go," he added, gazing up at her.

"Thanks for the tip." She watched the leggy gray in the show ring knock down a pole on the blue and white double oxer fence.

"You know I'm still your boss, and I want to make sure you win this."

"I realize that." She kept her eyes on the ring, evading his devastating gaze.

"So the least you could do is listen to me."

"What makes you think I'm not listening to you?"

"Because you're not looking at me." He slapped her right boot, making Rayne's eyes turn to him. "Take him slow through the course, and try to stay clean over the fences. You need a clear round to make the jump-off."

"I'm not an idiot, Trent. I know what I need to do."

He smirked at her. "Could have fooled me."

"Are you finished?"

"No...win this class, otherwise I won't show you my surprise."

Her heart skipped a beat. "What surprise?"

A round of applause from the audience kept Rayne from getting an answer from him.

"You're up," Trent clamored, and led Bob to the entrance of the show ring.

She leaned forward in the saddle to him. "What surprise?"

Entertained by her curiosity, his grin deepened. "Only if you win." He patted Bob's round rump. "Now get in there."

Rayne was glancing angrily back at him as she rode in the gate. She became so distracted by his promise of a surprise that she almost forgot which fence to jump first. Gathering up her reins, she straightened her back and took in a calming breath. Rayne reviewed the fences set up throughout the interior of the wide ring, going over the course in her head.

She could hear the murmur of the crowd, and smell the aroma of dust and horses in the air. Somewhere in the distance a single horse whinnied, breaking into the stillness of the show ring.

"All right, buddy, let's rock."

Urging Bob into a canter, she deftly circled him around the front portion of the ring, making the customary courtesy circle expected of all competitors before starting the course. When the first fence loomed before them, Rayne forgot all about Trent, Rebecca, Foster, and the world outside of that white fence railing. It was just her, and Bob, and all those jumps that mattered.

They cleared the first hurdle resembling the green and white barn of the host stables, and then cantered on to the water jump. After taking three more fences, she looked ahead to the touch and go Trent had warned her of. Trent. She wanted to laugh at loud at his last minute coaching. She cleared the first part of the touch and go, let Bob's feet just touch the ground, and encouraged him on to the very close second fence, not letting him take a stride. After clearing two more jumps, she spied the last one on the course; a big three-tiered monster that all the other horses had knocked down.

"Last one, Bob. Let's finish clean."

Bob's pace quickened when he saw the last fence. She held the reins steady, curtailing his exuberance, wanting him to let loose right before the imposing hurdle so he could use his energy to jump up and over. Three long strides before the fence, she slacked up on the reins to give him his head, and Bob responded. He charged the last three strides to the fence, and just in the right spot he took to the air, forcing his body upward with his powerful hind end.

Rayne always loved this feeling, the moment of flight when she and the horse were one over the jump. Making sure she did not put too much of her weight on his shoulders, she hugged the saddle with her knees as they descended over the other side of the wide fence. When his feet hit the ground, Rayne wanted to shout out loud. He had cleared the entire course, and they had the first clean round in the competition.

Applause roared through the air as soon as they were over the last jump. Rayne patted Bob's neck as they cantered to the ring entrance. Slowing him down, she performed the final customary exit circle to show the judge that she had complete control of the horse, and headed to the gate.

As soon as she left the ring, Trent was there, clapping enthusiastically. "Couldn't have done it better myself."

She directed Bob to the side of the entrance. "That's a first, admitting someone bested you, the riding master."

He came up to her and patted her black boot. "You bested me the moment we met, Rayne."

She dismounted and went around to Bob's head, keeping one hand on the reins. "Don't talk like that, Trent."

"Why not?"

Rayne removed her black velvet riding hat, letting her honey-blonde hair fall about her shoulders. "I told you, it wouldn't work between us."

"So you're just going to let Selene win."

She became acutely aware of his wide chest, and how the top buttons of his white polo shirt were open, offering a peek of his tanned chest. "What has Selene got to do with us?"

He folded his thick arms over his chest, distracting Rayne even more. "Lisa told me everything when she came over that day…about how Selene had arranged for her and Foster to be at that party. She also confessed that Selene had said I was anxious to return to Shelby Stables, and that's why she showed up with the offer. Lisa assumed I was interested in returning to her bed, as well. When I confronted Selene about all of her lies, she had no choice but to admit to it."

She shifted her focus to Bob, standing calmly beside her. "You confronted her? When?"

"The day after you ran out of my house. I threatened to fire her and then have Rebecca call her husband and let him know what she had been up to. After that, she was very forthcoming." He mashed his thin lips together in a disgusted grimace. "You were right about her. She was trying to drive a wedge between us."

The tension that had been twisting in Rayne's gut for the past few days eased a little. "Thank you for telling me, but it really—"

"So that's what you do," a woman's craggy voice intruded.

Rayne searched the crowd for the owner of that all too familiar voice.

Standing by Bob's rump and wearing a violet, long-sleeved A-line dress that hugged her frail figure, Estelle appeared painfully out of place.

"Mother? What are you doing here?"

"Surprise," Trent whispered in her ear.

She turned to him. "You brought her?"

"Trent and I had a long chat the other day when he came to visit me," Estelle disclosed, stepping forward. "He told me you had a show this weekend, and when I mentioned that I would love to see you in action, he offered to have me brought here."

"But you never wanted to come to my shows in the past, Mother."

Estelle wiped some dust from her low-heeled black pumps. "Well, now I do. I need to see what it is you find so damned fascinating about this sport."

Rayne's eyes glided over her mother's neatly coiffed blonde hair and perfectly made-up face. "I jumped a clear round."

"Which means you're up for a ribbon." She nodded her head. "Trent told me. He explained it to me while you were in the ring."

The clang of a pole falling inside the show ring made Trent careen his head around to see what had happened. A fat black thoroughbred had knocked a pole from the troublesome last triple fence to the ground.

"One more rider to go. You're definitely going to place in the top two," he pronounced.

Rayne took in the enthusiasm in his eyes. Determined to keep it professional, she tried to harden her heart against him, but it was not working.

When he saw her staring up at him, Trent cleared his throat and waved to the practice area beside them. "I'd better go and check on Selene and the other riders. They're getting ready to start the dressage portion of the show in the back ring."

"Sure." Rayne situated her riding hat on the pummel of Bob's saddle. "And thanks for the help."

He smiled at her, but it lacked his usual sparkle. This smile was all business. "That's my job," he gruffly replied, and then with one last pat on Bob's rump, he walked away.

As he ventured across the busy practice ring, his black hair bobbed about in the brisk October breeze as his short brown riding boots kicked up the dust around him. When Rayne's eyes settled on his firm butt beneath his brown riding pants, that familiar tingle came alive in her gut.

"So you want to tell me why you ran away from him? Seems to me you're still real interested, Raynie."

Rayne's right hand squeezed Bob's reins as she confronted her mother. "Why did you tell Foster about Trent and me? From the way he told it, you were trying to get us back together."

"Together? Ha!" Estelle cackled. "I got a hold of Foster to get information on real estate agents. He was the one who asked me about you and Trent. He went on and on about seeing you two at that party, so I told him the truth. I can't believe he said anything to you."

"He did more than that. He showed up at my house. Even apologized for sleeping with Connie, and pleaded for a second chance."

Estelle's nostrils flared. "I hope you told him to go to hell."

Rayne's mouth fell open. "I'm confused. Don't you want me to get back together with my rich ex-husband?"

"No, that's not what I want. Foster Greer never made you happy, and it's time you find someone who does."

"I didn't think you cared about my happiness, Mother."

Estelle's shrewd blue eyes studied her. "I know I haven't been a mother to you, Raynie. I won't stand here and pretend we've had a good relationship. I wish I could take back many of the things I've said and done, but I can't." She shifted closer to her daughter. "I'm not asking you to forgive me; I don't want that. I simply want to spend whatever time I have left trying to have a relationship with you that isn't founded in anger."

Rayne bit down on her lip, struggling to keep the tears from her eyes. "Why the sudden change of heart, Mother? We've been going toe-to-toe since the moment I was born." She sniffled. "Why now?"

Estelle tugged at the strap of her black leather purse slung over her arm. "When Trent showed up on my doorstep and invited me to this horse show, I laughed at him, knowing you would hate having me here, but after a while he made me see that perhaps I was wrong." She paused and watched as the last of the riders in Rayne's event entered the ring. "He told me a lot of things about you, and…he made me realize how little I know about you. We talked for quite a while about you and him, and about my drinking. He said it was never too late to try with you, and that my biggest mistake would be not trying at all."

Rayne played with the reins in her hand. "I can't believe he went to see you."

"I may be an old fool who has been blind to a lot of things in life, but I still know love when I see it." Estelle edged her daughter's head up. "And that man loves you."

Rayne lowered her mother's hand from her chin. "Even if he did love me, it can never last. He's a man who has been with a lot of women. He'll grow tired of me and move on, just like he has done in the past."

"You're wrong, Raynie. He's a better man than Foster. Foster was only motivated to help others when it suited his needs; Trent's not like that. He didn't visit me with the hopes of getting the two of you back together. In fact, he never mentioned it. He did it for you. He wanted me here for you, and all the things he said were for your benefit and mine. He gained nothing by doing any of this."

A loud crashing noise came from the center of the show ring. Rayne turned to see that the last entrant, a strawberry roan with a silver tail, had just knocked down two poles from one of the double oxer fences at the start of the course. Rayne's heart soared with relief; she had won the event.

"Does that mean you're the winner?"

"Yes, Mother. I've won the blue ribbon."

"Congratulations. Now don't you think there's someone you should share this victory with?"

Rayne contemplated the green and white barn behind her and then her eyes traveled to the back ring. In the distance, the dressage competitors were warming up outside of the white railings of their show ring.

"What if…?"

"Raynie, sometimes it takes the wrong kind of man to help you find the right one." Estelle patted her shoulder, encouraging her onward. "You'd better go and tell him the good news."

Rayne browsed the crowd outside of the show ring. When her eyes settled on her mother, she handed her Bob's reins. "Here."

Estelle was horrified. "Me?" She took the reins, eyeing the horse with utter panic. "What am I supposed to do with him?"

"Just hold him, Mother. He won't hurt you." Rayne took off running for the green and white stables.

"Raynie! What if he moves?" Estelle shouted.

But Rayne did not stop to reply. She ran in her black boots, feeling the rigid shoes fighting against her fluid motion. When she came to the main stables, she veered left, heading to the back show ring and the dressage events.

At the edge of the schooling field located outside of the main show ring, she scanned the plethora of horses in all shapes and colors practicing their difficult dressage routines. Trainers were scattered amid the horses, shouting instructions, while a few family and friends looked on. When Rayne caught sight of Trent's black, wavy hair and wide shoulders on the far side of the ring, her heart lifted.

"I'm an idiot," she softly berated, and then took off across the ring.

After ducking between horses and trainers, Rayne was within feet of Trent when a figure dressed in black stepped in front of her.

Wearing her everyday black riding breeches, black boots, and black T-shirt, Rayne was surprised Selene was not sporting the customary fitted black coat, white shirt with stock tie, and black dressage boots required in the show ring.

"My, my, what are you doing at this end of the world, Rayne?"

"You're not dressed out? Aren't you showing, Selene?"

Selene frowned, but quickly recovered. "I have to help—"

Trent came up to them, his gray eyes awash with worry. "What is it? Is it Bob?"

"No, it's good news…great news," Rayne told him. "I won. I won my event."

His features hardened, and then he directed his attention to Selene. "Get back to Mary Anne and make sure her boots are polished before she goes in the ring," he barked at her.

Selene's black eyes ripped into him. "Yes, sir," she snarled under her breath.

As she sashayed away, Rayne spotted the towel and brush tucked into the back of her jodhpurs. "Why isn't she showing?"

"Because I made her the team groom. After all the grief she gave me, I felt a little humiliation was in order." He offered her a businesslike smile. "You did well. I'm sure Rebecca will be pleased with your blue ribbon."

He was about to rush back to the riders waiting for him when she touched his arm.

"I was wrong," she blurted out.

He noted her hand on his forearm. "Wrong about what?"

She let go of his arm. "Us. You were right; I was scared. I shouldn't have run away. I'm sorry."

The impassive expression remained on his face. "Apology accepted. Now I have students to attend to." He twisted away from her.

"Wait! That's it? That's all you have to say to me."

He stopped and his shoulders flexed beneath his fitted white polo shirt. When he came around, the anger in his eyes terrified her.

"What else do you want, Rayne?"

She gazed about the ring, uncomfortable with the fact that a few of the riders around them were listening in on their discussion. "You know what I want, Trent."

He eased closer to her. "No, I don't."

"You honestly don't know?"

He took another step toward her, his features still cold and distant. "Perhaps you should just tell me so I can get back to work."

She waved her hand about the ring. "Here?"

"Tell me, Rayne," he bellowed.

"All right...I want you."

He leaned over to her and touched his ear. "Sorry, I didn't quite catch that."

"I want you," she exclaimed.

He brought his face right in front of hers. "I still didn't hear you."

"You son of a bitch," she muttered, and then she tossed her head back and yelled, "I want you!"

Trent's grin was slow in coming, but when it appeared, his face warmed and his eyes twinkled. "I didn't think you had it in you." His eyes rose to his students at the railing. "I'll be right back," he loudly asserted, and then took Rayne's hand. "Come with me."

He carted her back to the guest stables, and once beneath the shadows of the metal roof, Trent dragged her along the shaving-covered aisle to a row of tack room doors. He pushed open a door with a sign reading Southland Stables and shoved Rayne inside.

After he followed her into the tack room, he banged the door closed. "Now say that again."

"I want you," Rayne repeated.

"What's changed?"

"Changed?" Rayne shrugged. "I don't know. Before I was afraid if I got involved with you, I would end up being hurt like I was with Foster; but you're not Foster. I know that now."

"And what made you realize that?" His voice was tense and held none of its usual charm. "Ten minutes ago you seemed pretty dead set against getting involved with me."

She rubbed her hands together. "Ah, Mother told me about your visit. I guess if she believes in you, then I can, too."

"You guess?" His eyes probed her face, still not looking entirely convinced. "Now you believe in me. How do I know you won't change your mind again, Rayne?"

"I won't. I promise, Trent."

His gray eyes narrowed, considering her pledge. "Prove it," he finally said in a low rumble.

Rayne's eyes grew wide with uncertainty. "How do I do that?"

"You'll think of something," he assured her as a devilish grin rose on his thin lips.

Understanding what he was alluding to, she motioned to the tack room door. "What about your students?"

"They'll keep."

Rayne took in his cool eyes, and then shrugged. Slowly, she eased her black riding jacket from her shoulders.

"What are you doing?" he questioned.

"Proving that I won't change my mind."

He cupped his hands about her face. "That's not what I meant."

She wrinkled her brow. "It's not?"

"Rayne," he softly whispered, his lips inches from hers. "Just tell me how you feel."

How do I feel? She breathed in the scent of dust, horses, and the slightest trace of his citrusy cologne, and suddenly she knew the answer. It had been there all along, hiding behind the shadows of doubt in her heart. But now the shadows were gone, and all that was left was her love, shining through.

"I love you, Trent."

"See, that wasn't so hard, was it?"

He leaned toward her, closing in for a kiss, when she stopped him. "Wait a minute. How do you feel about me?"

He paused and his eyes took a turn of the tack room. "I thought that was obvious. I love you."

She smiled as her heart soared with happiness. "Nothing is obvious with you, Mr. Newbury."

"It will be from now on, Ms. Greer. I promise."

When his lips touched hers, Rayne knew she had made the right choice. His kiss made her heart race, her palms itch, and her toes curl inside her boots. This had to be love.

Suddenly he backed away, and a speck of worry crossed his handsome features. "Where's Bob?"

Rayne fastened her arms about his neck. "With my mother."

Trent's boisterous laugh bounced about the small tack room. "I want a picture of that. You'll never hear the end of it from Estelle."

"She'd better start getting used to it, because I plan on going to a lot more horse shows in the future."

His arms embraced her. "More shows? Don't you think you should check with your master rider first?"

"Nah. I'm sure I'll be able to talk him into it."

He kissed her neck. "How are you going to do that?"

She tilted back from him. "Would you like me to show you?"

His hands wandered down her back until they settled over her round butt. "Yeah, show me."

Epilogue

Rayne finished carrying the last of the boxes from her Highlander into Trent's wide living room. Placing the cardboard box on the dining room table, she took in the disarray of boxes scattered about the open room and felt something was missing.

"That's it for the bedroom, right?" Trent inquired as he came into the room.

"Where's Frank?" She looked past him to the bedroom hallway.

"Pool. He's been sitting in the shallow end since you arrived."

Rayne waved to the patio doors. "You do realize all that hair will clog up your filters?"

Trent shrugged. "So what? If Frank's happy, then I'm happy."

"I give that about a week."

Trent inspected the living room. "You've got a lot of stuff. Where are we going to put it all?"

"Be thankful I left the furniture with my mother."

"How is Estelle adjusting to living in your house?"

"I think she likes it. She's been a little down since the act of sale, but I know she prefers the money in the bank to the burden of that big old mansion."

He slipped his arms about her. "You sure you don't want to sell her your place?"

"Just because I'm moving in with you doesn't mean I'm giving up my house. Maybe I'll need it one day, if you ever get tired of me."

He kissed her lips. "Never, baby. Besides, I don't see you and Estelle living together. She may be sober now, but she is still Estelle."

"Hard to believe my mother's been sober for four months. I think that's some sort of record for her. Even Dr. Emerit is shocked at how well she is doing."

A loud "woof" followed by the thumping of four feet barreling in through the open patio doors distracted them. Frank, soaked from head to paw, began shaking his body and sending a spray of water all over the living room.

"Frank," Rayne yelled, and went running to catch his collar.

Trent laughed at her attempt to curtail the dogs zealous shaking.

"He's ruining the furniture," she roared to Trent. "Don't just stand there, grab a towel."

"It's fine, Rayne, let him enjoy himself."

"But the furniture?"

Trent came up to her and removed her hand from Frank's collar. "It's just furniture."

Frank went flying out the back door, heading down the steep deck steps and back to the pool.

She tossed her hands in the air. "How can you be so calm about this?"

He placed his arm about her shoulders. "Never mind that. I have a surprise for you."

She warily examined his features. "What kind of surprise?"

He ushered her toward the kitchen. "A moving in surprise." He led her to his built-in refrigerator. "Open it."

"My surprise is in the refrigerator?"

"Yep," he answered.

When she opened the heavy door, she was greeted by row after row of orange juice cartons.

"So when you come home from the stables, you will always have your orange juice waiting for you," Trent declared.

She threw her arms about his neck. "Thank you. That is the best moving in present I could hope for."

"Well, wait, baby. I have one more thing for you."

She stepped back from his embrace. "Another surprise?"

"But first...." He took a carton from the fridge. "We have to have a toast."

Retrieving two iced tea glasses from the cabinet overhead, he handed one to Rayne and placed the other on the stone countertop. Trent then unscrewed the top of the juice carton and nodded to her glass. "I want to ask you something?"

Rayne held up her glass, waiting for him to pour the juice. "What is it?"

He positioned the carton over her glass, and Rayne watched, a little bewildered, when not a drop of juice came out. Then, a light clang echoed in the kitchen. When she peered down into her glass, she saw a diamond ring.

"Will you marry me, Rayne?"

After the first instant of shock wore off, tears collected in her eyes. "Yes," she proclaimed. "Yes, I will marry you, Trent."

With the glass in her hand, she leapt into his arms. She kissed his cheeks, his neck, and hugged him tight.

When he set her down on the floor again, he held her back, frowning. "I know women love planning weddings, but when I mentioned I was going to propose to Tyler, he insisted he and Monique have the wedding at their house. I told them I would talk to you first. I'm not trying to — "

She touched her fingers to his lips. "I don't care where we have it as long as I get to officially make you mine."

"Yours? I think I've been yours since the day we met." Trent took the glass from her and tipped it over until the ring fell into his hand. "You were so stubborn and so damned distrusting. I never thought I could win you over." He slipped the engagement ring on the third finger of her left hand.

Rayne admired the two-carat, emerald-shaped solitaire diamond. "And I was convinced you were an arrogant ass."

"Still think of me that way?"

She cocked her head to the side, debating her answer. "I can't really say, since you're still my boss and all."

"I'm your fiancé now, darling, not your boss."

Rayne ran her hands up his chest, pleased with the way the diamond glistened on her left hand. "But you're still the riding master of Southland Stables." She nestled closer to him. "And I'm one of your instructors."

He touched his forehead to hers. "So?"

Her lips skimmed along his jaw as her hand pressed into the crotch of his jeans. "That means you're my riding master, and my boss."

"Your riding master?" Trent lifted her onto the kitchen counter. "I think I like the sound of that."

She slowly unzipped the fly of his jeans. "So how 'bout you take me for a ride, riding master?"

As she wrapped her legs about his waist, he uttered a contented sigh. "I think I've finally tamed you."

"You never tamed me, Trent." Rayne happily smiled into his exquisite gray eyes. "You simply gained my trust. Once we had trust, only then could we find love."

The End

Read the Next book in the Cover to Covers Series
The Bondage Club

About the Author

Alexandrea Weis is an advanced practice registered nurse who was born and raised in New Orleans. Having been brought up in the motion picture industry, she learned to tell stories from a different perspective and began writing at the age of eight. Infusing the rich tapestry of her hometown into her award-winning novels, she believes that creating vivid characters makes a story moving and memorable. A permitted/certified wildlife rehabber with the Louisiana Wildlife and Fisheries, Weis rescues orphaned and injured wildlife. She lives with her husband and pets in New Orleans.

To read more about Alexandrea Weis or her books, you can go to the following sites:
Website: http://www.alexandreaweis.com/
Facebook: http://www.facebook.com/authoralexandreaweis
Twitter: https://twitter.com/alexandreaweis
Goodreads: http://www.goodreads.com/author/show/1211671.Alexandrea_Weis
Pinterest: http://www.pinterest.com/apwrncs/
TSU: https://www.tsu.co/alexandreaweis

Made in the USA
Middletown, DE
11 January 2016